The Sword Bearer

The Archives of Anthropos – by John White

To Nancy, Paul and Stephen

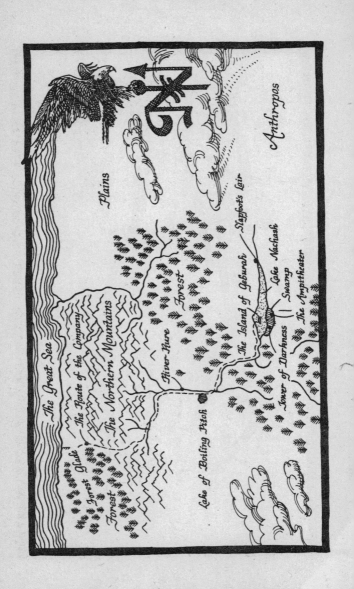

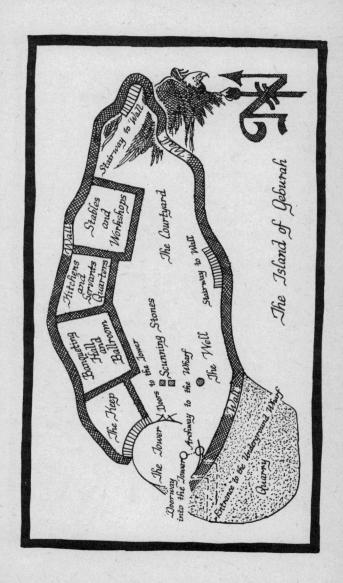

The Island of Geburah

1

The Birthday That Went Wrong

John Wilson was no good at whistling, but he whistled anyway. He whistled in spite of the fog, and the fog was one of Pendleton's worst.

Pendleton people used to call them pea-soup fogs because of their dirty yellow color. Scientists said the color came from pollution, the pollution caused by thousands and thousands of tiny houses. People warmed their homes with coal fireplaces in those days, and the coal sent smoke belching out of all those chimneys. And all the factory chimneys belched smoke too.

Pendleton fogs used to be so dense that sometimes you couldn't see across Ellor Street. Ellor Street was the street John Wilson followed most of the way home from school. The gathering darkness made it harder for John to see. He walked past a bus that was crawling along Ellor Street following a man who walked ahead waving a white flag to help the driver. "You might just as well walk!" one lady said indignantly as she stepped off the slowly moving vehicle.

John stopped whistling and laughed softly to himself. Then he thought of how he had tried to cross Ellor Street a few minutes before and giggled some more. He had stepped off the pavement (that's what they call the sidewalk in England), and like someone lost in a forest he had walked in a circle until he arrived back on the same side of the street. It was very confusing, but he got himself sorted out eventually, on the right side and going in the right direction.

As a matter of fact he had worked out a system. He had one foot on the pavement (that's the sidewalk, you remember) and one foot in the gutter. He could have walked beside the wall, touching it to be sure he was walking straight ahead. But everyone else was doing that, and they kept bumping into one another and saying things like, "Oo, excuse me! Isn't it *awful*. It's absolutely dreadful!" or, "Lors! I can't see a blessed thing! Am so sorry!"

John's plan was a lot better. The only things he had to watch out for were lamp posts. And since the lamplighter had just been lighting them ahead of John, he could see the eerie glow of a shining lamp several steps before he reached the lamp post. So he didn't have to touch anything or bump into anyone. At least, that was his plan.

So John Wilson whistled. It was his thirteenth birthday, and Grandma Wilson had promised to bake him a birthday cake with thirteen candles on it. John and his grandma had lived together for as long as John could remember. He could recall nothing about his parents, which was what made this day so special. Grandma Wilson had promised to tell him about his parents on his thirteenth birthday. Always before she had told him, "When you are older I'll tell you. You're too young to understand yet."

Sometimes John wondered whether his parents had been very wicked, and whenever he thought like that he grew angry and scared. At other times he thought he may have been bad when he was small and that his parents hadn't liked him and had left him with Grandma Wilson. But mostly he thought that his parents were on a secret adventure. Perhaps they were in the Secret Service. And now that he was thirteen he would find out. So he whistled his way through the fog, excited about the mystery that was about to be solved.

John Wilson loved mysteries. He borrowed mystery books from the library and went to the pictures (we would say *movies* now) as often as he could. He also spent a lot of time in a dream world where he was the hero in a hundred mystery stories he would make up himself.

He fumbled in his blazer pocket and pulled out a dirty piece of string from which a gold ring and a gold locket hung. Inside the locket was a faded brown picture of a World War I soldier wearing a moustache and looking very stern. (You were supposed to look stern in those days when you had your picture taken.) There was also a lock of curly red hair. The gold ring was a man's signet ring, but it seemed very old and it was impossible to read the letters on it. John was sure the ring and the locket had something to do with his parents, and he had often asked Grandma Wilson whether the photograph was of his father. But always she would make the same reply, "You're too young yet. Wait till you're a bit older."

"How much older, Grandma?"

"Stop bothering me, John. You'll know soon enough!"

But John continued to bother his grandma till at last she told him that if only he would stop, she would tell him at tea time on his thirteenth birthday.

He pulled the string over his head, tucking the ring and the locket inside his shirt and frowning as he did so. They were a source of trouble as well as a mystery. At first his grandma had insisted he wear them round his neck on a pink silk ribbon; yet the children in the earlier grades at school had made fun of him. After a number of arguments with his grandmother, a compromise was made. John could use ordinary string so long as he always wore them. But the teasing had continued until at last John had got into the habit of putting them into his pocket on the way to school and replacing them round his neck as he drew near home. He didn't bother to tell his grandma about the new arrangement and since she never asked, John felt he wasn't really disobeying.

Don't let me give you the wrong idea about Grandma Wilson. She was kind. She did all she could to make John happy. She was a smiling, fat old lady whose white hair had a yellow streak in it and was tied in a bun at the back. She always wore white blouses and dark gray skirts that came down to her ankles. She read John stories long after he could read for himself. There was something special about the way Grandma read which made the stories seem more exciting than when John read them alone. He especially liked the stories by Nesbitt, like *The Phoenix and the Carpet*. So for years he had coaxed her to read and had sat on the floor, snuggling against her knees and feeling the warmth from the fire as he closed his eyes and listened.

She was proud of John and even more proud after he had won his scholarship to Salford Grammar School, a sort of special high school for boys only. Salford Grammar School was a mile from Pimblett's Place, the side street John lived on, and he walked there and back twice a day. At that school they had forms instead of grades, and John was in a form called third form removed, a form for bright students who were skipping a year.

He liked the school, but soon after he arrived in form 1 (the equivalent of seventh grade) things became difficult, not at school, but on Ellor Street. No one from anywhere near where John lived had ever gone to Salford Grammar School before. It was a school for "toffs" and "snobs" and "sissies"—or so the boys on Ellor Street said. What made it worse was that John had won money with his scholarship so that he could buy things like the school uniform. And it was the uniform, just as it had used to be the pink ribbon, that caused the problem.

There were gray shorts and gray socks with green bands round the top. There was also a green blazer trimmed around the edges, and the collar had a bright yellow ribbon. On the pocket a yellow lion was embroidered, glaring defiantly. And from the front of the green school cap John had to wear, the same yellow lion clawed aggressively at anyone who cared to take notice.

And a gang of boys roaming Ellor Street were happy to do so, snatching the cap from John's head and tossing it from one to another. Grandma Wilson had taught John not to fight. But John soon found that it was fight or go under. He decided one day that a sudden and ferocious attack on the leader of the gang would be the best strategy, fists pummeling as accurately as possible on the gang-leader's nose. I don't know that he was right in his decision, but after a couple such attacks—all of which ended in victory—the gang became decidedly friendlier. There was no more hat snatching and no more name calling.

He held his head higher after that. He was not only clever. He was tough—or so he thought. Secretly he began to look down on the Ellor Street gang. Who else was smart enough to go to Salford Grammar School and strong enough to hold his own against this gang?

John Wilson continued to hobble, right foot in the gutter, left foot up on the curb and twelve more lamp posts to go. He also continued to whistle. He was not only happy about his birthday cake and the solution to his mystery, but about something that had happened in school that afternoon. The teachers, who were all men and were called masters, wore black gowns over their jackets, gowns that were something like modern graduation gowns, only much more full and having sleeves that hung low. And among the boys there was a competition to see who could tear the biggest piece of silk from a master's gown.

This was easier to do with some masters than with others.

The German master's gown was in tatters. The French master's gown looked perfectly new. The French master never smiled. He had a little black lump in the middle of his forehead that he could move. He spoke quietly, and you knew just by looking at him that to fool with him was to invite disaster. German lessons tended to be rowdy, whereas French lessons were orderly and subdued. You really got to know French, but even if you were good you barely scraped through in German. I *think* the German master enjoyed getting his gown torn and just pretended not to notice when it was happening. Or he would say, "Oh, confound it! I'm forever ripping this dratted thing!"

To tear a master's gown you had to wait until he stood beside your desk with his back to you. You then hooked his gown on a nail on the side of your desk, or else trapped it under your desk lid and leaned hard with your elbows on the lid. Some of the masters had the habit of moving suddenly toward the front of the classroom, and there would be a ripping noise as a new tear was made.

It took at least two and sometimes three or four tears before you could actually capture a ragged bit of black silk, and John Wilson had captured his first piece that afternoon. I can't say I approve, and I approve even less of the fact that he was hugely delighted.

In his dreamy mind it was not just a piece of black silk, it was a piece of King Saul's robe and John Wilson was David, waving it in triumph. Then it was a piece of yellow silk cut from the robe of an enemy of the Genghis Khan, who was telling him that from then on he would be given the fastest horse on the steppes of Asia and that he would ride beside his master in triumph to the very heart of China.

His dream began to fade as he stared into the deepening obscurity. The light from the next lamp had not appeared. He took off his glasses and rubbed them carefully with his dirty handkerchief. One lens was loose and he wiped it cautiously, taking care not to push it out. But he could see no better when

14

he put his glasses back on. Cautiously he edged forward into the foggy darkness.

What happened next took place too suddenly for John to realize what was going on.

He bumped against something or someone very solid, tripped and fell, banging his head against a lamp post as he did so, and knocking off his glasses. From above his head there came the sound of breaking glass. Pieces of glass fell on him and on the pavement around him. A familiar voice was muttering curses. He had bumped into Mr. Leadbetter the lamplighter, jerking Mr. Leadbetter's lighting pole through the glass of the lamp far above them both. (Mr. Leadbetter had a pole with a hook and a flame on the end of it, the hook to turn the gas on and the flame to light the mantle.)

"Oh, Mr. Leadbetter, I really am sorry," John said. "I couldn't see you."

"Is that young John Wilson?" the lamplighter asked. "I suppose it couldn't be 'elped, lad. Are you all right?"

John fingered his forehead where a lump was slowly rising. "I've knocked me glasses off," was all he said.

Carefully the lamplighter rested his long pole against the wall of a store beside them. Then he got down on his hands and knees with John, groping around in search of the spectacles. "I 'ope it's not smashed," Mr. Leadbetter said slowly. " 'Ere. What's this?"

In the dimness John could see his glasses in Mr. Leadbetter's big hands. "Thanks, Mr. Leadbetter," he sighed with relief. "One of the lenses is loose."

"Ay, an' it's not there now."

It took them a little longer to find the lens, and to John's delight it was not broken. "It's not even cracked, lad," the lamplighter said as John clicked the lens back into place.

Slowly they walked together, and John waited at each lamp post while the lamplighter pushed his flame-tipped pole up inside the lamp. With the hook he would turn the gas on, and

John could hear the faint hiss followed by a popping sound as the mantle suddenly glowed white and clear.

"It's me birthday today," John said after a while.

"Is it now? Many 'appy returns, lad! 'Ow old are you?"

"Thirteen," John answered proudly.

"Ee, bah gum! Thirteen! They'll be 'avin' you in long pants before you know what's 'appened!" English schoolboys wore shorts in those days.

"Me granny's going to get me a suit when she's got the money."

Soon they arrived at Pimblett's Place, where the lamps had already been lit. "Good-by, young John. Eat a piece of cake for me, will you? Don't forget now!"

His tall figure dissolved into the fog and John waited until his muffled footsteps grew silent before turning toward home. Pimblett's Place was a short street ending in a tall brick wall topped with broken glass. The terraced houses, blackened with grime and soot, huddled together as if to comfort one another. There were no gardens. Front doors opened directly onto the pavement.

John hurried down the street to his grandmother's house. Squeezed against a high brick wall, it was the last house on the left. He opened the door shouting "Hello, Granma! I'm home!"

But the house was in darkness. "That's funny. She must have gone to the shop for something," he murmured, groping his way forward into the blackness. "I wonder why she didn't leave the gas light on." His foot met something solid, and he pitched forward and fell for the second time that evening. He found himself lying on a cloth-covered mound. For a moment he did not move.

"Granny?" he breathed at last. His hands groped along the clothing until his fingers found her cold face, and he gave a gasp of fear.

"Granny!" Then louder, "Granny!" But there was neither sound nor movement. With a half sob, his panic mounting, he

pushed himself up and carefully found his way over her and into the kitchen in search of the matchbox which she always kept on the mantlepiece above the fireplace. With shaking fingers he pulled a match from the box but immediately broke it in his eagerness to light it.

Another match, fingers still shaking. Then the soft glow, the low hiss of the gas and a popping sound as the gas mantle burst into light. He turned and saw his grandmother, her skirt and legs in the kitchen where she had fallen at the entrance to the hallway and the rest of her beyond in the darkness.

"Granny—you'll be all right, Granny. Don't worry, Granny, I'm going to get Mrs. Smith." He knelt beside her body, his own body shaking as he tried to shake hers. "Granny, it's me, John. You're all right now."

He got up quickly and ran to the scullery. A flannel, that's what she needed, a wet flannel. That would make her come to.

But the flannel didn't make her come to, and as he turned her head toward him, he was shocked to see her eyes were wide open and staring, staring fixedly beyond his shoulder. "Oh, no! *No*, Granny! You'll be all right. I'll go and fetch Mrs. Smith. She'll know what to do. Just lie here a minute and wait."

He ran into the foggy darkness to rap on the door of the next house. "Mrs. Smith! Mrs. Smith! Something's happened to me granma! Mrs. Smith! Hurry, Mrs. Smith!" He continued to knock at the door.

" 'Ere, lad, what's tha' doin'? What's tha' makin' such a to-do about?"

"It's me granma! She's lyin' in th' hallway! She's ill! Please come, Mrs. Smith."

The tall lady wasted no time. She pushed past John and hurried into the hallway of his grandmother's house. A man's voice called from somewhere in the Smith's house. "Is she all right, Elsie? What's 'appened?"

John was standing in the corridor behind Mrs. Smith who was kneeling down by his grandmother. He could hear Mr.

Smith's footsteps walking hurriedly from the one house to the other.

"I think she's gone, 'Arold. I think she's gone. She must 'ave 'ad a stroke. Go an' fetch th' doctor. Tell 'im to come at once."

The man turned and began to run down Pimblett's Place toward Ellor Street and the nearest doctor. John was still shaking as he watched Mrs. Smith pull the woolen shawl from around her shoulders and lay it gently across his grandmother's head and shoulders to hide the staring eyes.

"Mrs. Smith!" John's voice was not working properly. "Is she—is she . . . ?"

Mrs. Smith rose to her feet and pulled him close to her, holding him against her warm body and rocking him gently from side to side. For a few moments she said nothing. Then, "It'll be all right. It'll be all right, young John. You see if it won't. You're goin' to be all right."

But John knew, knew by what Mrs. Smith had not said as well as what she had already said. *Gone* meant "dead." His grandmother was dead and Mrs. Smith didn't want to tell him.

His panic had left him, and he was strangely calm. His eyes were tearless and his mouth dry. He felt very, very wide awake, but at the same time felt as though nothing was quite real.

He let himself be held by Mrs. Smith who seemed to be talking to herself as much as to him as she repeated endlessly, "It'll be all right, luv. It'll be all right."

2
Troubled Sleep

They sent John upstairs, not as a punishment but because they said, "It would be better that way." Mrs. Smith promised to bring him some hot cocoa later on. "An' there's a birthday cake on th' kitchen table. Just imagine! On your birthday, young John. Well, well! These things do 'appen. Don't cry, lad. Don't cry."

Now though John did not feel in the least like crying, he was glad Mrs. Smith seemed to think he was. He knew he *ought* to cry. People in books always "wept piteously" when somebody died, and he felt guilty because he could not have wept piteously even if he had tried. He tried to read a book but gave up. Grandma Wilson was dead. His mind could not grasp the idea. Nothing seemed real. What would happen to him? Would they let him stay in the house by himself? Why was he not crying? He felt only fidgety, restless and strange. The whole world was different, dreamlike.

Absent-mindedly he pulled the string up over his head and began to fiddle with the gold ring and the gold locket. The ring was a heavy signet ring so worn that sometimes he thought the letters were not letters at all, but some sort of design. "It's a very old ring," his grandmother had told him. "I don't rightly know how old. It must be worth a lot of money, but *I'll* never sell it. An' don't you ever sell it, John Wilson, until you know what it's about. He owes you that much at least."

Usually he enjoyed dreaming up adventures about both the ring and the locket, but tonight something felt wrong about them. He frowned and tried to concentrate but found his thoughts flitting here and there, sometimes to Grandma Wilson, then to the mysterious sounds of busyness down below and then to what was to happen to him. Then his eyes widened and he stared with open-mouthed dismay at them. "She's dead—an' now I'll never know! She was going to tell me today!"

Fingers of fear stole round his heart. His mother and his father. Were they still alive? Where were they? How would he ever find them? He no longer felt like making up stories. He wanted the truth.

He opened the locket and touched the lock of hair. Whose hair? And the soldier. Was this his father? And if he was, why was there no photo of his mother? Why, oh *why* had his grandmother not told him before? It was wicked to feel angry with someone who had just died, and he was shocked by the strange tumult inside him. He loved Grandma Wilson. He always had loved her, but why . . . ? His thoughts chased themselves in circles.

They were interrupted by knocking at the front door. Footsteps hurried to open it and he heard Mrs. Smith say, "Come in, doctor. She'd gone when we found her. It was young John as really found her, but she was cold already." Their voices grew muffled as the kitchen door closed.

There were other comings and goings. John kept listening but grew confused. Mrs. Smith was saying something about "washing her" and "laying her out," and he supposed that "her" meant his grandmother.

Other phrases floated up from below. There was some talk about "the Methodist minister" and about "the lady almoner." John pricked up his ears when he heard someone say, "No. 'Is muther died when 'e was born, an' we don't know where th' father is. We don't even know if 'is father ever knew about 'im. They was married secretly but the old lady never did believe it, an' 'e was in Paris after the war. There was a rumor 'e was goin' to Canada. That's what the young couple wanted, but Mrs. Wilson lost contact with 'im. 'E was a right nice young feller. It's strange the old lady never took to 'im."

So his mother was dead. John felt no grief, only that it seemed as though pieces of himself were being taken from him one by one so that he felt smaller and less real. His father never knew about him? The thought was terrifying. Would he be in Canada? Or still in Paris? In Canada probably. Deep within him he clung to the thought that his father was still alive. But if he was alive, and if John did find him, how would he convince him he was his son?

Yet as the long minutes passed desperation hardened inside him. However long it took and however much it might cost, he would get to Canada. He stared at the faded brown picture, trying unnecessarily to memorize the thin features he already knew so well. Was it his father? Somehow, somewhere he would find this man. Even if the man wasn't his father, he would know something about him.

Other talk from below alarmed him even more. Words like "orphanage" and "*someone* will 'ave to look after 'im. 'E can't be let on 'is own. Oo's goin' to feed 'im?" made his stomach sink. Clearly he would have to get away if he was going to Canada. But how? He knew he must not stay in Pendleton but must leave early the next morning. How he knew he could not have told you. But he knew. He had a father. His father was not in Paris. He would be in Canada. In any case Canada would be the first place to go.

How much money did it take to get to Canada? He opened

his small money box and counted his savings again. Two pounds, ten shillings and sixpence-ha'penny. That wouldn't get him far. It might not even get him as far as Liverpool. Maybe he could borrow from his friend Peter who had four pounds saved up. Would that be enough? Or could he get a job as a cabin boy on a ship bound for Canada?

More words drifted up from below. "The minister said 'e would 'ave to come at eight-thirty tomorrow morning an' the almoner said it would be all right with 'er. They'll decide what's to be done with young John. Mrs. Wilson's all paid up for the burial. She paid regular into th' club, an' 'er account book is 'ere."

John was having a problem breathing and his head ached. The loss of Grandma Wilson had begun to frighten him. Somehow he would have to make his escape early the next morning before the minister and the lady almoner arrived. The train would be best for Liverpool. If he could get to the station before they found out that he was gone . . .

Footsteps ascended the staircase and Mrs. Smith came through the door. "You must be really 'ungry, luv," she said kindly, setting a cup of steaming cocoa and a slice of his birthday cake beside him. "I can fry you some eggs an' bacon. What d'you want, lad? Is there something you'd really like?"

She sat close beside him on the bed and put her arm round his shoulder. They had always been good friends. Her solidness and warmth comforted him, and he began to cry a little, tears rolling for the first time down his cheeks. He was glad he was normal enough to cry.

"There, there," Mrs. Smith said soothingly. "Don't cry, lad. Somethin's goin' to 'appen. You're goin' to be all right."

John told her he wasn't hungry.

"But you must eat, lad. You 'ave to eat, y' know."

"I'll eat the cake, Mrs. Smith. That'll be enough. I don't feel like eating."

"That's fine, lad. You eat your cake, then. You're goin' to

sleep in our 'ouse tonight. We're not goin' to leave you alone."

Later it seemed strange to be in a double bed in the Smith's back bedroom. John sat up shivering. He would *not* go to sleep. What were lady almoners? What would the Methodist minister say? Determinedly he shook his head. No orphanage. Absolutely no orphanage. Not tomorrow. Not ever. He cried a little at the thought of running away without saying some sort of good-by to his grandmother. But his grandmother had gone. *She hadn't said good-by.* Was it wicked to feel like that? But then there came a more dreadful thought. Perhaps she had gone away *because he was bad.* He was neither clever nor tough. He was wicked. It was all his fault.

He was still fully dressed. His savings were tucked into the top pocket of his blazer, the pocket with the lion on it. He got out of bed still shivering and looked out of the window that looked down on the Smith's yard. He would stay up all night and creep away before the minister and the lady almoner came. He would go to Peter Shufflebotham's house. Peter would lend him money. Then he would go to Victoria Station and get a train for Liverpool.

In spite of his best efforts he slept, lying half across the chair by the window and half across the bed. But in his dream he thought he was still awake and staring through the window. The fog had cleared away and a full moon shone.

John's eyes widened as he saw first a hand, than half an arm, then the top of a bowler-hatted head, and then the head and shoulders of a man climbing over the tall door of the Smith's tiny back yard. And as the man looked up at him John saw that it was Nicholas Slapfoot. John's heart beat sickeningly. Old Nick, as everybody called him, heaved himself to the top of the door and swung first one clubfoot then the other over it, dropped into the yard and perched himself on top of the dustbin.

Nicholas Slapfoot was feared by everyone in Pendleton. He lived in a hut in his scrapyard on the other side of the tall wall that blocked the end of Pimblett's Place. Every day he pulled his cart along the street shouting, "Any old iron? Any old iron! Rags and bottles and any old iron!" haggling with the neighbors for bits and pieces.

Yet people feared him. Some people said he was very rich, but that he was a miser. It was said that one boy who once climbed into his yard never came back. And certainly boys who did go after lost balls told some pretty gruesome stories. Some boys' mothers went to the police. But the sergeant laughed at them and told them there was no such person as Nicholas Slapfoot, and there was certainly no scrapyard on the other side of the wall. All there was was the ruins of an old mill.

John remembered Mrs. Smith talking about it. "The sergeant told 'em, 'Bring me a snapshot of 'im an' then I'll believe in this old Nick of yours.' A snapshot indeed! 'Ood ever 'eard the like! 'Ood 'av time and money to go round takin' snaps of Nicholas Slapfoot? If you ask me, 'im and the' police is in cahoots."

John had his own reason to fear Old Nick. On his twelfth birthday John had accidentally kicked a brand new soccer ball over the wall and into the scrapyard. Peter had let him stand on his shoulders to help him climb the wall. He could not see the ball but neither was there any sign of Nicholas Slapfoot. Taking great care to avoid cutting himself on the broken glass that topped the wall, he eased his way over, turned round so that his back faced the scrapyard and let himself fall.

But by the time he turned round Old Nick had appeared from nowhere. He was standing ten yards away, smiling. In one hand he held an iron crowbar, waving it gently. On the other hand he balanced John's ball which he extended tantalizingly. "Come an' get it, lad," he said. "Come on! Don't be frightened!"

John eyed the ugly little man in his greasy black suit and his dirty red neckerchief. He glanced at the heavy boots with their three-inch soles. Old Nick was moving slowly toward him with the peculiar rolling gait he knew so well, smiling diabolically, his dark eyes gleaming.

Out of the corner of his eye John spotted a heavy oil drum standing against the wall, only a yard to his right. Quickly he scrambled onto it and ignoring the broken glass on the top of the wall heaved himself up. With a roar of rage Nicholar Slapfoot dropped the ball and rushed toward him, the crowbar held high. John never saw the crowbar that flew like a bullet toward him. He was only aware of a tearing pain in his left shoulder, and of the ringing clatter the crowbar made when it fell to the ground.

As he squirmed over the top, he cut his hands and tore his clothes. "I'll get you, John Wilson!" Old Nick shouted hoarsely. "I'm comin' to get you one of these days. Just you wait an' see!" John never saw his soccer ball again.

His shoulder was badly bruised and the skin grazed. It was an injury that never healed but about which he said nothing to Grandma Wilson. And although he was the junior captain of gymnasium, from that day forward John frequently had to clench his teeth to fight back the pain in his shoulder. His coordination remained superb. But his joy in exercising it was gone.

And now in his dream (though as I told you John didn't know it was a dream) Nicholas Slapfoot was grinning evilly at him from the yard below. And though the window was closed, John could hear the words clearly when he spoke. "I'm comin' to get you tomorrow morning, young John." Suddenly the pain in his shoulder became almost unbearable.

He woke, and as the pain subsided he struggled to sit up to make sure it was only a dream. The little back yard was still shrouded in fog. There was no sign either of a moon or of Old Nick. "Thank goodness," John breathed. "This time I really will stay awake."

But try as he might, he could not, and before long he was dreaming a dream that had haunted him for months, a dream of an island where an enraged young dwarf killed another young dwarf and swam away from the island shouting, "Gold,

I will have gold! I go to join the Mystery. Now I shall live forever and hoard more gold than any being who has ever lived."

A voice in the sky cried, "Gold, gold for the Matmon Gold-coffin!"

He hated the dream and struggled to wake. But his brain was sluggish and his limbs were wrapped in the bonds of sleep. So his dreams continued, taking him where he had never been before.

3

John Makes a Dream Journey

Whoomph! John crashed through a thicket to the ground. He was startled, shaken, but unhurt, and bewildered he rose to his feet.

The night air flowed cool through his nostrils and into his lungs. A breeze washed his skin, the same breeze that made surrounding trees sigh to the clear moon above them. He was standing, feet firmly on the ground, at the edge of a forest glade.

Mechanically he began to brush the earth and leaves from his clothes, but as he did so he stopped, startled. He had expected to feel his flannel blazer beneath his brushing fingers, but instead his hand encountered soft velvet. He stared down in amazement at himself. He fingered the outer garment and said, "Just like a girl's gym slip without the pleats. Must be a costume of some sort." Around it was a leather belt. The moonlight made it difficult to determine the color. He thought it might have been light blue. Under it was a silk shirt, the sleeves of which were full and gathered at the wrists.

His legs were bare, the lower legs encased in the crisscross thongs of his sandals. Most startling of all, a heavy bejeweled scabbard hung on his left side from the belt. Cautiously he fingered the hilt. There was a place to grip, encased in smooth leather. The rest of the hilt was jewel encrusted.

He stared at the moon-washed glade in astonishment. "I think I'm dreaming," he breathed. "But everything is so real."

As was his habit in moments of perplexity, he reached for his glasses to clean them. But his glasses were not there. Yet his vision was sharp. Cautiously he felt for the string around his neck. This time his fingers encountered a fine gold chain and he pulled it over his head to inspect it. With a sigh of relief, he saw the ring and the locket hung from it. Puzzled, he replaced it round his neck.

"It is a dream. It must be." He could see wild flowers in the moonlight and knelt to pluck one, to test the dream hypothesis. He felt the stalk between his fingers, heard the snapping sound as he broke it, felt it tickle his nose as he raised it and the unmistakable scent in his nostrils as he breathed in. He threw the flower away and rested his hand on a tree trunk, feeling the rough bark under his palm. "Dreams aren't like this." But if it wasn't a dream—what was it?

As he stared at the hand against the trunk, he made another discovery. He could see, or thought he could see, the bark through his hand. Indeed the harder he stared, the fainter his hand became and the more clearly he could see the bark.

It was the same with his feet, through which he could now perceive earth and flattened leaves. Yet his body and the various parts of him all felt warm and solid. There was nothing ghostly or insubstantial about the way he felt, and certainly he had hit the ground with a wallop on his arrival. But where had he arrived from? His memory was patchy. He could remember nothing just prior to hitting the ground. He knew Grandma

Wilson had died, but he could not recall anything that happened after he had found her. He *was* dreaming. Yet the dream was like no dream he had ever dreamed before.

Whoomph! The sound startled him from his thoughts. Ten yards in front of him on the glade a strange old man lay sprawling on the grass, as though he had been dropped there from the skies. John was too surprised to do anything but stare.

The old man sat up, gaunt and withered, his eyes flashing with annoyance. He snatched a conical cap from the ground and placed it on his head so that his white hair flowed from under it to fall over the shoulders of his dark robes, there to mingle with the foaming cascade of a beard that tumbled over his chest. A wooden staff lay on the ground and he snatched it up and helped himself slowly to his feet, to stand tall and straight.

The added height from his conical cap made him an impressive but slightly comical figure. He raised his staff before him and stared at it wrathfully. "That was not the order I gave you," John heard him mutter. "Now, take me back!"

The staff slowly began to glow, increasing its light until it transformed the figure of the wizard (for that is what John took him to be) into a column of blue fire. Then he disappeared. The space he had occupied was empty. The glade remained as it had been before.

John reached for his glasses again and again found they were not there. "I wonder who that was—"

Whoomph! Once again the wizard lay on the ground at the same spot, his conical hat on one side, his staff on the other. Instantly he sat up. "Well!" Again he snatched up his staff, this time examining it closely. "I don't see—what in the name of sense? . . . Well, let's try again!" He reached for his hat, rose creakily to his feet, straightened his ancient frame, and again ordered the staff to "take him back."

The blue glow increased as it had on the first occasion. Then as it reached a certain shining intensity, the wizard, the staff

and the glow abruptly disappeared. John shook his head in wonder, staring at the empty spot. He felt lonely and hoped the old man would return again. He was not disappointed.

Whoomph! The wizard was back—sprawling on the grass as he had been the first time. John suppressed a snicker and watched the old man, fascinated.

This time the wizard did not stand. He sat up, then for several minutes sat shaking his head. He did not even collect his hat and his staff. "Humph. And humph again," he said. "This is indeed a pretty turn of events." He shook his head several more times. Then he said, "It is indeed. Yes, indeed. I haven't the least idea where I am."

He paused again as he reached for his hat and adjusted it carefully on his head. "I could, I suppose, try for some other place. But I have the distinct feeling, the *very* distinct feeling, that some large hand keeps throwing me back here. If the hand is the hand I'm thinking of . . . Ah, well . . ." He rose to his feet and picked up his staff.

John began to wonder whether he should speak to the wizard, but at that moment he saw the strangest trio approaching from the top of the glade. The dwarflike creatures, which one day he would learn to call Matmon, were accompanied by a female fox—a vixen. A thin circlet of gold crowned each of the Matmon, both of whom were broad, battle-chested and big-bellied. The one wore a long beard, white like the wizard's. He wore a leather jerkin, rough woolen pants and tall leather boots. The other, who looked like his wife, wore a leather dress and tall boots, while her hair was done in two white plaits falling over her shoulders. Five yards from the wizard the trio stopped with their backs turned to John. The wizard regarded them gravely.

The vixen advanced a pace or two. She behaved as though she was the leader of the party. To John's astonishment, either she began to speak or else one of the dwarfs was a ventriloquist. "You must be Mab, the magician," she said politely.

"For my sins, Madam, I am. But who are you?"

"Welcome, Sir Magician. I am the founder of our company. I present to you their majesties King Bjorn I, sovereign of all Matmon, and Queen Bjornsluv, who have joined me in my quest."

The wizard bowed gravely. "It seems that you were expecting me here."

"I summoned you."

The wizard was plainly startled. "*You* summoned *me*? By what power? In whose name?"

The vixen answered, "I had a vision last night in which one appeared to me named Mi-ka-ya, the Changer. He bade me take the stone from my left ear and use it to summon you. There is another stone like it, that hangs from my right ear. Look at it for yourself." Even from where John stood, he could see a strangely luminous stone that seemed to draw light from the moon and glow with soft beauty.

The wizard stooped to examine the stone between his fingers for several minutes. "It is a pross stone," he said slowly as he straightened his back. "A large and powerful one. I think I begin to understand. So you summoned me. I can't say I enjoyed the experience. What is it you want of me?"

King Bjorn spoke for the first time. "I and my wife here, along with a hundred faithful Matmon, have been joined by Folly, king of donkeys. We have renounced the service of the Mystery of Abomination. We travel to an island called Geburah and a lake called Nachash. We wish to serve the Regents. The prophecies say the Regents are to appear there—"

"That is correct."

"—that they will come from a garden inside a tower—"

"That is also correct."

"—and that they will do so at the close of this century."

The wizard's eyes were fixed on King Bjorn. "What is it then that you want from me?"

But it was Queen Bjornsluv who answered him. "We simply

want you to guide us to Lake Nachash and to protect us from the powers and malice of the Mystery."

The wizard sighed, and for many seconds he remained silent. Then he sighed again. "Sit down," he said, easing himself cautiously to the ground himself.

"I wish I could be more sure," he said when once he was seated. "But how certain can anyone be of these prophecies? If they are true, they must be fulfilled during the next three years. Ninety-six years of this century have now passed and as yet there is no sign that the prophecies will be fulfilled. Moreover several things must happen before the Regents can appear."

He frowned and shook his head. "Is there a tower on the Island of Geburah? I haven't been there for a couple of hundred years. But there was no sign of a tower when I was there last. And, about the Mystery, that evil being from whom you are trying to escape. You know better than I his power, his malice and his subtlety. The prophecies say he will attack the island persistently before the Regents come, from the vile swamps he will create along the shore of Lake Nachash. If the prophecies are true, we may have to cross those swamps to get to the lake."

He paused once more and his face was clouded with doubt and sadness. "I have, of course, a personal grief over the prophecies. Their fulfillment means my death. I have lived here since the dawn of Anthropos—for five hundred and ninety-six years. Even though the promise made to me remains unfulfilled, the coming of the Sword Bearer ushers in the time of my death—"

"The Sword Bearer?" King Bjorn interrupted.

"Yes, the Sword Bearer. When he appears we shall know that the rest of the prophecies will come to pass. And it is the Sword Bearer who will slay the prince of goblins, the day the Regents arrive. When the Goblin Prince is slain, the Mystery of Abomination will leave Anthropos—and on that day Mab the seer will die."

For a while nobody spoke. John did not want to intrude, but he felt a strange desire to talk to the little group on the grass. He stepped forward hesitantly and began to walk slowly in the moonlight toward them. As Mab caught sight of him he started, then struggled to his feet, his eyes wide with sudden excitement. He pointed at John and John stopped. John could see his face had become pale.

"There he is!" he cried hoarsely. "There he is! It is the Sword Bearer!"

"I see a shape, a ghostly shape, but that is all I see," Vixenia breathed.

Bjorn and Bjornsluv swung round, but it was plain to John that they could not see him. Mab brushed past them to stand facing John. "You are here, yet you are not here," he breathed, "for your body is transparent. I can also see that you see us, for you are looking me in the eye. Sword Bearer, what is your name? From whence do you come?"

"My name is John Wi—" John began. But he was interrupted by cries almost of terror from the pale lips of Bjorn and Bjornsluv, who heard a voice but saw nothing.

"Remember that voice!" the wizard cried, "you will hear it again! Now I can be sure that the Regents will come to the Island of Geburah."

But John could hear another voice, a familiar voice, the voice of Mrs. Smith. The glade, the wizard, the vixen and the Matmon king and queen began to fade from before his eyes. Mrs. Smith's voice was growing louder. "Young John? No—young John's still asleep, poor little lamb! But come inside!"

Suddenly he was back in the dingy little back bedroom at the Smith's house. Morning sunlight streamed through the window. He sprang to his feet. He had failed to get away in time. It was eight-thirty. He should have left by now. He must lose no more time.

But John Wilson's escape was to prove more difficult than he had anticipated.

4

Slapfoot Comes for John

"Mind you, Nicholas Slapfoot, I must say I'm a bit surprised to see *you* 'ere," Mrs. Smith's voice continued.

Nicholas Slapfoot? Old Nick? John was stunned. What could Old Nick want at the Smiths'? His heart rose slowly toward his mouth.

"It's about young John Wilson. I 'ear 'is gran'mother's passed away. I know I'm not much of a good neighbor. But there comes a time when everyone should giv' an' 'elpin' 'and, an' I think I'd like to give one now."

"Well, let me take you into me parlor—into th' sittin' room then. Parson and th' lady almoner's both in there. They come a little while ago . . ."

John leaped out of bed in a panic. His shoulder was throbbing furiously, but he gave it no thought. What in the world did Old Nick want? Suddenly his danger seemed to have doubled. He would have to move fast. But how could he get past the parlor door without being detected? He crept to the top of the stairs, still fully dressed and, checking to make sure his money was in his top pocket, listened cautiously to what was happening below.

The voices, though slightly muffled, were still clearly audible. And they were talking about him. A woman's voice was saying, "It's very sad, Reverend, but there's almost nowhere I can place him right now. Obviously something has to be done. I gather there are no relatives we can contact."

Mrs. Smith interjected. "This 'ere's Mr. Nicholas Slapfoot—'im as runs th' scrapyard. Excuse me interruptin' but 'e says 'e wants to 'elp."

"Er, good morning, Mr. er—"

"Slapfoot's the name, Reverend, an' I'm real sorry to 'ear what's 'appened. It's a pleasure to meet you both. I always did say neighbors was for 'elpin' an' if money can 'elp, I've got plenty."

"Well, that's very generous of you, I'm sure, Mr. Flatfoot." The minister had a high-pitched, preachy voice. "But I don't think we will need to avail ourselves of your generosity. There must be funds available somewhere."

There was a pause, and then the lady almoner said quietly but firmly, "There are no funds, Reverend. As I told you, I have contacted all the available sources in the city. There is still what we used to call the poorhouse—but he's only a child. And there's a matter of his education. The local orphanages are full, or so they claim. Even county funds are no longer available."

" 'Ow would five 'undred pounds 'elp? 'Ere's th' money in me own 'and. Take it an' count it for yourselves. Or is me money not good enough?" Nicholas was almost shouting.

John heard Mrs. Smith (who must have been listening from the kitchen door) give a loud gasp. In the front room there was only stunned silence.

"I know a special school on th' other side of Manchester. Friend o' mine runs it," Old Nick continued. Clearly he had everybody's attention now. "The discipline's a bit on th' firm side, but five 'undred pounds would give 'im food, board an' a good ed-you-KAY-shun for three years. I'll even take 'im there meself. It's not often I do good, but I want to do it for young John . . ."

"Mrs. Smith!" the lady almoner called. "Mrs. Smith, would you be kind enough to come and join us for a few minutes? I feel we need your advice. You know John better than any of us."

John heard Mrs. Smith scurry from the kitchen door into the parlor and close the door behind her. He was absolutely sure Nicholas Slapfoot was up to no good. The parlor door was now closed and he realized he could creep past it unseen.

Holding his breath, he started down the stairs. He stopped momentarily when a stair creaked, but he felt certain no one had heard. He crept in perfect silence past the parlor, silently opened the front door that led to the street and crept outside. It was a clear day. The sky was blue, and a wind was blowing. His heart suddenly lifted. He turned to close the front door as quietly as he could, but at that point tragedy struck. The wind pulled the door out of his hand and slammed it shut with a sound that seemed to John like a clap of thunder. He turned and ran for all he was worth for Ellor Street.

By the time he reached the corner voices were calling him back. "It's all right, young John. There's nothing to be scared of, lad. You're goin' to be all right." That was Mrs. Smith.

And at the same time the reverend was squeaking, "Come back, my boy, come back! No one is going to hurt you."

But worst of all was Nicholas Slapfoot, "Young John, young John Wilson! I said I'd come for you, an' I'm comin'. I'm comin' right now!"

John turned the corner and ran so that his feet seemed not to touch the ground. Peter's! Peter Shufflebotham's! He had to get to Peter's house for the four pounds. Peter would understand. He dodged down a side street and peeped back round the corner. No one had so far reached the corner of Pimblett's

Place and Ellor Street. He still had a chance if he ran fast enough.

In and out, down entries and among the winding streets he ran. At last he was hammering at Peter's door. "Mrs. Shufflebotham! Mrs. Shufflebotham! Is Peter there?"

The door opened and a fat lady looked at him in amazement. "John Wilson! Whatever's the matter, lad? There's no need to carry on like that!"

But at that moment John heard the voice of Nicholas Slapfoot. "There 'e is! 'Urry up, Reverend. 'E's right 'ere, the mean little brat!"

John turned, astounded to see how fast the cripple could move. How had he known where to look for him? John was sure he had shaken all his pursuers off. In the distance he could hear the high-pitched squeak of the minister, "Wait, oh, do wait! I can go no farther!"

John certainly did not wait but ran with all his might, running faster than he had ever run in races for his school or his city, dodging down side lanes, entries, climbing over walls as the cries died down slowly behind him. He was breathless but thinking clearly. He was now near the Cross Lane end of Ellor Street where his favorite secondhand bookstore was located. If only he could get inside it unobserved and hide among the bookshelves, he could recover his breath and have time to think. He would not be far from the bus stop for Victoria Station.

When he reached the bookstore the door was open, and he slipped inside unobserved by his friend Mr. Bloomenthal, the owner. Quietly he made his way to the shelves at the back of the store, pulled a book off the shelf and did all he could to quiet his breathing.

In the bookstore there was silence. John's heart began to beat more slowly. The pain in his shoulder had died away. He stared unseeingly at his book, listening intently. Minutes, seeming like hours, crawled by punctuated only by the occasional shuffling steps of Mr. Bloomenthal (who was still unaware of

John's presence) and the sounds of books being pulled and pushed on bookshelves. John's legs ached from standing so still.

When the door opened again, the bell rang loudly, and an agonizing jolt of pain shot through John's shoulder, causing him to drop the book he was holding. Old Nick's voice sounded, "We're lookin' for young John Wilson. 'Is granny died last night an' 'e run away. We know 'e sometimes comes 'ere an' we wondered if . . ."

"Eee, I'm right sorry to 'ear it. Nice young lad. Often comes 'ere but 'e's not 'ere now. Leastways I've not seen 'im. Shop's empty as far as I know . . ."

But at that moment John sneezed, and both men moved toward the shelves at the back of the shop. In panic John turned to see a stairway leading down to a cellar, and with his heart beating wildly he followed the steps into a dimly lit room filled with piles of unsorted books. He could hear the two men approaching the top of the stairs. The pain in his shoulder was excruciating. A door at the back of the cellar seemed his only hope of escape and he seized the handle. It vibrated startlingly in his hand, but he turned it and advanced in desperation, suddenly finding himself surrounded by strange blue light. He closed the door behind him.

Everything changed. His pain was gone. It was as though he had been dreaming and that now he had suddenly woken up. Or as though he had been awake but had walked into a dream.

His panic melted and in its place came the kind of feeling you get when you are inside a very large cathedral (if you've ever been in one). Although he could still faintly hear the voices of Slapfoot and the shopkeeper they sounded as though they were so far away that they no longer had anything to do with him.

His heart was still beating and he had the feeling that he ought to keep still and quiet, not because he was scared that someone might find him, but because he was in an important place, the kind of place where you are supposed to stand at attention and not move.

In spite of the blue light (a light that was inconceivably lovely) he could see nothing, nothing, that is, except the light itself. Yet he knew without being told that he was standing in a very large place. He could not even see his own feet, though he could feel vibrations on the floor beneath him.

Then came the gentlest rumble of thunder, the thunder of a quiet voice speaking. "Welcome, John Wilson. I am glad you have come."

To his surprise John began to cry. At least tears began to flow down his cheeks silently and his nose began to run a little. He fumbled for his handkerchief and used it.

"Are you afraid, John Wilson?" The thunder boomed majestically, echoing and re-echoing.

It was a thunder you had to answer. John found he was trembling, just like the floor to which his feet were rooted. "Yes. No—I mean, I don't know." And, silently, he cried more, releasing tears that were filled with relief and with other feelings he could never have named. He was afraid with a kind of fear he had never felt before. Yet in spite of his fear and his flowing tears he felt sure that all was well and that this beautiful, terrible place was also a place of safety.

"Why are you crying?"

"They're going to put me in some sort of orphanage and I don't want to go. Me granma died last night." These were the only reasons he could think of, but he was not sure that they explained his flood of tears. His handkerchief was getting wet and soggy, and he held it loosely in his trembling hand.

Suddenly he felt it being taken away from him, though he could detect neither movement nor sound around him. Indeed he could still see nothing except the impenetrable blue light. Then warmth touched both his cheeks.

"What. . . ?"

"This is my bottle. You can feel it against your face," the

thunder rumbled. "I am collecting your tears in it."

"Me tears? Why?" The words had slipped out of his mouth before he could stop them.

"Your tears are important to me. I intend to keep them so that they will never be forgotten."

There was a long pause. He did not dare to ask more. If anything the strange words made John's tears flow faster, and yet the warmth against his cheeks was comforting. Slowly he became aware that the rest of his face was dry and that the warmth was gently moving up his cheeks, drying his face as it did so.

"Who are you, . . . please, sir?"

"I am the Changer, the Unchangeable Changer. I am the Beginner-Who-Never-Began." The words made no sense, and John dared not ask for an explanation but trembled all the more. "You now know your mother died, John Wilson. Yet of your father I will not speak at present."

The warmth was just below his eyes now, and though he broke into a smile even at the word *father* he could feel that his tears, if it were possible, were flowing faster than ever.

"When . . . I mean, when will you speak of him, sir, . . . please?"

"When the time is fully come," the Changer rumbled.

For a moment John thought of his Grandma's words, "When you're old enough." But the Changer's words sounded different. They made him a little more certain, more hopeful, that his father would be found. But doubts still lingered. He was suddenly conscious of the string round his neck.

"Please, sir, will I have to go to the orphanage? I don't want to. I really don't. Please, sir, if you don't mind."

"That is why I called you here," the thunder replied.

John wanted to say, "But you didn't call me. I just came." Instead he said, "You mean I'll have to go back to them? I don't mind Mr. and Mrs. Smith (though Mr. Smith gets drunk every Friday night) but that Slapfoot . . ."

"No. You will not go there. You will not return to Pendelton for many years."

"What's going to happen to me?" He began to do his best to speak "proper" English.

There was a long silence. John began to fear that the Changer might be angry with him. But after a few moments the low rumbling thunder continued. "You are going to learn about things that can be changed and about other things that cannot. There are things that I change and others that I do not change. Perhaps I will let you join me in changing some things I intend to change."

John felt bewildered. He was trying hard, desperately hard to understand what the Changer was talking about, but in the end he sighed and shook his head.

"Please, sir." His voice was unsteady. "Please, sir, I don't understand." He was working hard on his accent, though the thunder didn't seem posh in any way. But school habits died hard.

"No, John Wilson. The time has not yet come for you to understand."

Again there was a pause. John began to feel a little less afraid. "Where will I live? Who will look after me?"

"I will look after you. As for the place where you will live for a while, I took you there last night."

"You took me . . . ?"

"You thought you were dreaming," the thunder echoed, "but as you will see the moment you go through the door, you were really awake."

"The door? The door behind me?" John could still faintly hear Nicholas Slapfoot. "He's in there, that Old Nick . . ."

"There is no door behind you now. It was a door I made for you. No other eyes could have seen it. When the mist ahead of you clears you will see two lines of cherubim and beyond them a door. At the foot of the door lies a sword. Pick it up, open the door and go through it."

John took a deep breath. "Please, sir, what's on . . ."

The rumble of thunder began almost as soon as he had opened his mouth, "You will see when you open it."

John had the feeling the Changer was smiling and he laughed a little nervously. "Sir, I'm scared. Not very scared. Just a bit."

The air around him was clearing and the warmth was gone from his cheeks. His flow of tears had ceased and his face was dry. He could see that a floor of the palest blue marble was spreading outward in a circle around him as the blue mist withdrew. Fear seized him. "Sir," he shouted, "are you going away?"

"No," the soft thunder rumbled from somewhere close to him. "You will not hear me often, and you will certainly not see me. But I will always be near you."

The circle of marble was now huge and John began to wonder how long it would take to cross it.

"Sir, what do cherubim look like?"

The thunder sounded more distant, and John felt that in spite of his promise the Changer was leaving him.

"Start walking forward, John Wilson!" the voice was more distant yet.

Tremblingly John began to place one foot after another. He was still shaking and found that he was sweating too. A sudden thought came to him and he shouted, "Sir, you didn't forget your bottle, did you?"

Then he heard the warmth of a thunderous laugh that seemed to fill the universe with merriment, and though it grew ever fainter he found that without lifting him up from the marble floor, the laughter caught him up into itself. He began to run, laughing as he did so, laughing helplessly and stopping from time to time to hug himself with inexplicable joy, before running on again, laughing and knowing that the laughter was a kind of link between them, a link which would never be broken.

At first he hardly noticed the two columns of flaming fountains, lined like rows of burning poplars on either side of him. When he did so he realized that under normal circumstances he would have been terrified. But the terror had been burned out of him for the time being and he ran forward, still laughing, between the burning giants.

The door was ahead of him. He could see it clearly now. It was a small door, hardly big enough even for a boy to get through, and like everything else around, it glowed with pale blue light.

Now he had reached it. "Pick up the sword!" the mighty voice of the nearest cherub called.

He had almost stepped on it in his mad rush. It lay at his feet, its handle jewel encrusted and its blade smooth and shining. It was heavy to lift. But the door was in front of him, and he leaped forward, the sword in his right hand. He seized the handle and turned it, lunging forward into total darkness.

5
The Lord Lunacy

He was sure that for an instant there had been light as he came through the door. But it was certainly pitch-black now. Blackness enveloped him. Sword in hand, he leaned back for a moment against the door through which he had come, wondering what he was to do next. A faint current of air on his face told him that he was under the open sky. Cautiously he extended his right foot and slithered across the ground, which proved to be rough and stony.

Holding his left arm across his face as protection, he took a cautious step forward. So far so good. But where was he? Where was he supposed to go? The Changer had told him nothing. He extended his foot again to test the ground in front of him, and this time sensed earth, stones and dead leaves.

A sudden thought crossed his mind. Could he be in the woods he had dreamed about? It was a pleasing idea, and it injected hope into the situation. If he was in the woods he dreamed about, then he was the Sword Bearer. And if he was the Sword Bearer, something was certain to happen before long. He extended his left hand straight ahead into the darkness, groping to find what was ahead. Two more steps and his fingers brushed something solid. A tree trunk.

A sudden stirring of the breeze brought to his ears the unmistakable sound of swaying branches and rustling leaves. He was in a forest. But was it the forest of his dream? He caught his breath as yet another idea occurred to him. If he were in *that* forest, if he were the Sword Bearer, *then there would be a scabbard on his left side,* a scabbard into which he could insert the sword the Changer had given him.

For a moment he did nothing. For some reason he could not have explained, he wanted the scabbard to be there. But what if he was about to be disappointed?

He felt for his blazer, and his heart leapt as he discovered he was no longer wearing it. Instead of the familiar flannel, his fingers encountered the velvet. Then as his downward-groping hand encountered the rough solidity of the scabbard, he gave a cry of delight. Trembling, he lifted the sword and in the darkness both felt and heard it slide into the scabbard with a ringing *shish* and a click. He was exultant. He *was* in the same forest. And he was the Sword Bearer. Excitedly he fingered his velvet clothing. Once again his legs were bare except for the long crisscrossed thongs of his sandals.

Both his hands were now free. Holding them in front of him to protect his face from tree branches, he continued to make his way cautiously forward. A twig cracked loudly and he stopped. He glanced around, uncertain what to do. No twig had cracked under his own feet. The sound had come from his right. The wind had dropped and silence and blackness still wrapped him round. He could hear the air in his own nostrils.

Yet he knew he had heard the twig crack. What was it? He strained his ears and eyes. He thought he could make out the dim shape of trees, but he could not be sure.

"Hello! Is anyone there?" he said softly. There was no response. Gathering his courage he called out more firmly, "Hello! Hello there! Where are you?" But his words were swallowed by the oppressive stillness.

After a few seconds he groped his way forward again. From time to time the breeze stirred the leaves around him and he strained his ears to distinguish any other sounds of movement. Once he tripped over a root, stubbing his toe and narrowly avoided falling. Then suddenly he froze. He was sure this time. Something or someone *was* following him. A cold trickle of perspiration made its way slowly down his back.

"I can hear you!" he called out loudly. "Who are you?"

For a moment nothing happened. Then his legs doubled from a hard blow to the backs of his knees. A heavy mass struck his chest and with a startled yell he crashed backward to the ground, the breath knocked out of him by his fall and by the ponderous weight on top of him. Hands seized his arms and legs, and course ropes bound them painfully together. He could hear the heavy breathing of more than one assailant and struggled fiercely at the feel of the ropes. But his struggles were useless. With surprising efficiency his captors quickly trussed him into helpless inactivity.

"Light the lamp!" a gruff voice ordered. There was the sharp sound of a flint being struck. Then a second or two later the soft yellow light of an oil lantern lit the long beards and the rugged faces of two Matmon. They stared at him from above, John on his back, and the Matmon standing beside him, one of them holding the lamp high.

Bildreth knelt beside John, fumbling with John's belt and pulling belt, scabbard and sword from him. John's lips were pressed tightly together. He was both frightened and enraged. He never knew what made him say it, but suddenly the words came with surprising firmness and clarity, "The Sword Bearer and his sword cannot be separated for long. And those who try to separate them meet an ugly fate!"

Bildreth struck him sharply across the mouth, glaring hatred. Strange as it may seem, the blow drove John's fear away. Though he was bound and helpless, he felt a burning rage. He licked his lips, tasting blood that had already begun to trickle from the side of his mouth. Again he found himself talking, wondering where the impressive words came from. "He who strikes the Sword Bearer will encounter the wrath of the Changer."

Bildreth's arm shot skyward to strike him again, but before the blow could descend, the lantern bearer seized his wrist. "He is bound, Bildreth. And he is the Sword Bearer. Beware lest wrath overtake us. It is enough that we have bound him and taken his sword. Those were our orders. Beware that we meddle not with the great powers. The Lord Lunacy wishes only to speak with him."

Bildreth snatched his wrist from his companion. But he made no further attempt to strike John. Placing his fingers in his mouth, he whistled piercingly. "Folly!" he cried, "come hither!"

John stared at his captors. He could not remember seeing either of them in his dreams. The lamplight shone on their yellow leather jerkins and their bottle-green stockings. Their hair and beards were dark. Bildreth was lean and his mouth, twisted and cruel. The lantern bearer was heavy, his stomach ballooning ahead of him. It was the lantern bearer's weight that had pinned John to the ground.

The sound of trotting hooves drew nearer and suddenly a donkey's gray muzzle loomed over John's head. The donkey eyed him with a mournful expression. "I must not presume to question the judgment of the Lord Gutreth," it said in deep and fruity tones, turning to the Matmon with the lantern, "but discretion—ah, I mean—ah—mistakes, as it were—if you take my meaning. No offense?"

"You do what we say and you ask no questions, King Folly," said Gutreth the lantern bearer with a smile. "Pick him up,

Bildreth, and place him gently on Folly's back."

With surprising ease Bildreth lifted him, dumping him face downward across the donkey's back. His face pressed on the buckle of one of the donkey's saddlebags. He felt both uncomfortable and desperately unsafe. It was hard to breathe and he had the sensation that he would slide to the ground any minute. It was frightening to have no hands with which to hold on.

The donkey repeated endlessly, "Quite so. Quite so. We must respect authority. I know that it is foolish of me even to mention the matter. But we must not put our heads into a noose, must we? Yes, yes, I know. Who am I to make suggestions? Ah, well. Such is life. Young heads on old shoulders. A stitch in time. It's an ill wind, etc., etc., etc."

At any other time John might have been amused by the donkey's endless patter. But at the moment he was more concerned about his extreme discomfort and the helpless sense of being about to tumble off the donkey's back.

By a miracle he did not slide off as they made their way by lantern light along the twisting pathway that led upward. Only Folly the donkey spoke, in a dreary muttered soliloquy which the Matmon ignored. "Matters too high for me, of course. Humpty Dumpty and all that. How great shall be the fall of it. Pride goeth—and so on. I was a fool to say anything . . ."

At length they stopped and Bildreth lifted John from Folly easily, propping him in a sitting position against a tree. He then began rummaging through the panniers at Folly's side. But a startled cry from Gutreth arrested his movements.

"Hsst!" he cried, pointing. "Is it another, or is it the same? What magic is this?" John followed the direction of the Matmon's finger and perceived in the dimness just beyond the sphere of the lantern light a flat rectangular object that stood alone and erect among the trees. Gutreth approached it cautiously, holding the lantern high. It was a flat gray door bearing the number 345. John could see it was a door because it bore a handle. No wall surrounded it. Nothing appeared to support it. It led nowhere but stood erect like a sentry on duty.

"It is the same," Gutreth said, turning to John. "It bears the same numbers. What is it doing here?" He stared hard at John. "You drew it here by the power of the Changer, didn't you?" he said, his voice heavy with fear.

John said nothing. He had no idea what the door was, but he could tell that Gutreth was worried. "You came through that door—came through it from nowhere. What lies beyond it?"

So that was it. Could it be? He had scarcely looked at the other side of the door through which he had passed and had never seen the outside of it.

"What lies beyond it, Sword Bearer?"

John was about to reply, "The Changer is on the other side of that door"—but he changed his mind. "It would be simple enough to find out. Why don't you open it?"

Even in the lantern light he could see the pallor on Gutreth's face. Still with his hands on the saddlebag Bildreth laughed. "Afraid, my friend?" he said, addressing Gutreth. Nothing was said for a moment. Then slowly Bildreth withdrew his hands from the bag, flipped the leather cover into place and walked to the door.

He hesitated for a moment, then gripped the handle with both hands. At once he screamed and his hands flew into the air as he fell backward to writhe on the ground crying, "My hands! My hands! Oh, Mi-ka-ya! My hands!" But John was staring at the door. For a moment it seemed to wave like a curtain blowing in a breeze. Then it faded from view and disappeared. No sign of it remained.

Bildreth's hands were badly burned, and for several minutes Gutreth, still pale and shaken, anointed them with ointment, binding them with linen bandages from one of Folly's saddlebags. Then taking an axe, he strode up an incline behind John. Bildreth followed him, cursing softly as he looked at his bandaged hands.

John stared at Folly. "Who are they?" he said, "And what do

51

they want with me? Where are we, anyway?"

"Where are we? Of course. Exactly. We are—how shall I put it—in a wood, among trees, if you know what I mean—"

"Yes, but what place is this? Does it have a name?"

"Ah yes, a name, how stupid of me. My poor scattered brain. A name you say. The name is Anthropos. You have heard of Anthropos, no doubt?"

John shook his head. "No, but it doesn't matter. What are they going to do with me?"

The donkey rolled his eyes, waggled his ears and sighed. "Wheels within wheels. Plots and counterplots—if you follow me." (John didn't, but he said nothing, hoping that Folly would eventually get to the point.) "We are—how shall I put it—reverting back to Mi-ka-ya, the Changer. Bildreth and Gutreth are against the idea. The Lord Lunacy told them you were coming and told them to capture you, shut you in the cave just above us. They are to cover the mouth of the cave with branches to conceal it. Lord Lunacy wants to talk to you."

He rolled his eyes once more. "We're all kings, you know. I am King Folly, king of all donkeys. My stupidities entitle me to the high dignity. Bildreth and Gutreth are not of royal descent. But they are—how shall I say it—entitled to their opinions. Don't you agree?"

John said nothing. After a moment Folly said quietly, "I will tell Vixenia and King Bjorn of your whereabouts. Have no fear. You will be rescued."

There was no time for further conversation for the Matmon returned. This time Gutreth lifted John and within two minutes he had been bundled into a rocky opening in the hillside. Both Matmon remained silent. Gutreth released his bonds and the two withdrew, taking their lantern with them. A heavy boulder was rolled against the opening, and for a few minutes John could see chinks of light around it and hear the muffled sounds of the Matmon as they sought to disguise the cave mouth. Then came darkness and silence.

John scrambled to his feet, rubbing his wrists and ankles gently. He groped his way to the cave mouth, felt the coldness of the rock in the entrance and traced the outline of the huge boulder that was rolled against it. For a while he strained his ears for sounds of the Matmon and Folly. But he could hear nothing. Then straining his muscles to the utmost he pushed against the boulder. It rocked a little. Again he pushed and yet again. He began to perspire and breathe hard. Then grunting desperately he strained until his head and heart were pounding. But he could move it no farther. The task was beyond him.

Slowly he groped his way farther into the cave. In a few minutes he would explore it by feel. For the moment he would rest. He squatted on the dry sandy floor and leaned against a smooth wall. Curiously, he was not disheartened. His rage had subsided. Somehow Bildreth's injury at the mysterious door, coupled with Folly's remarks, had heartened him. He was not glad that Bildreth had been hurt, but encouraged to know the Changer's power was near. Warm memories of the Changer flooded his mind.

His old shoulder injury, the injury inflicted by Old Nick's crowbar, began to trouble him again. A throbbing ache grew in his shoulder until he winced with pain. Suddenly light danced faintly before his eyes. As he stared, it took shape, forming a tall column, then resolving itself into the giant robed figure of a hideously beautiful man. His deathly pallor illuminated the floor and walls of the cave. He was exceedingly tall so that his feet rested below the floor, and his head and shoulders could be seen through the rock above the ceiling of the cave. "I am the Lord Lunacy, disturber of moonlight." The voice was cool and musical.

John said nothing. He could feel the slow thumping of his heart, another trickle of cold sweat down his back and the awful stabbing of pain in his left shoulder. He stared at the strange figure before him, wondering why it seemed as though life was being slowly pressed out of him. His mind began to freeze. A power greater than his own was taking control of his thoughts and feelings.

"I am indeed sorry about all that has happened to you," the cool voice continued. "You have had a difficult time—a *very* difficult time."

Suddenly as the words left the lips of the Lord Lunacy, John began to feel sorry for himself. Yes, he had indeed had a difficult time.

"It's such a pity about the Changer," Lord Lunacy went on.

"A pity? What do you mean?"

"Well, he doesn't exist, you know. There *is* no Changer."

"But I've met him! I heard his voice," John said, struggling against the power.

"Yes, yes, of course. You've met him and you've heard his voice. It must have seemed very real to you." The voice of the Lord Lunacy seemed compassionate and concerned.

"Oh, it did! It felt wonderful!"

There was a pause. Then, "It was only a dream, you know."

John's heart sank. "It didn't seem like a dream," he said anxiously. "I mean it was so—well, like you said, so real."

"That's the sad part about it. You see, it wasn't real. It was just a dream. I know all about dreams. They belong to the night, you see, and I'm the ruler of night."

John remained silent, his thoughts powerfully shaped by the being before him. The Changer not real? What was real? Dismay softened his bones and weakened his muscles.

"You're angry with the Changer, aren't you?" the Lord Lunacy asked quietly.

"Angry? No. I'm not angry. What makes you say that?"

"It's natural that you should be angry with him."

John struggled to resist feelings that threatened to sweep him into darkness.

"You just said he didn't exist. How can I be angry with him if he doesn't exist? You can't be angry with someone who's only a dream!"

"You certainly can. And you are, aren't you? Don't be ashamed of it. Anger is normal. It's human."

He felt trapped. The throbbing of his shoulder was almost unbearable.

"I'm not angry!" he almost yelled.

"And yet you shout."

"But if he doesn't *exist* . . ." His voice was even louder.

"It makes no difference. Let yourself be angry with him— *even if he doesn't exist!* What does it matter whether he exists or not? The dream creature has given you false hope. It has pretended to comfort you, then thrown you to the wolves." Furiously John struggled to cling to what he knew was true. The Lord Lunacy reached down a cold white hand and touched his forehead, and at his touch something exploded inside him and John's confusion left him. Everything was revealed in clear lines. The Changer did not exist. And John *was* angry. A few moments before he had felt almost stifled. Now a cold rage filled him, a rage with the nonexistent Changer, with his dead grandmother, with his father and his captors.

"He abandoned you, of course."

"Who abandoned me?"

"Your father. He didn't want you. He was and is an irresponsible drunk. You hate him."

"Yes." Of course he did. Why had he never realized it before?

"You despise him."

"Yes!"

There was a pause. John's heart beat with fierce exultation.

"In fact you hate him!"

"Yes."

"You never want to see him. You will not seek him."

"No, I won't."

"Then pull the chain from your neck and throw the ring and locket away."

Mechanically John groped round his neck. He was mildly surprised to find the string had become a fine gold chain.

Pulling it over his head, he looked dully at what had once been his most treasured possession.

"Give it to me!" John looked up at the specter. Its hand was extended to him. For the first time he noticed that the white glow was tinged faintly with yellow green. John's head began of itself to shake from side to side. He didn't want it to, but it was shaking. The shaking would not stop. Did he imagine it— or did a look of rage flash across the face of the Lord Lunacy? Slowly John replaced the chain round his neck. He had really wanted to give it to him and could not quite understand what was happening.

The Lord Lunacy smiled slowly. "You know it is bad to hate and despise people? You despised the boys in Ellor Street, didn't you? You thought you were better than them. You hated them, didn't you? Face it. You are evil."

John said nothing. The pain in his shoulder, as fierce as ever, had become strangely pleasurable. The Lord Lunacy continued. "So this means you are bad."

Bad? So he was bad. But after all, what did it matter? What had he to lose? In fact, why not be bad? A feeling of strength grew inside him. It felt good to be bad.

"You are feeling the power of evil within you. You always were evil. But until now you didn't know it."

Still John did not speak. His exultation did not change, even though the Lord Lunacy's words grated on him. He stared at the dead white figure before him, wondering vaguely how his head and shoulder could be seen through the rock when there was no hole. Solid things were not solid after all. The figure before him seemed to switch itself off, just like a light bulb, and velvet blackness touched his eyes again. The presence was gone. Yet John was gripped with a wild exhilaration. He was evil. It was a new sensation to him, a sensation he had never before dared to let himself feel. He was different. What adventures awaited him now? The pain in his shoulder slowly subsided to a dull and throbbing ache.

6
Death Sentence

The sun's glare dazzled John. He squinted at the strange trio in front of him, King Bjorn and Queen Bjornsluv seated on boulders, and Vixenia, her brush curled neatly around her feet. On either side of him stood two Matmon with swords. A fly persisted in buzzing round his head, settling annoyingly on his face from time to time so that he was obliged to wave it away constantly.

To his left, on slightly lower ground in the forest glade, an assortment of Matmon sat on the grass and watched them. John had looked eagerly for Folly, king of donkeys, but Folly was not there. He realized with dismay that his rescue from the cave was not through Folly's intervention.

It had been a huge relief when first he had heard the sound of the boulder being removed. It had been glorious to be hit by a burst of sunlight from the cave's mouth. But his rescuers had been surly and uncommunicative. Hungry and thirsty, he had asked them about food and drink, but they had ignored him, bustling him unceremoniously along a narrow forest trail. Three hours later they had reached the very forest glade he had dreamed about in Pendleton.

"You say you are the Sword Bearer," Bjorn said in measured tones.

"Yes, I am."

"Then where is your sword?"

Out of the corner of his eye, John had seen Bildreth's bitter twisted face among the little assembly on his left.

"The one you call Bildreth took it from me. He took the scabbard and the sword—and my belt."

Bildreth sprang to his feet, his thin lips curling in a sneer. "He lies! He had no sword—"

"Silence!" Bjorn shouted. "You have already spoken. You will not speak again unless you are bidden, Bildreth son of Baldon!"

Then turning to John, he asked the same question, "Where is your sword."

John felt sorry for himself, resentful and a little frightened. "He took it," he said, "I'm not lying. There was another one with him called Gutreth. He told him to take it from me. Gutreth said I was the Sword Bearer and it would be safer if they took my sword."

Again Bildreth stood, crying in agitation, "It is false! It is false! I was alone when I captured him. I, Bildreth alone, subdued him! Alone I imprisoned him in the cave! I speak truth!"

Bjorn's face was purple. "Silence, I said! You will be sealed in the cave yourself if you speak out unbidden again."

Queen Bjornsluv's merry eyes were fixed on John's face. "He has the same voice," she said.

"And the same shape," Vixenia barked.

"—and he has not the face of one who is accustomed to lying. Where were you going, young one, when you were captured?" Bjornsluv continued.

"I don't know."

"You don't know? Explain yourself," demanded the king.

"I came through the door. When I opened it, it was dark, very dark. I couldn't see anything and I had no idea where I was. I thought it *might* be here, so I felt for the scabbard—"

"You came through *what* door?"

"Oh—er, from the Changer—"

"You say you came from the Changer?"

John hesitated. *Was* there a Changer? The Lord Lunacy had said it was a dream. Was everything a dream? Was he dreaming now? If he was, then he was dreaming that his mouth was parched. He was also dreaming that he was sick with hunger, that he felt dizzy and confused, and that a fly kept landing on his face. He waved it away angrily. "I don't know."

"You don't know?"

"I *thought* it was the Changer," John sighed. "It was beautiful. But maybe I was dreaming."

"What is your name?" King Bjorn asked.

John thought quickly. He knew his life might depend on the answer. "I am John the Sword Bearer," he replied.

"So you are John the Sword Bearer without your sword," Bjorn returned evenly.

"It was stolen from me."

"And you were unable to defend yourself, Sword Bearer."

"I told you already," John said, "I didn't even know where I was. It was pitch-black. Two of them knocked me down before I knew what was happening. The one called Gutreth weighs half a ton." Suddenly he felt very sorry for himself. "Besides, I'm only a boy," he pouted.

Bjorn's voice was cold. "I have no idea what a *boy* is. But I know you are a Sword Bearer without a sword. A magical Sword Bearer unable to defend himself against an ordinary Matmon. Not a spy, of course. Not a spy acting under orders from the Mystery of Abomination."

His rugged face was set in stone. A breeze sighed through the boughs of the surrounding trees and rippled in fluffy moving waves of light across the grasses of the meadow. The faces of the watching Matmon and animals were intent on the six participants in the trial. Far above them a summer cloud of cotton wool floated toward the sun.

Bjornsluv touched her husband's hand. "My lord must not be too hard on him. I perceive from his face that though he may be troubled, he has been reared in truth." Turning to John she said, "Where is your home, John the Sword Bearer?"

John sighed. "It's—it used to be—in Pendleton."

"It *used* to be?"

"Well—my granma died last night—at least I think it was last night, and they were going to send me away, so—"

"So you ran away."

"Yes, how did you know?"

Bjornsluv smiled. "And where is your grandmother's home?"

"Er—Pimblett's Place, Pendleton." He had the feeling that the words would be meaningless and he could see from their faces that they had not understood. "Pendleton—" he said, hopelessly. "It's in Lancashire. You know—in *England*."

"These words are empty. Such places do not exist." Bjorn's face was still set and to John he suddenly seemed stupid. After all he was small and fat.

"Idiot!" he hissed. "Of course they exist! I was born there. It's where I lived. What do you know of geography?" A surge of the exultation he had felt in the cave began to rise inside him. He felt contempt for the three in front of him and for the guards at his side. The summer cloud crossed the face of the sun, and a shadow swept over them all.

Bjorn's eyes burned with anger. His tone was carefully controlled, but his voice shook a little. "I know only that the young respect the old, and that death awaits spies from the Mystery of Abomination."

For the first time John saw beyond Vixenia and the Matmon king and queen the sinister figure of a hooded Matmon shar-

pening a heavy bronze axe on a whetstone beside a low tree
stump.

"The block is prepared," Bjorn said. "The teeth of an executioner's axe bite keenly, and young though you may be, your
own head will be severed from your body if you prove to be a
spy from the Mystery. And if you are nothing more than an
impudent runaway, you will be lashed with whips."

John's heart beat faster. Anger exploded inside him. He
could feel his upper lip curling. He said nothing, but held his
head high. Bjorn continued. "Tell us where you are from!"

The rage inside him came to a boil. His head swam and the
scene before him seemed shrouded in red curtains. Suddenly
he lost control. "You idiots!" he screamed. "You stupid, ignorant idiots! I go to Salford Grammar School! I come from *Pendleton!* I can't help it if you don't know where it is! Don't ask
me how I got here. I don't know! I had come the night before
in a dream. A magician was here."

The red curtains were lifting before his eyes, and unexpectedly his rage began to subside as swiftly as it had come. He
sighed again and continued more slowly. "The one you call
Vixenia had summoned the magician through some kind of
stone. He pointed at me and told you I was the Sword Bearer.
And I said my name was John."

Anger had now drained from him like a retreating wave on
a sandy beach. He was hungry, hot and depressed.

"It is very strange," Vixenia mused. "Clearly the child is not
lying. Yet his words explain nothing. *He* knows from whence he
is, and the place must surely exist. And it *is* his voice we heard.
So far as we are concerned, he comes from a place unknown.
In any case, has anyone ever seen a creature of this sort before—unless the magician is one of the same species?"

Below them there was a stirring and an excited murmuring
among the watchers. The cloud floated away from the sun,
which broke over them warmly again. But Bjorn's face was
impassive. "You say you came through a door from the

Changer," he said. "What does this Changer look like?"

John's depression deepened. "How do I know? I never saw him."

"Were you lying then when you said you came from him?"

John groaned. "It was all blue. And the ground was shaking. His voice was like an earthquake—but nice, really nice." He paused and frowned. "He even touched me. I couldn't see him because of the blue. Then he told me to go between the cherubim and pick up the sword before going through the door. And I already told you the rest." He experienced a tug of longing to feel the shaking again and a touch of the Changer's bottle drying his face.

"And you no longer have the sword."

John did not reply. He wished the questioning would end and that someone would offer him something to eat.

"Who told you to give us this story?" Bjorn persisted.

John's knees felt weak. Suddenly he sat down. "I'm tired. I don't understand where I am. I've had nothing to eat or drink. I'm sick of answering questions."

"Who told you to give us that story?" Bjorn repeated.

John sighed and lowered his head. "No one told me. It isn't a story. If it didn't happen, how did I get here? Maybe it was all a dream. But if so, then this is a dream too."

"Stand up, child!"

"No, I'm tired."

"Stand up!"

John raised his head and looked at King Bjorn. There was no exultation in him now, only weariness. He no longer cared about anything.

"Go and eat coal," he said. Bjorn would understand his tone even if he did not understand the words.

The queen had her hand on her husband's shoulder. "Be calm," she said softly. "The child understands no more than we ourselves. Whatever has brought him here is beyond his comprehension. His bewilderment is real." She paused and looked at John with compassion. "We must feed him or he will grow faint. If he is a runaway, then he ran away in another world than ours. There are legends about doors that connect with other worlds, and who knows but that he came through such?"

Vixenia nodded. "Large as he is, he is no more than a cub. And there is something else. He named the name of Gutreth. And plainly he felt his weight. How did he know that name if he did not in fact encounter him? Where is Gutreth now?"

But Bjorn was not listening. He turned to the small gathering of his Matmon followers and said, "Is there counsel from the rest of you? What are we to do with this child?"

For several seconds no one spoke. The silence weighed heavily on the afternoon air. Then Bildreth rose slowly to his feet. "I may speak again, majesty?" His tone was humble, but his face contemptuous. King Bjorn nodded.

"He has had traffic with the Mystery of Abomination, majesty."

"How do you know that?"

"He told me so, majesty. He said that we could not keep him in a cave because he would call on the Mystery to release him. He said he could enter the presence of the Mystery whenever he chose."

John stared sullenly at the cruel face. Plainly he was being accused of something. Who was this Mystery?

"Is this true? Do you traffic with the Mystery?"

"Is that another name for the Changer?" John asked. "I already told you I thought it was some kind of dream."

"He traffics with the Mystery!" Bildreth cried. "I saw a pall of deep darkness moving into the rock to follow him into the cave!"

Bjorn stared hard at John. "With whom did you speak in the cave last night?"

Then a strange and dreamy mood fell over John like a net. "Oh, *him!*" he heard himself saying. "He called himself the Lord Lunacy. His head went through the rocky ceiling, and his feet went through the floor. He touched me on my forehead and told me I was evil—you know, *bad*. And I suppose I am. I think I like being wicked."

"The Lord Lunacy is one and the same as the Mystery," Bildreth shouted.

The dreamy mood lifted from John as suddenly as it had descended on him. He glanced at Queen Bjornsluv to see that profound shock had taken all the merriment from her eyes. There was a haunted look on her face as she stared at him. Bjorn's own face was pale, his lips parted.

For a long time no one either moved or made any sound. When the king spoke finally, his voice was unexpectedly filled with compassion and dismay. "I placed the executioner there to frighten you. It was never my intention to use him. A spy is one thing, but to traffic with the Mystery itself!"

He shook his head wonderingly, his lips still parted as he stared in amazement at John. "So young," he mused. "Yet such a knowledge of evil! Young sir, you will have to die. You have left us no choice." His mouth remained open, and from time to time he shook his head as if he was stunned. Finally he drew in a deep breath, sighed and said wearily, "Seize him! Lead him to the executioner's block!"

There was a murmuring and a stirring among the animals and Matmon, all of them rising to their feet. If John had been watching Bildreth's face, he would have seen that it registered a smile of triumph. But at that moment John's arms were seized and he found himself being hustled unceremoniously forward. The royal trio had also risen. All three stared at John in horror as he passed them.

Though he was startled, John felt no fear. Rather, he seemed to be bathed in warm self-pity. Somehow it insulated him from reality. He was forgotten by the Changer, friendless, forlorn and rejected by an uncaring father. He was also hungry and thirsty and no one cared. A sob shook him and tears rolled down his cheeks. He found that he was no longer walking but that his feet were trailing along the ground as he was half carried, half dragged toward the tree stump that served as an executioner's block.

He was flung down to kneel before the tree stump. His body fell forward and his head dropped across it. He was vaguely aware of a commotion around him. Then came a silence, and into that silence King Bjorn's voice rang grimly.

"Executioner! Sever his head from his body!"

The executioner took a firmer grip on the handle of his axe.

7

The Prophet and the King

"Hold! Hold still! Stay your hand, executioner!" Bjorn's voice rang loudly across the glade.

He was staring, startled, at a giant eagle that swept across the treetops toward them. The vast spread of its wings filled him with dread. From one of its claws hung the ancient figure of Mab, while from the other a donkey and a Matmon were suspended, dangling like dolls. Instinctively the Matmon began to flinch as the monstrous bird swooped menacingly toward the glade. And when it landed the ground trembled.

Mab and the donkey both struggled to their feet, while the Matmon remained motionless on the ground. Mab turned and looked up at the eagle. "My thanks, good Aguila! You have done well," he said. The eagle ruffled her feathers and began to preen herself.

"Whence come you, wizard? And who are these?" Bjorn cried. Slowly John raised his head and stared uncomprehend-

ingly at the strange scene. He was still wrapped in the warm self-pitying dream, little realizing the danger in which he found himself. But he recognized Mab, and he could see that the donkey was Folly, the donkey on whom he had pinned his hope of rescue from the cave. The eagle's wings were folded and her head rose to half the height of the trees, dwarfing Matmon and terrifying the horses.

Mab raised his right hand which clutched a large wineskin. "I bring the wine of free pardon your majesty requested," he said coldly. "And here," raising the belt from which the Sword of Geburah hung, "is the Sword Bearer's sword. I found it buried in the earth by the body of this sorely wounded subject of your majesty. I recognized it from my dream."

John glanced at the Matmon lying between the giant eagle's claws and saw that it was none other than Gutreth. The Matmon's face was deathly pale. His clothing was bloodstained and a gaping wound crossed his forehead.

Folly brayed loudly. "Wheels within wheels! Wheels within wheels!" he cried.

Bjornsluv stared hard at the donkey. "What is the meaning of this?" she asked.

The donkey brayed again. "I was deceived, your majesty. Wheels within wheels! Your subjects Bildreth and Gutreth bade me in the name of Mi-ka-ya to accompany them into the forest last night. They said they were to capture a servant of the Mystery. Ah, the treachery of it! Wheels within wheels! A stitch in time—if your majesties take my meaning. People who live in glass houses gather no moss."

Bjorn interrupted impatiently. "Spare us your proverbs. What happened in the forest? Bildreth informed us that singlehandedly he captured this servant of the Mystery." He stared at John, a worried frown on his face. For once Folly spoke sense.

"One who is the Sword Bearer appeared through a door bearing the number 345, a mysterious door that stood alone in the forest. It moved, and for a second blue light lit the forest as—" He paused, startled, as he stared at John. "—as he who now kneels before the executioner's block, and who is the Sword Bearer, came through it bearing in his hand the sword you now see. A stitch in time is like apples of gold in baskets of silver."

"Never mind apples. What about the door?" Bjorn asked sharply, still staring with uncertainty in his eyes at John.

"Doubtless a door that led from the presence of the Changer himself!" interrupted Mab, whose eyes had taken in the hooded executioner and the kneeling John Wilson. "It would appear that your majesty was about to behead the hope of Anthropos. How can you expect the aid of the Changer when you plan to kill his servants?"

"He is a servant of the Mystery! He told us so himself, wizard!" Bjorn countered.

"He could have told you no such thing. For he has come from the Changer according to the prophecies. He is the Sword Bearer!"

"He is an imposter!"

"An imposter? We shall see!" Mab had placed the wineskin on the ground, but his left hand, which held the belt and the sword in its scabbard, was still raised. "This sword will find the bearer! He to whom it will be drawn is the true and only Sword Bearer."

If it is possible for silent things to become more silent, then the Matmon did just that. Their bodies stiffened. Their eyes widened. Mab released the sword, and the crowd gasped as they saw it hang in the air. The magician looked at it intensely. Then he said, "Go sword! In the name of the Changer I command you—find your master!"

For a moment the sword still hung in space. Then, as if pulled by invisible strings, it floated across the glade toward John. Hardly knowing why he did so, he rose to his feet. As the sword reached him, the belt curled round his waist and buckled itself. Once again the scabbard and the sword hung from his left side. Bjorn, Bjornsluv and Vixenia stared at him, stunned.

"We were tragically mistaken," Vixenia murmured.

"But he has spoken with the Lord Lunacy," Bjorn spoke quietly, a troubled frown creasing his forehead still. "He told us so himself. He even seems proud that he is evil!"

"You know nothing," Mab said wearily, picking up his staff and the leather wine bottle. "Doubtless the Lord Lunacy searched him out, trying either to confuse or to destroy him. The Lord Lunacy well knows that the coming of the Sword Bearer presages the doom of the Goblin Prince! It is even foretold that he will cause a tower that controls the earth and the planets to sink beneath the swamp!"

He turned to stare at the unconscious Matmon who was lying on his back with his mouth open. "Now let us see what this creature can tell us!"

He removed a cap from the mouth of the bottle. He then stooped and squirted a few drops of the wine of free pardon between Gutreth's parted lips and then replaced the cap. John, whose self-pity was subsiding slowly, watched him. He was beginning to take more interest in what was happening. He recalled the tussle in the darkness with the Matmon. He also remembered Gutreth's protection from the blow Bildreth had been about to give him. What would become of Gutreth? The Matmon's eyelids fluttered. Slowly he sat up, then shook his head bemused. And as John watched him, he saw his gaping wound close and disappear. A look of comprehension stole across the Matmon's face, and he rose to his feet. For a moment he hesitated. Then he strode toward Bjorn and knelt before him.

"I come to ask your forgiveness, sire!" he said.

"Forgiveness? Forgiveness for what?" Bjorn asked quietly.

"Forgiveness for having broken my vows to you by continuing to serve the Mystery of Abomination!" Gutreth's words were sharp and clear.

"Your majesty's servants Bildreth and myself went last night at the bidding of the Mystery to capture the Sword Bearer, who was to emerge from a magical door in the forest. We thrust him into a cave and robbed him of his sword. All this we did at the bidding of the Mystery."

"You say you did this *at the bidding of the Mystery?*"

"Yes, sire!"

"Then you admit you had traffic with him?"

"To my great shame, yes, sire!"

"And it was he who bade you capture this John who now wears the sword?" Bjorn pointed at John, and Gutreth started as for the first time he saw him.

"Yes, sire. He is indeed the one whom we captured."

"And the sword?" Bjorn asked.

"We buried the sword two leagues from here, your majesty," he said.

"And it was there that we found them," Mab interrupted. "As we journeyed back from the north, Aguila the eagle with her keen eyes saw Folly bending over a wounded Matmon. And it was Folly who told us where the sword had been buried. Bildreth had tried to kill Gutreth, that he might become the Sword Bearer himself."

"It is even so," Gutreth continued. "Bildreth, my companion, wanted to have the sword. He did indeed try to kill your servant."

His hands rose to where the wound had been and his fingers probed unsuccessfully to find it. "Your majesty, I have done a great evil—"

But Bjorn's eyes were searching the group of Matmon. "Then Bildreth is lying. Bildreth—" he said sharply, "where is he?"

But Bildreth was nowhere to be seen. For at the sight of the eagle's descent with Folly and Gutreth hanging from its claws, he had stolen into the forest to flee. Quickly Bjorn sent a search party to capture him.

The Matmon king then turned to the kneeling Gutreth. His eyes narrowed as he stared at him. "It is easy to repent when the game is up," he said. "How do I know that yours is a true change of heart?"

Gutreth's head bowed low. "Your majesty . . ." he faltered.

"Those whose stomachs retain the wine of free pardon," Mab interposed, "those who absorb it and do not reject it are changed. They know evil and good. And they reject the evil. Your majesty may rest assured that this one will be a loyal servant, both of your majesty and of the Changer. I am presuming, of course, that it is still your majesty's wish to serve the Changer." There was a hint of scorn in Mab's voice, but Bjorn ignored it.

"I need every follower I can get," he mused thoughtfully. He stared at the kneeling Matmon for a full minute. Then he said, "Raise your head, Gutreth son of Gyndror. Now do you swear by the bones of your ancestors that you will be true to me to the death?"

The Matmon's face was white and drawn. His eyes were fixed on those of the Matmon king. He drew in a trembling breath and in a barely audible voice said, "I will be true to you, sire. I swear it by my ancestors' bones."

King Bjorn continued to hold the Matmon in his level gaze, almost as though by an act of will he was willing the loyalty of his subject. Finally, he said, "Then rise from your knees. You are pardoned. Henceforth you will flee at the very approach of the Mystery of Abomination!"

Gutreth stood, bowed low, then stood erect. "Your majesty is gracious far beyond my desserts," he said in a trembling voice, before turning slowly to join the group of watching Matmon, his legs shaking a little as he did so.

John had watched the proceedings with a growing sense of the danger through which he was passing. He could see Gutreth's agony and terror. And though he still felt a little sorry for himself, his mounting anxiety was driving self-pity away. He stood by the tree stump on which his head might still be severed. He glanced at the hooded executioner, now leaning nonchalantly on his axe, and shuddered. Surely Bjorn would let him go, now that the magician had so clearly shown him to be the true Sword Bearer. Then he saw that Bjorn's keen gaze had turned on him.

"We now know that he is what he says he is—the Sword Bearer," he said quietly, the troubled look still on his face. "What we do not know is whether the Sword Bearer remains loyal to Mi-ka-ya. It would be better for him to remain as our captive until we are sure of him."

"The prophecies are clear enough," Mab returned evenly. "The Sword Bearer is to slay the Goblin Prince, lieutenant and chief to the Mystery. His coming presages the arrival of the Regents. He is the destroyer of the tower that controls the planet. His loyalty is never in question. So much the prophecies make clear."

"I know nothing of prophecies, wizard," Bjorn said slowly. "But I know the child has been in contact with the Lord Lunacy—"

"A matter I have already explained," Mab interrupted testily. "I am myself a seer, a prophet. I am insulted by those who call me wizard, sorcerer, magician. I am none of these. I serve the Changer. My powers are to do his bidding. And as for the Changer's prophecies—*they never lie.* You should know this if your intention to serve the Changer is real. The Sword Bearer is to remain loyal to the Changer!" He stamped his foot in irritation and seemed about to break into speech again. But he changed his mind and bit his lower lip.

"I am sorry," King Bjorn sighed wearily. "I do not doubt your wisdom. But I must be sure. Seize the Sword Bearer, guards, and chain him to a tree!"

The guards, who still stood on either side of John, reached out to take his arms. But in that instant John was deafened by a terrifying noise and blinded by a flash of brilliant blue light. When he was able to see again, the guards were lying on their backs stunned, while Mab stood erect, his staff held high and his eyes blazing. "Do not lay a finger on the Sword Bearer!" he cried. "If you wish me to aid you, you will leave him at liberty!" For a full minute nobody moved. The Matmon seemed stunned by the power that had burst from the wizard's staff.

John's heart was beating furiously. His breath came in frightened gasps. He glanced at Bjorn whose face was pale and set, his lips pressed tightly together. Bjornsluv's fists were clenched at her side, and Vixenia's brush was low on the ground. The guards began to climb uncertainly to their feet. Hardly knowing what he was doing, John snatched his sword from its scabbard, and instantly a low but penetrating hum filled all the glade, while from the sword came a flashing blue light that rivaled the light of the sun. The guards drew their own swords, looking to Bjorn for further orders. For several more seconds no one moved or spoke.

At last Bjorn said to Mab, "Unhappily I know not the extent of your powers, nor yet of his," nodding at John. "But understand, magician—or prophet if you must so call yourself—that I am responsible for the lives of this company. I do not wish to fight with you. I need your aid. Yet so long as I fear for the Sword Bearer's loyalty I must take precautions. Know, O magician—which surely is no different from prophet—that however much I fear your power, I fear much more the powers and malice of the Mystery. I must secure the Sword Bearer, even if it takes every Matmon in my company. So take him, guards!"

The guards eyed John uncertainly. John raised his flashing sword above his head and cast a desperate glance in the direction of the magician. And this time he saw the flash at its source, for from Mab's still raised staff twin lightning streaks of blue fire roared into the ground on either side of him.

"Entrust him to me if you cannot trust the prophecies!" Mab cried in anger.

"How do I know . . . ?"

"You have seen my powers! They are greater than his! You would be in no danger, even if he were a follower of the Mystery, which he is not. No harm will come to the company if you commit him to my care."

Bjorn drew in a worried breath.

"And you will bring us to the island?"

"I will bring you to the island."

Bjorn paused. "And give us the wine of free pardon?"

"And give you the wine of free pardon."

This time there was a longer pause. Bjorn was frowning. At last he nodded. "Let it be so then." He glanced at the guards. "Sheath your swords," he said. And then he turned to John and said, not unkindly, "Go then to the magician, Sword Bearer, and do as he bids."

John discovered his legs were unstable columns of gelatin, as he stumbled, sick with relief, to where the seer was standing at the foot of the giant eagle. He hardly glanced at the sloping ceiling of white eagle feathers above his head, but as he looked up instead at the ancient face above him, he found himself staring into a pair of friendly blue eyes that were wrapped in wrinkles and lines of laughter, hooded by shaggy white eyebrows. The white hair from Mab's head tumbled over the shoulders of his blue velvet gown. "You must do all I say, for perils surround you," he said quietly.

John nodded, his throat too dry to speak.

"And the child must have food and drink," Bjornsluv cried, relief written large on her grandmotherly face. "I go to prepare something. He is but a child." She turned and strode energetically toward a small square tent at the edge of the forest which she shared with her husband.

The Matmon had come to life and were moving slowly here and there, relieved that the tension was at an end. The relief had softened even the hard character of the prophet, for suddenly he called again to the Matmon king, striding across the grass toward him with John at his side. "Food—yes—food! And wine of the best! Let us feast tonight as we make our plans for the journey. There will be perils enough ahead."

"Food? Alas, we have barely enough. And as for wine . . ." Bjorn began.

Mab laughed, and turning his head to the gargantuan bird behind him, he called, "Aguila! A feast, Aguila! Fetch us a feast that is fitting for a company of kings!"

The eagle spread her wings until they seemed to span the glade. Lazily she leapt upward, sweeping the great wings powerfully downward so that the wind rushed about their eyes and the branches of nearby trees bent and creaked. A moment later she was shrinking in size as she surged into the sky.

8

John Behaves Badly

John should have been happy but he wasn't. Bjornsluv had given him a meal that any boy would have enjoyed. He had feasted on cheese and sausages, fried bacon and eggs, hotcakes and honey, nuts and fruits of many varieties. He had then washed everything down with fresh, creamy milk.

But he was not happy. You would have thought that to be rescued from execution would have done something to his mood. But the relief of his rescue had lasted only minutes. Even the strange business of the Gaal tree had failed to shake him from his petulant self-centeredness.

Mab knew all about Gaal trees. He had invited John to "share his tree," and John had supposed that he was being invited to some kind of tree house. So when they had stopped at a large oak tree on the edge of the glade and Mab had said, "This is it!" John had stared up into the branches.

But Mab had raised his staff and talked to the tree in the

name of the Changer. And as he talked, a door in the tree trunk had swung open. "In you go!" Mab had said to him. And John, shrugging his shoulders and trying to behave as if doors on oak trees were an everyday occurrence, stepped nonchalantly through.

To his surprise he found himself in a large and comfortably furnished room—a room that was larger on the inside than the trunk of the tree on the outside. But he was determined not to show his surprise. After all, the Sword Bearer ought to know all about Gaal trees. And since Mab seemed to take no further notice of him and did not bother to explain how something could be larger inside than out, John had to stifle his curiosity. But he felt resentful. Somebody, he felt, ought to explain things like this. Shouldn't the Changer have told him? But then, there was no Changer. Bitterness twisted his lips.

He had dozed fitfully on a couch for a little while, waking from a brief sleep to find Mab still silently perusing a parchment scroll.

I wish he'd talk to me," he thought. Yet for some reason he could not explain, he was reluctant to break the silence himself.

He strolled to a window that looked out on the glade. As he did so, it occurred to him that no window had been visible on the outside of the tree. The more he thought about the matter, the more puzzled he became. He decided he would go out to see again what the tree looked like from the outside. "Perhaps if I go quietly he won't notice," he thought. But when he turned to the door, there was no sign of it. The room was a room without a door. Anger boiled inside him as he stared with hard eyes at the glade.

Mab was probably laughing at him. The Sword Bearer was still a prisoner, the prisoner of a wrinkled old man who did nothing but read a parchment scroll and mutter to himself from time to time. "He was very excited when he saw me in my dream," John thought resentfully. "Why does he ignore me now? After all, I am the Sword Bearer."

The remainder of the afternoon proved exceedingly boring. The monotony was broken only by the news brought from two Matmon that the search party sent to find Bildreth had returned empty-handed. This, of course, did nothing to improve John's mood.

But at last as the sun began to go down, Mab raised his head and said, "Aguila should be back soon. Let's go outside and see if we can see her. Sorry I've been busy with the records. Hope you've not been lonely."

John said nothing. "He's treating me just like a boy, and I'm the Sword Bearer," he thought. Mab crossed the room to where the door had been, and as he did so it not only reappeared but opened itself. "There you are!" he said cheerfully. "After you, young sir!"

Outside John stared at the tree trunk. Once the door had closed again, the trunk became like any other tree trunk. There was no sign of either door or windows. But Mab was striding on across the glade, and he hurried after him, hardly noticing the warm sense of summer, which normally would have intoxicated him, and ignoring the crowd of Matmon the seer joined.

The Matmon all stared expectantly at the western end of the glade where the sun hung low on the trees. A clamor of cawing rooks could be heard above the Matmon talk, and from time to time a restless crowd of the birds would boil up over the distant trees.

But finally they saw what they were looking for. The powerful silhouette of Aguila, flanked by fourteen other eagles, seven on either side of her, moved steadily toward them, their wings driving rhythmically. They were large birds, though not nearly the size of Aguila, each carrying some load. But below Aguila was suspended the largest object of all. Excited chatter filled with speculation arose as to what it was. Finally as the giant eagle came closer, several voices cried, "A table! It's a table! She's bringing an enormous table!"

The wrinkles in Mab's face deepened in a broad and com-

placent smile as if he knew all about the eagles and what they
were bringing, as indeed he did. John concentrated on looking
unconcerned, glancing at the birds from time to time with su-
perciliously raised eyebrows. The Sword Bearer would surely be
used to unusual events. Whatever happened he was determined
to establish his superiority. So as the exclamations over the size
of the table grew in volume, he said to no one in particular,
"Well, what do you expect? How can you have a feast without
a table?" The seer threw him a worried look but said nothing.

The table, long enough to seat more than a hundred people
and low enough for them to sit on the grass, landed a little
bumpily. But it seemed none the worse for wear, and the moment it was on the ground, the first pair of eagles, carrying a
long white linen cloth between their beaks, spread it in less
time than you would take to throw a tea cloth over a card table.
And in pairs several more eagles set down linen napkins, silver
flagons and goblets, silver bowls and platters, and silver knives
and forks which several Matmon arranged quickly on the table.
The remaining eagles then loaded the table with steaming roast
geese and ducks, whole roast boars with apples in their mouths,
cheeses, wine, fresh and dried fruit, cakes, pies and fruit-fla-
vored sherbets.

"Have you further orders, my lord seer?" Aguila's voice was
harsh and unmusical.

"Nothing except to ask whether you have arranged for lights
when darkness falls," Mab said.

"All is arranged," the giant eagle croaked.

The old man bowed to her courteously. "Go then to your
aerie," he said, "and accept our gratitude for your provision.
You have done well." All the eagles with Aguila then flew silently back toward the setting sun, which was now hidden by
the trees.

And so a hundred Matmon feasted in the gathering dusk
along with Mab and John. Folly the donkey begged to be ex-
cused for any seeming discourtesy, explaining that he was a

vegetarian and would prefer to nibble a little grass beside the table. Vixenia, on the other hand, played gingerly with a large goose leg on a silver platter. The Matmon tucked their linen napkins around their necks and seized the meat with their fingers, ignoring the knives and forks. They ate noisily and gleefully.

Mab ate thoughtfully with knife and fork, his napkin resting on his knees except when he raised it carefully to wipe his lips, his mustache or the top of his beard.

Out of the corner of his eye John watched him. He had never before experienced such a feast and was not sure how to behave. But he was determined not to show his ignorance and carefully copied Mab, dabbing his lips delicately with one corner of his linen napkin (which he called a serviette) and glancing scornfully at the vulgarity displayed by the Matmon.

Wine was poured, and an air of merriment enlivened the party. Then as darkness fell, the scene was slowly transformed. A million fireflies converged on them to form a dancing canopy of light above the table. This was the illumination Aguila had promised. Firefly light softened the faces of the feasters and gently burnished the silver bowls and plates. And from nowhere onto everyone's ears gentle music fell sweetly and soothingly to mingle with their talk and laughter.

At any other time John would have been entranced. But now he was sulky, resentful of everybody around him, including the prophet, and profoundly discontented. What point was there in being the Sword Bearer? Swords were for cutting and killing. Swords were for heroic action. When was he going to be able to show them what he could do? Resentment welled inside him as he looked at Bjorn. One day Bjorn was going to be sorry.

Then as he stared at the two bearded young Matmon seated by Bjorn and Bjornsluv, he started, staring at them closely. Yes, he was sure. These were the two he used to dream about, in the dream where one murdered the other for a gold chain. Later he was to learn that the murdered one was Bjorn's grandson, Rathson, and the murderer, his grandson's cousin, Gold-son.

Only Mab seemed aware that all was not well with John, and for the most part he was too busy conversing with Bjorn to pay much attention to him.

"So the bird exists," Bjorn said. "We had heard tales of her but dismissed them as empty legends. Never have I seen such magic."

"What you call magic is the mystical power of the Changer. It might solve a problem for you. Tell me, from whence will you get supplies for the long journey you propose?"

Bjorn's face grew solemn. "That is indeed a problem. When I proposed a feast I had nothing such as this in mind. We carry our supplies partly on what few horses we have and partly on our backs, and our weapons at our sides. But our stores are meager. We hunt. There are also nuts and roots in the forest. But I feel we may go hungry ere long. A feast like this . . ."

He left the sentence unfinished, reached for a duck and tore off a leg and a wing with his fingers as he spoke. Mab watched him in silence. Then after some moments, as the Matmon king ate on, he said, "To the Changer it is a small matter to provide a daily feast."

Bjorn looked at him sharply. "You are still going to accompany us then? And you would command her to do this thing every day?"

But the seer did not reply.

They ate and drank for an hour or more, their joy arising more from the surprise of the feast and the abundance of good food than from the wine. Yet they sang and toasted one another until the table was bare of food.

And at that point Mab rose to his feet and rapped on the table. A wave of silence passed slowly through the company. Firefly-lit faces turned expectantly toward him. He straightened his shoulders and lifted his head in defiance of his great age. "Your majesties! Rebels against the dark powers! The feast you have enjoyed reflects the kindness of my master, Mi-ka-ya, the Changer and Maker. You have chosen to forsake the Mystery of Abomination and wish to serve my Master. Your willingness to seek and serve the Regents on the Island of Geburah, risking the malice of the Mystery, is proof enough of your change of heart. But know that before you can enter my Master's service, you must drink the wine of free pardon."

From beneath the table, he withdrew a small wineskin. "Already you have seen in Gutreth's body and mind what effect the purifying fires of this wine can have. I call on you now to drink of it with me!"

A blanket of silence fell over the group. Slowly, to the strange music of the fireflies, the prophet moved around the table pouring wine from the small wineskin into their goblets. Small though it was, it never appeared to empty of the wine of free pardon. Mab continued to fill goblet after goblet until he had completed a full round of the table. He raised his own. "Drink!" he said quietly. "Drink freely of the Changer's pardon!"

The Matmon raised their goblets and began to drink. Most of them drank deeply. A few, including the murderous Matmon of John's dream, coughed, spat and angrily flung the contents of their goblets onto the grass. But still nobody spoke. Vixenia sniffed at the wine and then slowly began to lap.

John stared at the firefly-lit faces. A few bore scowls. Plainly they were displeased with the wine. Others began to tremble. He stared at these, fascinated. The silence seemed to deepen as the firefly music grew fainter. Before long, his attention was arrested by a Matmon facing him, whose hands and arms were shaking as though he had a fever. Perspiration glistened on the Matmon's upturned face so that it seemed almost to shine while from his eyes tears streamed.

For the moment or two John looked away, embarrassed. What had the wine done? Could he have become drunk so quickly? He looked at him again. No, he didn't seem drunk. His arms rested on the table in front of him. He made no attempt to dry his tears, and the look on his face was not a look of pain, but of joy, as he gazed at something he alone could see.

For the moment John forgot his restless discontent. He drew a deep breath, and before he realized what he was doing he had asked the Matmon, "Are you all right?"

There was no reply, and John repeated his question. Slowly the Matmon lowered his face and looked at John, his lips apart and his tear-filled eyes shining. He nodded. "Yes. Yes, I think so." He seemed bemused with wonder.

"Why are you shaking?"

There was a pause. "I don't know."

"Are you scared?"

"No. No, your lordship, I don't think so."

"And why are you crying?"

"Because—because I am happy."

"*Happy?* But why?"

The Matmon slowly shook his head from side to side. Fresh tears fell from his eyes. Turning his face upward again, he murmured, "Such kindness. Such great kindness. Who would have dreamt it could be . . ."

John's eyes swept the table. Many of the Matmon seemed to have been affected by the wine in much the same way as the one facing him. Some trembled more violently. Others were perfectly still. But all those who had drunk deeply had their faces transformed by joy.

He became aware that the seer was staring at him, and he grew uncomfortable. The eyes were searching his mind.

"Have you drunk of the wine, Sword Bearer?"

"No. I've never drunk wine in my life."

"Then drink!"

"But I'm only a boy . . ."

"You are the Sword Bearer. So drink!"

John raised his goblet with both his hands, staring at the liquid inside it. He raised it further, to his lips, and tasted. Bitterness and fire exploded in his mouth and throughout his body. Disgusted and afraid, he spat and spat again, wiping his mouth feverishly with one hand. "Ugh, it's *horrible!* You're playing a joke on me. You think you're funny, don't you!"

The frustrations of the previous twenty-four hours boiled up inside him. Tears stung his eyes as he stared at the wizard, and rage threatened to take his breath away. In a thin, shaky voice he cried, "Here—take your filthy wine!" and flung the contents of the goblet in Mab's face, hurling the empty vessel onto the table.

Then he turned and ran into the darkness, sobbing with rage as he ran.

9

The Goblin Prince

The next morning John stared gloomily through the window of
the Gaal tree. His feelings were confused. The previous night
Mab had found him where he lay in the grass at one end of
the glade. He had pounded his head and fists into the earth
until he was exhausted. Wearily John had accompanied the old
man to the Gaal tree and accepted a cup of liquid from him.

"What is it? It's not that pardon wine, is it?" he had asked
suspiciously.

"It's medicine," Mab had replied gently. "It will ease the hurts
and griefs in you. You will rest better if you drink."

He had watched John sadly as he took the cup, and after a
moment he had said in a low and trembling voice, "No one can
make you drink the wine of free pardon. You must want to
drink it yourself. And until you do, John the Sword Bearer, your
sword will prove useless to the cause. Indeed, if before drinking
the wine you should ever try to kill the Goblin Prince with it,

your sword will surely fail you."

John had remembered no more. He had lain back on the couch on which he was sitting and sunk into a dreamless slumber. Now staring out of the window, he was ashamed of his behavior. But he was also defiant and determined not to apologize. He was the Sword Bearer.

He scarcely saw the glade, washed in the morning sun, or the Matmon washing themselves in the stream and cooking breakfast on fires before their tents. Here and there the tethered horses contentedly cropped grass. When at last his attention was arrested by the scene in front of him, it was not by any movement, but by the sudden absence of movement.

They had all stopped. It was rather like a movie that suddenly freezes on one frame. Some still knelt by their fires. Others stood motionless in a variety of postures. The horses had ceased to eat. But this was not the stillness of death so much as of intense watchfulness. All of them were staring, gripped by what they saw.

John drew in his breath when he spotted what they were looking at. A bear had emerged from the forest, a bear larger than he had imagined any bear could be. Though from where John stood it appeared to be black, it was in fact a grizzly, but greater in size than grizzlies of our modern world. Even on all fours it stood taller than the horses, and clearly was of far greater weight and bulk. John wondered what it would look like when it stood on its hind legs.

The bear was the only thing in the whole glade that moved as it slowly shuffled with apparent aimlessness into the opening. Even the leaves on the trees did not stir. Matmon and horses watched the bear as though transfixed. But eventually one of the Matmon did move. John saw him draw back a spear. For several seconds nothing happened. Then the arm flashed forward, and the spear sailed through the morning air to glance lightly across one of the bear's shoulders. It swung its shaggy head to stare at the Matmon, who had dropped to his knees.

Then it turned to look at the spear.

The grizzly was no ordinary bear as John was to find out. Grizzlies cannot pick up spears with one paw. But this grizzly did. Then it raised itself to its full height of fifteen feet, held the puny weapon above its head in its two paws, snapped it in two and tossed the pieces away. A growl came from deep in its chest, a growl that made even the window of the Gaal tree rattle, and then it moved on its hind feet toward the cowering Matmon.

There was a sound of hurried footsteps behind John. The wizard had seen what had happened and was tumbling through the door. "Oso," he cried. "Oso! Let him be, Oso. He is a friend! He does not understand! Oso!"

John followed the old man through the door. As he emerged he saw that the bear had dropped to all fours and was now bounding like a great eager dog in the wizard's direction. John backed nervously to the tree, only to find to his dismay that once again the door through which he had just emerged was no longer there. Instead of going through it he slipped behind the tree.

Mab stumbled forward. As the bear reached him, it again reared to its terrifying height, dwarfing the fragile figure of the old man. "Welcome, old friend!" Mab cried, opening his arms widely as though to hug the large creature.

"I come from Aguila," the grizzly rumbled. "She thought I might be of use to you!"

Then, as if a signal had been given, Matmon began to move again and the tethered horses to eat grass.

That night under a full moon, after a day of preparation to strike camp for the long journey ahead and after yet another feast provided by Aguila, John sat somewhat sulkily with Mab and Vixenia between the haunches of Oso.

"You are still of a mind to accompany us then?" Vixenia asked the old man.

"I fear to say what I will do," Mab replied.

"You fear?"

"The moon is full."

"And what of it?" Clearly Vixenia was puzzled.

"The Goblin Prince is said to walk abroad at times when the moon is full. I fear that if I declare my intention to join you, some great evil will befall you all."

"Let evil come!" Vixenia barked. "What do I care about the wrath of the Mystery? Let it do its worst, full moon or no full moon!"

"Hsst—it has ears—"

"Then let it hear and do what it may!" Vixenia returned.

The pain was growing in John's shoulder again, throbbing relentlessly and slowly worsening. He rubbed it, frowning. Mab turned to see what he was doing. "It hurts," John said. "It doesn't hurt all the time—just when Nicholas Slapfoot seems to be around."

"Who is Nicholas Slapfoot?"

John tried to explain.

"Does it hurt at no other time?"

"Just once," John found himself flushing. "I felt it the other night when the Lord Lunacy came to the cave where they imprisoned me. It really hurt then."

"And what about now?"

"It's—it's getting worse. It's certainly not dying away." Oso growled deeply as John continued.

The old man drew in a breath. "Perhaps it accepts your challenge, Vixenia. At any rate, evil is abroad in the camp. And I would advise you to return to your den to be with your mate and your little ones."

"You mean the Goblin Prince is *here*?" Vixenia asked.

"I only know that evil is near. My staff tells me that much. And it seems that the Sword Bearer's shoulder serves the same purpose."

"I don't know about the Goblin Prince. But Nicholas Slapfoot can't be *here*," John said. "I mean, it's not possible. He—he doesn't belong to this sort of place. He just doesn't."

Pendleton, Pimblett's Place and the old rag-and-bone man seemed impossibly remote. Yet suddenly the night was filled with memories, the moonlight cold and deadly, and the stillness—the sort of stillness that made you think of invisible dangers waiting to strike. All the Matmon were asleep. Folly had retired with the horses.

Mab rose to his feet, pushing himself upright with the vibrating staff. "Come, Oso," he said, "we shall follow the edge of the glade. If there is anything brooding in the woods that surround it, I shall know by my staff." He turned to John and looked at him uncertainly. Then he nodded as if he had made up his mind. "Go with Vixenia," he said, "and see that she gets back safely. You think you could find the tree again?"

John nodded.

"Well then, if I have not returned, unsheath your sword and bid the door open in the name of the Changer. I shall be back before long."

John wanted to ask what was likely to happen, but the pain in his shoulder made conversation difficult. In any case, the old man did not wait for questions. Oso had rolled onto all fours, and as Mab headed toward the northern end of the glade, the bear followed him.

John looked inquiringly at Vixenia. "Our den is in the opposite direction," she said, rising to stand on her tiny, delicate paws. "We were lucky to find it. It hadn't been used for a couple of years."

She turned from the trees and John followed. "You said 'we'?" he murmured. "Is there more than just you?"

"I have a mate and cubs," Vixenia said. "My husband was at first unwilling to come on this expedition. Life for him is a matter of hunting birds and bringing them to the den for food. But he came in the end."

If his shoulder had been hurting less, John would have been delighted to accompany the vixen to her den on a moonlit night in the woods. As it was, the pain grew steadily the further they advanced, and it was all he could do to follow her, his lips tightly pressed together and his forehead creased.

Vixenia moved through the woods following no pathway that John could detect. He was obliged to force his way between thickets and undergrowth, crashing noisily in the woods in the wake of his silent and agile guide who would wait for him whenever she got too far ahead. There was less light under the trees, and at times he would be on top of Vixenia before he realized she was there. He felt clumsy and awkward.

From somewhere ahead they heard the sound of a fox's bark and Vixenia stiffened. Then in the silence came the awesome and ponderous crashing of a falling tree. Both of them froze. They heard another tree crack and then crash to the ground. Then another and yet another. In all, a dozen trees must have fallen only a few yards from where they stood.

"What is it?" John whispered.

"It is the Goblin Prince," Vixenia replied. "He alone has the strength to fell trees with his fists."

For about a minute they heard nothing more, until at last came the chilling sound of a yelp, a thick scream and a pitiful squealing.

Vixenia was gone. Soundlessly she disappeared into the dense thicket. John's heart beat sickenly. It was all he could do to suppress a whimper because of the pain. Stubborn pride struggled to assert itself. He was the Sword Bearer. If evil was abroad, could he not deal with it?

Another thought gripped him. Was he not himself evil? Did not his strength lie in evil? Gritting his teeth, he plunged into the bushes in the direction he thought Vixenia had followed. The same fierce exultation that he had first experienced with the Lord Lunacy inside the cave flushed his body again, filling him with scorn for the danger ahead. He forged ahead determinedly crying, "I am the Sword Bearer!" But his voice sounded thin and unconvincing.

A second later the fleeting exultation left him. A peal of diabolical laughter sounded from a few yards ahead. It seemed to cut through his muscles and make his shoulder jump with agony. He stopped abruptly and gasped in pain. Peal after peal of laughter sent jolt after jolt into his shoulder. There was no exultation left.

In misery and pain, shivering with cold and fear, he emerged into moonlight, into the confused chaos of fallen trees and the source of the devilish laughter.

At first his mind could not take in what he saw. A man stood behind the foliage of a fallen tree. He was holding the limp form of Vixenia high above his head. The voice of Nicholas Slapfoot cried, "Yes, Vixie, me sweet, you'd like me to kill you, wouldn't you? But I want you to live."

He shook her furiously but her body remained limp and flaccid. He lowered her, cradling her in his arms as though she were a baby and rocking her gently. "There, there, sweet'art. You must tell that young John 'ow I tore your husband's 'ead off and murdered all your cubs. You mus' tell 'im I felled these trees with one blow from me fists." Then he took the limp Vixenia by the tail and flung her into the bushes.

John sank to the ground, sickened with horror. He dropped his head onto his knees and closed his eyes. He crouched without moving for at least two minutes and then slowly the pain began to leave his shoulder. Nicholas Slapfoot was here— wherever "here" was—and Nicholas Slapfoot was called the Goblin Prince. He didn't belong to Pendleton after all. This was the strange world he came from. Nicholas Slapfoot had found his way into this other existence and seemed more powerful than ever. John opened his eyes and looked up, half expecting his tormenter to be grinning down at him, but his eyes met with only the foliage of a fallen tree in the moonlight.

Cautiously he rose to his feet. Nicholas Slapfoot was no longer present, and the pain in his shoulder was gone entirely. Scarcely daring to hope, he began to scramble over and around

the fallen trees in the direction where Vixie might lie. He forced his way over a thick branch, groping with his foot for firmer ground. Instead he felt something soft. Was it Vixenia? He bent down, pushing leaves and branches away from his face, awkwardly trying to feel with the fingers of one hand what his foot had encountered.

And at last he did. He felt the warm and shaggy coat of a fox. He had stumbled on the body of Vixenia's mate. He turned and dropped to his hands and knees. For several minutes he remained crouched among the fallen trees, shaking uncontrollably.

10
The Secret Plan

That night in the Gaal tree John scarcely slept at all. Nightmares haunted the fringes of his sleep, terrible nightmares of Nicholas Slapfoot. In the morning he was feverish, confused and suffering from a severe headache.

Mab and Oso having heard the sound of falling trees had been quick to find him. They found Vixenia, too, shivering, silent, but apparently suffering no injuries. She did not weep and would say only that the Goblin Prince had killed her mate and her cubs, and would then retire into a tormented silence in which she made no response either to questions or to kindness.

Gray skies and a slight drizzle of rain did nothing to lift the pall of gloom that had fallen on the company. In the afternoon there was a funeral. Most of the Matmon attended the burial of Vixenia's mate and cubs. King Bjorn made a speech at the graveside while Vixenia with horror-filled eyes sat shivering and remote, wrapped in a grief she could share with no one.

John was not present at the service. He had stayed in bed during the morning and toward lunchtime had fallen into a troubled sleep.

He struggled in his dreams to lift Grandma Wilson to a chair. If he could but get her to sit up, she would tell him about the ring and the locket. So he struggled and struggled. Sometimes she would almost be in the chair. Then mysteriously she would slip back onto the floor again.

She was heavy, so very heavy. He would heave and heave and heave, now from behind, now from in front, now pushing, now struggling to lift. Then the chair would move magically farther away. From the dream he would struggle into wakefulness to find himself sitting on a feather mattress straining his muscles at nothing. His body drenched in perspiration, he would lie back with a groan. He never saw the tense figure of Mab who watched him anxiously from the shadows.

John's dream continued to repeat itself. Each time he would exert all his strength. He would almost get her into the chair only to let her slip through his arms again.

Finally, as he woke, he saw that Mab was beside him, the wrinkles in his ancient face delineated like tiny chasms in the moonlight. "Here, Sword Bearer, drink this!" he said, holding out a silver cup.

"What is it this time?"

"Drink it! Never mind what it is. It will help you to rest."

John tasted it. "It's *horrid!*"

"Drink it! The faster it goes down, the less time you'll spend disliking it!"

John tilted his head back and gulped the potion down, shuddering and retching as he did so. "Ugh!" But even as he said the word, the taste in his mouth had turned to honey, and a warm glow enveloped his body and limbs.

"Now lie down and try to rest."

There were no more dreams of Grandma Wilson. For several

hours he slept deeply, and Mab left him to attend the funeral. But soon John was dreaming again.

Like the dream in his last night in Pendleton, it seemed too real to be a dream at all. He sat on a rock in a beautiful circular cove. A soft breeze brushed his skin and ruffled his hair. The rock was the tallest of a circle of green rocks that jutted like sentinels from the glass-clear water, their pale green splotched with brilliant orange patches of lichen. Through shadowy pine woods surrounding the cove a pathway led from a small sandy beach. No undergrowth cluttered the woods, but rocks of all sizes stood boldly among the trees as though, like the rocks in the cove, they were soldiers on guard watching him. Turning his head he saw a narrow rocky entrance to the cove behind him. Beyond that the lake stretched, its waters a glittering slate blue.

Then electric needles shot through his body. The Lord Lunacy (where had he come from?) glowed motionless as he stood beside and above him, his great body dominating the whole cove. He was not looking at John but staring intently into the clear waters below him. For a moment John was too shocked to breathe. The glowing alabaster beauty magnetized him. Awesome power flowed from the proud head down the deathly white robes to the marble feet.

One foot was resting on John's leg, but he felt no weight. When he stared, he could see only the Lord Lunacy's foot. At other times he could see only his own leg, and occasionally he could see both his leg and the wide foot simultaneously. It reminded him of his first dreamlike experience of Anthropos.

Relief filtered slowly through him. Evidently the Lord Lunacy would not be able to perceive his presence, any more than the Matmon king and queen had done. Very slowly he began to drag his foot away. But the alabaster figure made no move. All its attention seemed concentrated on the water below.

John would have preferred to get away, but there was nowhere to go, unless he swam to another rock. And that might draw attention to him. It would be better to stay. He looked down to see what it was that held the terrible being's gaze.

The lake bed, a world of rocky peaks and valleys, was visible in sharp detail, even though the water must have been anywhere between six and twenty feet deep. An occasional trout moved slowly among the valleys.

"Aha! So you came!" Again needles seemed to shoot through John's body at the sound of the Lord Lunacy's deep voice. Swiftly he looked up, but the attention of the terrible presence was still focused on the lake bed. As he followed its gaze John perceived a man-sized creature swimming rapidly upward. A moment later Nicholas Slapfoot broke the smooth surface of the water.

He seemed to float like a cork, a small cork when you compared him with the presence that looked down at him. His ugly little head and shoulders bobbed above the water, and John could see a scaly black body below.

"So you came within yards of the Sword Bearer last night and you never saw him. That was careless of you."

Old Nick shrugged. When he spoke it was as though he was saying something like, "I think it might rain tomorrow." What he actually said was, "I'll kill th' boy. We shall meet once more, and it'll be for th' last time. It'll be his last encounter with anyone!"

John found it unnerving not to be near them but to hear that they were talking about him.

"*His* last encounter, you say? Or yours? You will kill *him*? Or *he* will kill *you*? You know what the prophecies say. Only a human boy can kill you. And *this* boy has apparently been chosen to do so!"

Nicholas Slapfoot replied by spitting. Then after a moment he said, "Why have you summoned me, O Lord? Why do you do me this honor of approaching my hiding place?"

"The boy is to come here. He will come with the bear and the eagle. The bear will flush you out of your den and try to destroy you. The eagle will watch from above and will attack you as you escape the bear. But the boy—and his sword—will accompany them both. You must be prepared and on your guard."

Suddenly the rock was empty. Old Nick's eyes shot hatred at it. "Let 'em come!" he muttered. "I shall kill 'em all!"

And John awoke. Mab stood at his bedside, staring at him curiously. The funeral was over and it was late afternoon. "You were dreaming," he said.

"Yes, I . . ."

"I tried to enter your dream but I failed. What was it you dreamed?" Mab's voice was urgent.

"I—it was very vivid. I . . ." But suddenly all memory of his dream had been wiped clean away. "I can still sort of feel it, but I can't remember what it was—"

"Keep trying!"

But try as he might, John could remember nothing. Even the feeling of the dream slipped through the fingers of his mind like water. Nothing remained.

Mab's eyes were half closed. "I must enter your dream," he murmured, half to himself. "It can be done, and I think I know how."

Later, feeling better, and wandering around the camp as the rain lifted and a watery afternoon sun eased its way slowly through the low, shifting clouds, John encountered the grizzly staring into the stream that flowed through the glade. By now he had lost all fear of him.

"Hello, Oso, what are you looking for?"

The grizzly settled to his haunches and looked at him. "Looking for fish. Not hungry though. Don't really need one. You all right?"

John nodded.

"You met Goblin Prince last night."

"You know him too?"

"Never met him. Everyone knows him. Bad lot. *Very* bad lot.

Not surprised you couldn't kill him."

John flushed. "I didn't get there in time," he said, suddenly ashamed and irritated by Oso's remark.

"Not your fault," Oso rumbled. "Prophecies say you'll get him. Sword Bearer, aren't you?"

John nodded.

"Like to get him soon?" Oso asked in the tone of someone issuing an invitation.

A pang of fear shot through John, and for a few seconds a fierce struggle went on inside him. Part of him longed to prove to Mab and to the Matmon that as Sword Bearer he could perform acts of heroism. He suppressed his fears. "Yes, I'd love it!" he lied.

Oso looked at him for several minutes. "Discuss it with Mab?" he asked suddenly.

John remembered Mab's words about the sword being useless unless he drank the wine of free pardon. He shook his head, and his heart began to beat. "We'd better not. He might worry about me," he said, half elated, half terrified, feeling he was heading down a slippery slope but determined to show no fear.

"Lives at the east end of Lake Nachash. No one can find the lair. Some kind of underwater cave. No one knows."

John's feeling of excitement increased. "Oh—I think *I* might know—it's coming back—my dream—yes, I *dreamed* about it! I dreamed about the place where his den must be!"

Eagerly he described the way Old Nick had emerged from the water in his dream. Oso listened intently. At length he said, "Could be two entrances—one land, one water. If Aguila took you, think you might spot it?"

"Aguila?"

"Flying, like . . ."

"*Flying?* On that big bird's back? I'd be scared—no I wouldn't. I don't mean that. I'm not scared of anything. But how—?"

"Coming tonight with supper. I'll talk. I'll arrange. Probably dawn tomorrow. Let you know."

Oso stood, stretched, dropped to all fours and ambled away. John's head was spinning. Waves of fear came over him. What had he done? What if his sword *was* of no use? What if he fell off Aguila's back when they were flying? "Oso," he yelled in panic. But by then Oso was twenty yards away and apparently did not hear him.

"Oso!"

The great creature lumbered on unheeding.

"Never mind," John murmured shakily. "He'll think I'm scared if I . . . well, I am scared. But I'm not going to be. It's a magic sword. It's sure to work. And there's prophecy. I'm the Sword Bearer." Wasn't a prophecy always supposed to come true? If so, wouldn't he be safe? He—he John Wilson—was to kill the Goblin Prince so that the Regents would come. The thought of meeting Old Nick was still frightening, but it was going to be all right.

Or was it? What else was prophesied? He frowned. Then it came to him. When he killed the Goblin Prince, *Mab was going to die.* For both the coming of the Regents and the death of Mab would hinge on the slaying. Nausea twisted his stomach, and sweat cooled his forehead.

John ate little at the magical and magnificently spread supper table. Indeed few of the company did; their spirits were low, too low to be lifted by soft firefly light and the gently flowing music. But the music did have the effect of taking his fear away and making him drowsy.

"Be with you at dawn," Oso murmured as John was later trying to catch up with Mab on his way to the Gaal tree.

John stopped. "But I don't know how to open the door," he said anxiously.

"Slip sandals off!" Oso ordered.

John obeyed, pushing the thongs down to loosen them and slipping them off.

"When you close door," Oso said, "make sure one thong hangs through. At dawn, push above the thong." Then he ambled away—and John ran barefoot to overtake the old man.

He slept lightly that night and awoke the moment he heard the gentle growl outside. He slipped from his bed, already dressed. As he buckled on his sword belt, he could see, sketched in moonlight, Mab's huddled form. The old man's breathing was soft and regular. He crept across the floor, picked up his sandals, noted the place where the one thong seemed to go through the wall and pushed. Silently the door slid open, and he stepped into the cool dawn.

He felt uneasy when he saw the giant eagle so close, her neck lowered for him. Oso swung him up as high as he could reach to place him among the feathers between the wings. He sank into the softness, gripping the feathers with his sweating hands and noting the warmth that surrounded him.

Oso left them, and before he knew what had happened he felt himself rising. Enormous wings spread on either side and they surged forward, soon to rise above the treetops and into the still dark sky.

They were on their way. It was an errand of death—the death of Nicholas Slapfoot. And John was going to kill him.

"Cling with your claws to my neck feathers," the eagle shrieked. But John was already clinging as if his life depended on it—as indeed it might have, though he showed no tendency to slide off.

Soon they were high above the glade. Though the feathers half covered him, John enjoyed a clear view. Over the east the sky was rimmed with a haze of soft light. Aguila circled until she faced south and east. She then flew in a straight line.

"Oso travels swiftly," she called to John. "He will arrive soon after we ourselves. He too has magical strengths."

For a while she was silent. Then, "I am surprised that Mab allowed you to come. Sword Bearer or no, you are young." John said nothing.

The flight was strangely quiet and smooth. The wind tugged at his hair and face as they drove forward. Aguila's wings shifted a little to catch the rising currents of air. Light spread slowly over the sky, and then the sun pushed splendidly over the horizon. The day was glorious. Trees poked through the mists below them. There was no great sense of speed. Rather they seemed to be sweeping in stately leisure far above the forest.

About midday they came to a lake with a rocky island and a stone tower at one end of the island. In another hour they reached the eastern end of the lake. The sun was now high.

"Do you see anything?" Aguila screeched back at John.

He peered down at the shores of the lake, and for a while, as Aguila crossed and recrossed its eastern end, wondered whether his dream had played him false. Then he saw tiny and circular, the seven green rocks now like seven tiny candles on a birthday cake.

"There it is!" he shouted, pointing.

Aguila saw the cove and dropped through the air like a piece of lead. John's breath left him, and for a few giddy moments he felt as though his stomach was still in the sky far above. They glided smoothly to the small sandy beach where the path led to the pine forest.

Aguila lost no time. "The land entrance to this lair must be close by. The path may lead to it. I shall look out for Oso and guide him here. He travels fast and should not be too far away."

Then without more ado she spread her enormous wings and circled back into the sky, evidently expecting John to find the entrance to Old Nick's hiding place. But John was troubled. Would Nicholas Slapfoot be expecting him? Might there be a trap? Had the dream been just a dream or had what he dreamed really taken place? He shivered in spite of the warm sun.

He *had* been there before. Everything was exactly as in his dream, if dream it was. The pale green rocks were still splotched with vivid orange lichen. The rocks among the trees still looked like sentries watching him suspiciously. Whether because the wind had dropped or because of something magic in the air around the cove, there was no wind. The water was glass smooth. The woods were silent.

It was a silence that added to John's uneasiness. No birds sang. There was no sound of rustling leaves or creaking branches. Nervously he began to creep along the path which led him within yards to a cleft between moss-covered, fern-sprouting rocks. The sand scrisched softly under his sandals, however lightly he trod.

The cleft in the rock turned a corner. He could hardly squeeze through. "Old Nick would be too big to get through here," he thought. Ferns kept brushing his face. There was another turn ahead, and then he heard it—slap, slap, slap. Something—or someone—was coming.

How he turned, he never knew. But turn he did, brushing past ferns, scraping himself against rocky walls and darting back around the corner. But where to hide? A large rock ahead seemed to invite him to climb. Somehow he thought he would be safer up high. His sword. He could use his sword. He scrambled quickly up, found himself on a flat surface ten or twelve feet above the forest floor and quickly lay down, looking back at the cleft in the rocks. Ferns crowned the rim of his rock, and he could peer through them with little danger of being seen.

And then he saw him. Nicholas Slapfoot. He saw Nicholas Slapfoot, not wearing boots or clothes, but naked, his body covered with black scales and his feet large and webbed. He scuddered this way and that before slapping his webbed feet as he wandered deeper into the forest.

What was he doing? Where was he going? More important, what should John do now?

Confusion filled his mind. He began to wonder why he had come. He did *not* hate his father. He wanted to find him. What had all these strange adventures got to do with finding his father? Was there a Changer? Was it really nothing more than a dream? Nothing seemed to make sense. Yet he knew that Nicholas Slapfoot was to be feared. He also knew now that he had found one entrance into his lair. He could not imagine what good the knowledge would do, since a fifteen-foot grizzly could never squeeze between rocks to get inside the lair, whether it was above or below the lake. And in any case, did Nicholas Slapfoot not expect the grizzly to come? Or had Nicholas Slapfoot left to escape?

"I'll kill 'em all!" Old Nick had screamed in John's dream. No, he was not escaping. And John was at that point in no mood to tackle him, sword or no sword. He would wait till Oso and Aguila came to support him. And then he would kill Old Nick.

He eased himself into a more comfortable position. Aguila might be back fairly soon. John would need to be where he could be seen. He looked up and was surprised to see clear sky above him. The rock was not hidden by the pines. Shafts of sunlight cut down through delicate curtains of leaves around him. The far corner of the rock was sunlit.

Something made him think of the Changer and of the strange laughter that had united them as he left between the columns of cherubim. Indeed as he looked up at the sky he almost thought he could hear the laughter ringing again. At the thought his heart was warmed and his confusion dissipated.

"They can both see me from above," he thought. "Aguila will be able to see me and perhaps the Changer can too. Maybe he does exist." He paused a little. "I must keep a lookout and wave if I see Aguila. We could all meet right here."

He put the puzzle of how Oso could penetrate the lair out of his mind and for the time being ceased to worry about what Old Nick was doing. He would keep watch for the eagle. Carefully he looked around to make sure he could not be seen from below and to be sure that old Nick was no longer around too. But there was no sign of him. The ferns that sprouted round the edges of the rock would curtain his bed.

The rock on which he lay was crinkly with soft dry moss. He lay back on it and gazed up at the blue heavens. He would have felt nervous and restless, except that as he rolled onto his back to look up, something strange happened. He heard again, or thought he heard, the Changer's laughter far above. And the memory of that laughter, the laughter he and the Changer had shared together, the laughter that had seemed to link them, brought a sense of shame to him. He tried to put the matter out of his mind.

The slow circling dot above grew larger as Aguila weaved downward, her wings stretched wide. A minute later she lighted on the rock beside John. "Oso is coming along the path," she said. "I told him where you were, and he'll be here soon."

11

Oso and Aguila
Attack

The tension began to mount as they waited for Nicholas Slap-foot to return. Oso pattered on all fours to and fro on the rock. Sometimes he would raise himself to his full height and turn slowly, ponderously looking this way and that. Aguila sailed up into the sky several times. At last she turned, saying, "He comes. He approaches from the east. He will be here before we know he's upon us."

Oso stepped with surprising grace from the rock to the ground; then he stood upright beside the rock, being partly covered by a wall of ferns. "Me first crack," he said. Then turning to Aguila he ordered, "You next."

John dropped on his stomach, crawled forward and peered through the ferns. Aguila remained far above. Nothing moved. No birds sang. The unnatural silence began to oppress John again. He became conscious of his own breathing and his beating heart. He was only too glad to let Oso have the "first crack."

Then came the dreadful sound as the slap, slap, slap of Old Nick's flipper feet began to break the silence. At first the trees hid him. When John eventually saw him, he seemed to be walking toward them with no concern, apparently unaware of their presence, ignorant that a towering giant Oso was waiting to strike him down and kill him.

John held his breath. He was fearful of what he would see, yet too fascinated to turn away. He desperately hoped Oso would kill his enemy for him. In less than a minute Old Nick had reached the rock, turned his back to where Oso stood and stepped toward the cleft from which he first emerged.

As he turned, Oso lifted himself to his full fifteen feet and with a terrible growl rushed forward, flashing one of his mighty forepaws downward as if to knock the creature to the ground. Yet even as he moved he shrank in size. Before John's eyes, he was transformed in the fraction of a second from a terrifying grizzly to a small and petulent bear cub, chasing behind the demonic form of Nicholas Slapfoot like a puppy stumbling after its master.

Old Nick swung round with a laugh. He lifted the struggling little creature into his arms and disappeared into the cleft with him.

Events had taken place too quickly for John to take it all in. One moment Oso had towered above the rock itself. The next, he was a small cub carried off by a scaly goblin whose laughter still echoed faintly from between the rocks. Then silence descended again.

John was stunned. He was alone. Oso, Oso who had magical strength, was helpless before the powers of Old Nick. Even the grizzly's weight and strength were useless—gone.

John stared at the space between the rocks as if his staring could change matters, as if it could bring them both back again. What would happen? Would they come back? Horrified, he watched the truth take shape in his mind. A bear cub could never kill someone so formidable as Old Nick. And if Oso could not kill Old Nick, Old Nick would certainly destroy Oso.

John groaned, groaned from fear, from rage, from despair. He glanced up at the sky, once so reassuring with its echo of the Changer's laughter, now so bare and silent. Where was the Changer? Was he just a dream as Lord Lunacy had claimed? Was the laughter merely a hallucination? Where was Aguila? Had either seen what had happened? Would Aguila come back? Or would she from the skies hunt the evil demon herself?

Half sobbing, mainly with anger but also with fear, he scrambled madly down the rock, flung himself into the cleft that faced him and forced himself once more along the pathway leading to Old Nick's lair. He never knew what made him do it, only that he felt a desperation he had never felt before. In seconds he had reached the narrow section, squeezed himself through it and broken through into a sandy opening before a cave mouth.

He hesitated for a second, then stepped boldly and angrily into its cool dimness. Almost at once he encountered water that filled a narrow cave. It seemed to become deeper the farther the cave went back. But lying on his side half in the water and half on the damp sand of the cave floor was the huge body of Oso, his fur matted and bloodied.

"Oso!"

John's shriek echoed hollowly. He dropped to his knees beside the bear and stared into the half-opened eyes. His eyes were glazed, but something told John that Oso could see him. "Oso, are you all right? What can I do?"

A barely perceptible sigh escaped the bear. He was still alive.

Not knowing why he did so, John ran to the cave mouth, flung back his head and lifted his face to the sky. "Changer!" he screamed. "Changer who never changes! I thought I heard you laughing before! Where are you now? *Where are you?*"

He continued to stare upward, his fists clenched, his feet planted wide, but the sky was empty and silent.

He drew in a breath and stared into the cave mouth beyond

the body. Was Nicholas Slapfoot farther in? Had he heard his shouts? Was it now up to John to use the sword and kill him? For the first time in his life he felt his knees knocking together and knew what real fear was. His mouth was dry and the blood was pounding in his head. He could hear the rhythmic rush of it in his ears. The passage ahead was dark, but trembling he stepped round Oso's body and waded into the shallow water, gripping his sword hilt as he did so.

The tunnel narrowed and took a bend. Beyond the bend an evil red light glowed. John followed it cautiously, taking care to make no sound. The tunnel widened into a sizable cave whose roof was reflected in the still waters. He searched it with his eyes but could see no one. The floor beneath him was firm and sandy and the water shallow.

With infinite caution he moved forward into the cave. The farther he proceeded, the deeper the water became. Soon it was up to his hips. A horrible thought crossed his mind. What if Nicholas Slapfoot were waiting for him *beneath the water*? What if he were to be seized by the ankles and dragged into deeper water?

Farther ahead, in the center of the cave, a rock rose above the water. He would be safe if he could clamber onto it. Better still, a sloping ledge on the righthand side of the cave led to a sort of rocky platform about ten feet above the surface of the water. He waded to the ledge, pulled himself onto it and climbed up to the platform. He was obliged to crawl, for the roof of the cave was only a few feet above him. He squatted awkwardly on the ledge, uncertain what to do next.

If Nicholas Slapfoot was not there, then John could not kill him. A wave of relief swept over him. Perhaps, after all, he should leave the cave.

He was still shaking, partly from fear and partly from cold. He felt he had been very courageous to have come this far. And he certainly had been. It takes a lot of courage to do things you are scared of doing.

Suddenly his eyes were caught by a gleam of blue light beside him, the same color of blue that had surrounded the Changer. When he groped to feel the source of the light, his fingers encountered a stone the size of a pigeon's egg. Excited, he laid the stone in the palm of his hand, and as he did so he both felt and saw the thin chain attached to it that was draped over his hand.

The stone radiated light, a strangely reassuring light that filled him with hope.

Curious, he fingered the chain and let the stone hang from it, delighting in the beautiful light that reflected on his body and that glittered in dancing blue specks of light on the walls of the cave. He slipped the chain over his neck. Instantly everything changed.

He was at once filled with terrible shame and a sense of unbearable guilt. His fear of Nicholas Slapfoot was gone, and in its place there was a terror of the Changer. Suddenly he *knew,* knew with absolute certainty that the Changer existed, knew also with horrifying clarity that he would have to hide from the Changer if ever he encountered him in the future.

What came as an even greater shock was the discovery that he was invisible. His body had disappeared. He knew he was still there. He could feel the cold rock beneath him and the inrush of air into his nose as he breathed in. But when he brought his hand in front of his eyes, there was no hand to be seen.

It was distinctly unpleasant. The sense of shame and guilt, the fear of the Changer and the unnerving invisibility made a dreadful combination. He pulled the chain over his head, and at once the shame and guilt fell from him, and to his relief, he could see his own body again. Curiously, the power of the blue stone did not surprise him. He was growing accustomed to magical powers.

The chill of the cave now seemed to enter his bones. He was shivering all the time now, and he decided to leave the cave.

He glanced at the water below and as he did so, terror gripped him. Nicholas Slapfoot was sitting on the rock in the center of the pool. John lay flat on his stomach on the platform and peered cautiously over the edge. The creature was staring at something in his hand. John saw again the dark fish scales that clothed his body from the chest down. The arms were light in color, and like his face, his neck and his shoulders seemed to be covered with human skin. The lower limbs terminated in large webbed feet. The light was too dim for John to see clearly what Old Nick was staring at. It looked like a feather.

The silence was broken by the sound of his voice. "So that's the end of you. There's just the boy now. An' I'll get 'im sooner or later. Eh, Aguila, my sweet? There'll be no more feasts at your magic table!" He continued to stare thoughtfully at the feather.

But John was filled with dismay. What did he mean? That was the end of whom? Of Aguila? Had something happened to her? Plainly "the boy" that Old Nick talked about was himself. And just as plainly Old Nick was unaware of his presence in the cave.

What was he to do? He realized at once that with the blue stone he had found there was a good chance of escape. He could become invisible. But once he was invisible he could also behead Old Nick. Which was it to be? Escape? Or kill his enemy?

Now that he faced the possibility of killing the creature that sat only yards away from him, he felt sick with fear. Silently he slipped the chain over his head and at once the sick fear was gone. His heart leapt. He would kill Old Nick! Somehow he would get back to the camp and he would be a hero! He was the Sword Bearer.

The sense of his own evil was strongly with him now. He was ashamed, but he despised the shame. Silently he crawled from the platform, making his way very cautiously down the ledge. When he reached the water, he was able to stand upright. He turned to look at Old Nick, and to his surprise saw that the upper part of Nick's body had been transformed. The head was now the head of a shark, the great mouth slightly ajar, with one unseeing eye staring vacantly at John. The arms were gone, replaced by two small fins.

John knew, without being told, that he was seeing Nicholas Slapfoot for the first time as he really was, seeing him by the power of the blue stone. Fascinated, he stared. He thought of the bowler-hatted man with the red neckerchief and the greasy black suit. He remembered the thick-soled boots and realized that the three-inch soles must have been hollow so webbed feet could be folded in.

Then resolution filled him. He gripped the sword hilt firmly and pulled. But the sword refused to leave the scabbard. He pulled again, tugging at it with all his strength. But it might as well have been welded into the scabbard. "It couldn't have been rusted that quickly," he thought, "even if water did get into the scabbard." Then he remembered Mab's words, "No one can make you drink the wine of free pardon. You must want to drink it yourself. And until you do, John the Sword Bearer, your sword will prove useless to the cause."

So that was it. He was not to be allowed to kill the Goblin Prince. Magical power was holding the sword in the scabbard. His excitement sank to nothing, and in its place came the sense of shame and guilt that he had felt when first he had placed the stone round his neck.

The shark-headed creature on the rock stirred, shook itself and dived smoothly into the water, leaving scarcely a ripple. A minute passed, then another. No sound broke the oppressive silence. Was the creature lurking below the surface? Or had it retired to a deeper level in the lake? "Well, at least I'm invisible," John thought. And buoyed by the courage the stone gave him, he entered the cold water cautiously, paused, then made his way slowly toward the passage. A minute later he was at the cave mouth, having clambered over the body of Oso to stand dazzled in the sunlight. Only then did he remove the stone from around his neck and loop the chain through his belt. As he looked back at Oso's body, dismay filled him. He was sure the grizzly was not dead. But what could he do? The Changer would surely take pity on him. He began to talk quietly, almost to himself.

"Changer, it wasn't his fault. Don't blame him for what I did."

A quiet voice spoke three times before he heard it, "I am not he. But I am here!"

When he finally heard the voice, he stared in front of him at a green-gowned woman with flowing white hair. Though he heard no sound save that of her gentle voice, her presence itself was like a clap of thunder.

"What did you say?"

"I am not he, but I am here."

"Who are you?"

"Does that matter? I am Wisdom. My name is Chocma. He sent me."

"Who sent you? The Changer?"

"You were calling to him, were you not?"

John stared at her, speechless.

"I have come to teach you how you may restore Oso, the bear."

"Me? Restore him?"

The lady in green repeated her previous words without changing them. Power flowed from her like waves of heat from a furnace. But it was not heat. It was power. It made him feel dizzy.

"You can teach me? To restore Oso?"

"Even so, I come to teach you."

"How? Who are you? What do you mean, 'restore him'?"

"You may restore him either by the deep power or by the herbal remedies that the Changer has implanted in the earth around you."

A streak of stubbornness rose in John. In spite of all he had

115

seen of strange powers he said, "I believe in science."

"Then doubtless you will choose the herbal remedies."

He continued to stare at her. "You mean he can be *cured?* With herbs? How?"

The lady turned and plucked a berry-laden twig from a bush behind her. From the folds of her dress she drew a wooden cup. Clutching the purple berries in her hand, she squeezed them, letting a few drops of juice run into the cup. "Here," she said, holding the cup out to John. "Find and squeeze these berries until the cup is filled with juice. Then moisten the lips of the bear with the juice until he tastes it. When he does so, he will open his mouth. Pour the juice down his throat, and he will be healed. It is sanavida, the juice from which the wine of free pardon is fermented."

John took the cup from her hand. "Sanavida?" he repeated. But the lady was gone. She had disappeared as mysteriously as she had first come. And the world seemed suddenly normal again. Yet changed. For she had impressed him deeply.

"Perhaps I shouldn't have said I believe in science." Would the berries work?

The drops of sanavida had barely stained the bottom of the cup. But around the small clearing by the cave mouth, John could see three or four bushes with similar berries. And after staring at them for a few moments, he approached the first. The berries were in clusters, surrounded by long and piercing thorns. He plucked a cluster of berries and squeezed a few drops into the cup as the lady had done.

It took him half an hour to fill the cup. Both his hands were badly scratched, sticky and purple-stained before he was through. When he licked them, the taste was bittersweet, but it startled him into wakefulness. It gave his body the same feeling you get when you've come out of a cold shower and have just rubbed down. The half-hour of squeezing seemed to last only one exciting moment. The pain from his scratches did not trouble him.

But as he approached Oso, his wooden cup now brimming with purple juice, his excitement subsided a little. Were the glazed eyes still looking at him? The bear's head lay sideways on the sand.

He knelt, moistened his finger in the juice and rubbed it over the side of Oso's black upper lip. The lips seemed stiff and cool, and he shuddered a little as he touched them. Again he dipped his finger and again rubbed the lips. There was no response. He repeated the process a third time and then a fourth and again a fifth. On his sixth attempt, Oso again heaved a sigh. On the eighth try Oso rolled his head back and opened his mouth wide. John was exultant.

His hand shook as he held the cup over the gaping mouth. It was going to work. He was sure of it now. He tipped the cup carefully and poured its contents between Oso's jaws. A trickle of purple mingled with the bristly fur beside the lips.

Oso gulped. Coughed. Gulped again. Sneezed and coughed violently.

He half rolled over. Then his trunk hinged forward suddenly on his hips so that he swung into a sitting teddy-bear position, holding his great head between his forepaws and shaking it from side to side.

John was half laughing, half crying. "Oso! Oso! It's me, John. Are you all right? This lady came from nowhere and told me about the berries—sanavida she called them—"

"The devil! That demon had magic! Could have torn him to pieces! Wretched little thing! He shamed me."

"But you're all right now, Oso. The juice has made you well! I never thought it would work—"

"*Shamed* me! I was a cub! A *cub*!"

"But you're not a cub now! You're well!"

"Cub. Tiny cub. I'm shamed, shamed, shamed!"

The bear continued to shake its head, unreachable in its bitterness. His body was well, but his spirit was crippled with humiliation. Suddenly John thought of Aguila. "What about

Aguila, Oso! Aguila must be hunting it now! I'm sure she would hunt Old Nick and try to kill him if she thought he had hurt you! We must help her. She could be in danger!" He did not believe his own words, but he felt he had to say something to get the bear's mind off his shame.

The head-shaking stopped. Oso rolled over onto all fours. He shook himself, tested each limb carefully. "Come!" he said, finally. "We comb skies. Search shores." John sighed with relief. The crisis—at least this crisis—was over.

John thought Oso could not return by the way they had come. But the narrowness of the rocky passage proved no obstacle to the bear who leapt up the rock. John then found his own way through the narrow passage. Once on the shore, they began their search. But where to look?

For a long time their eyes vainly combed the heavens. Finally Oso said, "Alive she would circle and search for us. Therefore dead or hurt. If dead, she will wash on shore. We begin with northern shore."

It was slow and tiring work. There was no way in which John could keep pace with the bear. He stumbled far in Oso's wake. The beach was covered with rocks of uneven size. The bear would climb up a steep wooded slope from time to time to a higher point from which he could survey a whole stretch of shore. And John would barely catch up with him as Oso loped easily down again. Each time John would wearily ask if Oso had seen anything. And eventually Oso did.

"Up ahead. Quarter of a mile. Like a heap of bones."

This time Oso seemed in no hurry. Indeed it was John who led the way, Oso moving slowly and ponderously on all fours behind him. Soon John saw something, something dark and shapeless at the edge of the water, being lifted and dropped gently with each succeeding wave.

He quickened his pace to a half run. His eyes never left the thing at the water's edge, and so he tripped and almost fell several times. The nearer he came, the more his legs faltered and his strength failed him, less from physical weakness than from dread. For the mass was indeed a mass of feathers and bones that—he knew it without being told—once had been Aguila.

Eventually he stood before her, or before what was left of her, trembling and breathing hard. There had been hope for Oso. Oso had not been completely dead. But Aguila no longer existed. All that remained were water-logged feathers, many of them scattered about the beach, crushed, torn and distorted wings, and a twisted neck. The giant head lay apart, a few feet away, the beak open and one eye staring skyward. The bird had been savaged with inhuman ferocity.

A shadow fell over Aguila's remains, the shadow of a tall man. Slowly John looked up and found himself staring into the face of Mab, staff in hand, standing ramrod straight, his long white hair blowing in the breeze.

"So this is what you were dreaming about, John the Sword Bearer."

"Yes, well not this exactly—but it all came back when—"

"Yes, yes, I know. I was able to break into the dream myself just as you left. It is as well for you that I did."

John said nothing. He felt ashamed and dropped his head. He knew now that he should have told Mab of their scheme. Mab knew about magic, power and the Changer. He seemed to know more than any of them about these things.

"I repeat, it is a good thing for you that I did."

John had no idea what could be "well" or "good" about Mab coming now. How could anything change what had happened? Oso was already alive. Mab had had nothing to do with that. But Aguila was dead.

A searing flash of blue blinded him. The dismembered carcass of the eagle came alive with liquid blue fire. For several seconds the light burned so fiercely that John could see only the barest outlines of the eagle's remains. He glanced up. Mab's face was alive with rage. From the staff he held up high there streamed a continuous arc of blue fire.

Then from Mab's throat came a roar, "Aguila, arise! Arise by command of the Changer! In his name I bid you, live again!" Flaming feathers and head were drawn to a center as by a magnet. The fire was molding, shaping, forming. It was hard to say what was fiery light and what was eagle. But suddenly it was over. The light was gone. The staff was lowered, and Aguila stood there, preening herself unself-consciously before Mab, John and Oso.

12

The Two Towers

Aguila did not spend long preening her feathers. Suddenly she looked up. Her eyes were clouded with pain. It was clear that though she was alive, she would never be as she once had been. Her movements were stiff and awkward. For the rest of her life she would never be free from pain. She glanced in turn at John, at Oso and finally at Mab. There was a long silence between them as the waves lapped on the rocks. Finally Aguila croaked softly.

"I am alive! How can it be? I am alive! I had trusted the keenness of my eye. I had trusted the sharpness of my claws and the magical powers in my wings. Oh, how he seized me, so little, yet so terribly filled with evil power . . ." She shook violently standing among the rocks, her proud head bowed low.

"He pulled me down and down into the waters of the lake and began to tear my wings from my body and the flesh from my chest . . ."

There was no need for her to say more. All of them became aware, terrifyingly aware, how awesome were the powers opposing them. If the goblin Nicholas Slapfoot was as powerful as this, how great must be the power of the Mystery of Abomination! Oso trembled. John's throat was dry. Only Mab seemed certain of himself.

"Events move quickly," he said slowly. "Aguila's powers should have been more than a match for those of the Goblin Prince. Something has happened. The power of the evil ones has increased." He paused. "There can be only one explanation. The Mystery must now have transferred his headquarters here. He has begun to build his tower. He may even have completed it. Why have I been so slow to suspect it? And how can we find out? How?"

John and Oso stared at him. For several minutes he stood, his eyes clouded and his ancient forehead creased with concentration. Then he said, "*I must know whether the tower is built.* Once it is completed he will be able to control the planets. And we cannot know unless we enter the swamp. Yet even if we were to enter it by using my staff our entry would be detected and our lives imperiled. Only by using the Old Way can we gain access unobserved. But who controls the Old Way now?"

He turned to Oso and Aguila. "Return, both of you, to the camp. Use your powers to get back with all haste. Let them know we are well but that our mission to the swamp could be perilous. Bid Vixenia and their majesties prepare for the journey as quickly as possible. We dare not lose another day."

Something about the way Mab spoke awoke a still greater fear in John. Oso seemed to have lost all his confidence. Enormous as ever, he stood like a humbled statue. Aguila shifted her feathers painfully. Mab addressed her directly.

"You can still fly. Leave at once. Tell them that for the present we are well. You and Oso are alive. The Goblin Prince has failed. Now go! Be on your way, both of you."

Aguila waited for no further instructions. She spread her

wings stiffly and swept skyward in widening circles. Soon she was a distant speck receding into the northwest. Oso hesitated for a moment and then turned without a word, gathering speed as he loped into the trees.

John's fear had not abated. He was especially afraid of the swamp. He looked again at Mab. "How will we get back?" he asked. "With your staff? And what did you mean about the tower?"

"The prophecies speak of two towers—the Mystery's tower in the swamp and the Changer's tower on the island from which the Regents will emerge. The Mystery will concentrate all his power in his tower and project it outward to control the movements of the planets. He hopes by this to defeat the Changer's purposes for Anthropos."

"And will he?" John asked. "I mean will he do what the prophecies say?"

Mab frowned. "Their meaning is disputed," he said. "Certainly he will complete the tower. And just as certainly he will control the planets from it. But whether he will defeat the Changer's purposes for Anthropos . . ."

His voice faltered and he stared at John, his eyes hard. John flushed. Mab's eyes were twin accusations. "A good deal depends on the Sword Bearer," Mab breathed, his voice as soft as his eyes were hard, "for only the Sword Bearer can bring about the ruin of the Mystery's tower."

John's heart beat unpleasantly. He was sorry he had asked. Suddenly he didn't want to know anything more about the two towers. He even wanted to forget he was the Sword Bearer. The notion of bringing about the destruction of a tower was terrifying but too absurd to be true. He thrust it to the back of his mind. But Mab's eyes did not leave him. "We must go, you and I, to see this tower for ourselves if indeed it exists. And if it does we must know how soon it will be finished. I must take the risk of summoning the Guardian of the Old Way."

The old man struck the rocks with his staff, and a loud crack whipped the air. The rocks split and a chasm opened at their feet. Steps led down into a gloomy subterranean passage. At its head stood a tall blue-robed figure holding a naked sword with both hands above its head, as if about to attack them. The face was distorted with rage. "Who dares . . . !"

"In the name of the Changer, in the *name—I* dare!"

A flash of blue from the magician's staff knocked the raised sword from the creature's hands. The look of rage on its face was replaced by one of uncertainty.

"You are one of his servants, are you not, Guardian of the Old Way?" Mab's voice trembled with suppressed anger.

"He is—the power of Mystery is—"

"The power of the Mystery is as nought to the might of the Changer," Mab continued. "And it is in his name, in the name of your rightful Lord, that I demand passage along the Old Way."

There was a pause. "I . . . dare . . . not." The words fell hesitantly from the lips of the Guardian. Mab's voice was low and quiet. "It appears that you have yielded allegiance to the Mystery. Leave your sword where it lies."

He spoke again. "I could destroy you now, treacherous one. The power of the Changer himself flows from my staff. But either you will accompany us and show us the way to the swamp that lies at the end of the Old Way, or we shall leave you in the open to the tender mercies of your new master."

The Guardian turned slowly. "Be it as you wish," he muttered and began to descend the steps into the passage below them.

"Can we trust him?" John asked fearfully.

"It will be the better choice," Mab replied, stepping in the wake of their new guide. "It is clear now that the Mystery is at present in the swamp. Our only hope of penetrating it undetected is this way. The Guardian of the Old Way is the one who knows the secrets of the swamp."

The Old Way was like no way John had ever trodden. At first he thought they were descending steps. But before long he was sure they were climbing. Then after a while he could feel nothing under his feet. Yet he was walking, walking on nothing. Ahead Mab went on eerily into soft blue space, his feet falling on a firmness John could neither see nor feel. And ahead of the seer the Guardian glided mysteriously.

The blue light was around John again, the light that took his fears away but made him guilty and ashamed. It was like a curtain hiding everything else from him—floor, ceiling, walls. He could only see ahead as far as the Guardian. He had the sensation that rock and earth no longer surrounded them.

"Mab," he called softly, looking ahead again, "Mab—where are we? Where is this?"

Mab's reply did not help. "This is everywhere. Or nowhere. Take your pick. It is the Old Way. It has nothing to do with time and space. It is where time and space come from." But he said the words with no expression, as though he were thinking of something else, as indeed he was. And as John looked beyond him again to the Guardian, he saw that the Guardian looked more like a ghost than a man.

For one thing he kept changing color. Shifting grays, pinks and soft yellows. Delicate lilac shades fluttered across and through him. An eery green halo surrounded him. Mab was muttering to himself and John thought he caught some of the words, " . . . too late . . . too late . . ." One phrase came through clearly, "Damned, forever damned, and therefore treacherous . . ."

But for the moment John's fears had left him. Only the shame and the guilt continued to haunt him. He could never afterward tell whether the whole thing had lasted for days or only for minutes.

At length he felt steps beneath his feet, steps leading down. A moment later the Guardian cried strange words in a loud voice. Smoke surrounded them, smoke that slowly changed to the ugly yellow of a Pendleton fog. And as the fog faded John saw that they were in the open air again. But the stench! The canals of Lancashire smelled sweet in comparison with the choking foulness that made him retch.

The sun was dull red in color, and the sky a faded blue gray. He tried not to breathe but could not help himself. They were in the middle of the swamp.

They stood on a slimy pathway winding among the foul gray sludge that spread into a dull yellow mist around them. Here and there the skeleton of a dead tree rose gaunt and naked.

The sludge was not still. Bubbles were slowly rising like miniature domes, as though rotting soccer balls were oozing their way upward. Then they would burst wetly, leaving a hollow which slowly filled. The vapors that came from the bubbles were the source of the stench that sickened John.

But there was little time to observe their surroundings. Fear was back. It fell like an icy cloak around John's shoulders as he slipped and slithered after Mab who seemed to be hurrying to stay close behind the Guardian. The Guardian's pace had suddenly changed. Mab's eyes never left the creature.

"Keep close behind me!" Mab called over his shoulder.

For an hour they hurried forward, twisting this way and that. If anything, the pace increased. But the sun was growing clearer. Occasionally they could see patches of slimy water, and once or twice fingers of clear water poked their way into the sludge. Mab turned around, his old face alight with pleasure as he said to John, "Not far now!" And then it happened.

As soon as Mab turned, the Guardian shot a long arm around him to snatch at the sword hanging from John's side. John gave a wild leap sideways, landing waist-deep in the sludge. There was nothing solid beneath his feet, and he felt himself being drawn down. "Mab!" he shrieked. Mab was wrestling with the Guardian. The cold mud rose to John's neck. It compressed his chest so that he could not expand it. He was sinking rapidly. Before he could cry out again, it had risen to his mouth and nose. Blackness surrounded him. His head seemed to swell like a balloon, and his lungs fought helplessly for air. His mouth

and nose filled with suffocating foulness.

Searing heat suddenly burned his body. For a few seconds he was blinded by light. But he could breathe again. And with his first lungful of air he screamed.

He was back on the path. And miraculously he was dry and clean. Clean, dry, but trembling and panting, his head and heart pounding. In front of him Mab was a flaming blue giant. But of the Guardian there was no sign. Slowly the light faded from Mab, and he was his tall and aged self again. "He is no more," Mab said. John supposed, and supposed rightly, that Mab was referring to the Guardian.

As they stared at the yellow curtain of mist that shrouded the deeper parts of the swamp, a rush of wind came from behind them, driving the foul vapors inward. Then for a moment the curtains parted, and they saw a tall tower, piercing the sky like a long white needle. It was wider and more solid than it seemed, but its extreme height gave the appearance of fragility. But there was an asymmetry about the top of it that suggested it was still uncompleted.

Mab's arms cradled John's shoulder, pulling him down protectively. "Lie flat," he ordered. "Never mind the mud!" For several minutes they stared. "So he's here," Mab breathed, nodding at the tower. "The Mystery of Abomination has come. It has taken up its abode in the swamps as the prophecy said. And it has almost completed the Tower of Darkest Night, the tower that controls the planets. Before long radiations from the tower will bring the planets to a standstill, and darkness will cover the land."

The tower stood surveying them, proud, contemptuous and in spite of its fragility, menacing. "Can they see us?" John asked, shuddering.

"They might, but I doubt it," Mab answered. "However we must not delay our departure. Our time is short. We must get to the island to see what the situation is there." He looked thoughtful. "Who can be in the Tower of Darkness with him?

It is rumored that some of the Matmon disloyal to Bjorn set out for the swamps to find him. Others have long been his slaves, working as laborers on his projects. The tower could house an army."

The wind had dropped and the curtain of mist closed again so that John almost wondered whether what they had seen was real. They rose to their feet. "This time I must use my staff," Mab said. "We have no other choice, and speed is essential." He raised the staff above his head and seized John by the arm. A moment later John felt himself rising and whirling through darkness.

The whirling sensation slowly subsided, Mab's grip relaxed, and light warmed John's curtained eyelids. He could feel he was sitting on a gently rocking seat. On opening his eyes he discovered he was sitting with Mab in a tiny leather coracle that bobbed on waves a couple of hundred yards from an island, the same island he had seen from the air some hours before.

About a hundred and fifty yards in length, its cliffs rose sheer on all sides from the water. A majestic gray stone tower soared massively from the cliffs at its western end. It was the tower from which the Regents were to emerge, the Tower of the Garden Room.

Anxiety and urgency were written on Mab's face as he dug a paddle viciously into the water. "I can see an opening in the cliffs over there below the tower," he breathed. "The sooner we are sheltered inside it, the better I shall feel." Quickly the little vessel skittered across the waves. As they entered the cave, he drew in his paddle, and John listened in awe to the water's gentle whispers as they echoed along the smooth cave walls.

Indeed it was more of a tunnel than a cave. As he looked more closely at the walls, he saw that they were built of smooth stones. "Matmon work," Mab said, stroking his beard slowly. "King Bjorn will be interested. Servants of the Mystery have been here already, and here for some time."

"Where's all the red light coming from?" John asked,

puzzled. A red dimness filled the tunnel, but no light source could be seen. The water beyond them danced black and soft crimson.

"It is a sign of the Mystery. He has stamped his mark on this place!" Mab replied. "I can only suppose it has abandoned this place to make its headquarters in the swamp. It wanted a tower of its own." He dipped his paddle into the water again, directing the coracle round a bend and then through an arch into a more spacious subterranean cave, also lined with smooth stones and filled with red light. There was a low stone wharf on the right. Mab attached the coracle to a ring on it, and they scrambled on shore.

Two stairways led up from the wharf, one from the end and one from immediately in front of them. Mab headed for the one at the end and, followed by John, made his way up the narrow winding stone staircase to a heavy oak door at the top. His staff was glowing blue. "This must lead into the tower," he said slowly. "It is a door we may not enter. We must try the other stairway. It probably will take us to the surface of the island."

He was right. Moments later they were back in the sunlight, standing at the cliff top and staring at the stone tower that stood in splendid isolation. Close-up it was even more impressive. Surrounded on three sides by steep cliffs, it rose sheer and imposing from the western point of the island. Dominating the island, it seemed to ignore them, guarding its own secret counsels, hiding its thoughts behind the blank windows that served as its eyes.

The island was a sort of giant's table in the middle of the lake. It was longer than it was wide. Wiry grass clothed the undulating surface. Here and there gorse and heather exploded into brilliant splotches of yellow and purple. And standing like two sentries twenty yards from the tower, two gray rocks seemed to watch them with the same solemn intensity of the tower.

"What are they?" John asked Mab.

"Can you hear the humming?"

John listened intently. As he did he was able to discern a low, undulating murmur, rising and falling with a dim throbbing light that came from the rocks.

"What do they remind you of?" Mab asked.

"Chairs, grandfather and grandmother chairs—but the light and the sound—"

"They are chairs—of a sort. They are the Scunning Stones."

"The *what*?"

"The Scunning Stones. They were made at the dawn of time. Touch them at your peril. Any who sit on them die instantly. Only the Regents may sit on them and live. That is how we will know the Regents when they come."

The wonder and the mystery of the island had begun to work its spell on them. "So it is true," Mab said slowly. "The tower is really here, built by no human hands. And from these walls will come the Regents who will sit on the Scunning Stones." He drew in a deep breath. "We must return to the company. It is essential that we establish ourselves here. We must be here to welcome them when they arrive. And we must entrench ourselves here lest the Mystery come again. Clearly his agents have been here already. We may have to defend the island. We must get back, John the Sword Bearer. We must get back at once."

With one hand he seized John's sword belt, and with the other he raised his staff. "By the Changer," he cried, "take us back to the company!"

Then once again John saw the staff glowing blue. It spread along Mab's outstretched arm until the old man was himself aglow. Indeed John, too, felt a burning inside, and suddenly the earth seemed to turn topsy-turvy. He was drifting dizzily through midnight skies as Mab hung onto his belt. Stars and moon spun round them. Yet amid the blackness and the whirling stars two towers stood motionless, one on their right and one on their left, the one enormous, white and thin, the other solid and built of rock.

13
The
Seer

It took the little company two months to reach Lake Nachash. They had to leave the coastal forests and cross the northern mountains to where the River Rure flowed into the heart of Anthropos. And night by night Aguila and her eagles would bring a freshly prepared table for the company so that they could feast on fresh meats, and drink again and again of the wine of free pardon. As the darkness fell each night, the fireflies would come and their multicolored lights and delicate music would fall gently over the feasters.

As they drank free pardon the Matmon would sing songs about Anthropos. Their voices were deep and the melodies enchanting. In spite of himself John found that he was picking the songs up and joining in. They sang about the day when the Changer made their world out of darkness and emptiness. They sang about the coming of the Regents who would rule them for ages to come. They sang songs about someone called Gaal who would one day destroy everything evil. There was even a song about the Sword Bearer—but John would close his ears and turn his face when they sang it.

Sometimes when the food and wine were finished, they would climb on the table and dance their wild and vigorous dances, shouting and clapping their hands above their heads.

For at least a month there was no sign of opposition. Nicholas Slapfoot remained in his underwater lair. The Lord Lunacy appeared to no one. The Mystery of Abomination was all but forgotten.

On the whole tempers remained good and spirits high. But Vixenia spoke little and grew thin, bearing herself with quiet dignity, saying only, "I shall be avenged one day. The Lord John will slay the Goblin Prince and I shall be content. In the meantime I shall play my part in the company's ventures."

John would grow uneasy whenever she spoke like that. Ever since he had been in Nicholas Slapfoot's cave, his sword had remained firmly fixed in its scabbard. He thought more than once of telling Mab about it, but did not do so, fearing that Mab would try to make him drink the wine of free pardon. Indeed he fought against a growing conviction that the sword would not be released until he drank. And he had no wish to drink. Nor had he any wish to encounter Nicholas Slapfoot again. His heart would beat and his forehead sprout drops of sweat whenever he thought of the shark in the cave. The momentary courage he had felt when he had hung the blue stone around his neck had gone completely.

He told no one about the stone, fearing it might be taken from him. Nor did he try to wear it. The appalling shame and guilt that stole through him whenever he did so had taught him to leave it alone. It remained hidden within an inside pocket in his tunic.

His mood varied. Mostly he was bored and discontented. He avoided Mab whenever he could. He grew more self-conscious than ever beneath Mab's searching glances.

He began to make friends among the Matmon. There was a group of them that held themselves a little apart from the rest who were led by the Matmon prince, the murderer of John's dreams. He had been drawn to the group initially by his fascination with Prince Goldson. But little by little the impression from his dreams had subsided, and he found himself wanting both the prince and his Matmon followers to let him be a part of their group.

He could not have said what it was that attracted him. Several times Mab questioned him. "They do not drink of the wine of free pardon," he said thoughtfully. And John, saying nothing, had thought to himself, "No, and neither do I." Somehow Mab's disapproval and the occasional anxious glances that King Bjorn threw his way increased his determination to be a part of the group.

So as they wound their way through spectacular mountain passes and descended toward the Valley of the Rure, John found himself spending more and more time with what he began to regard as the rebels. As for the rebels, they seemed delighted that he chose to be with them. To John's pleasure, the Matmon always addressed him as "your lordship." Even Prince Goldson did so, though John could never be sure whether there was mockery in the prince's voice.

Two strange events marked their passage through the highest pass, both events concerning night. As they camped high and cold in the thin air, King Bjorn claimed everyone's attention with the words, "This is now the third night in succession on which we have seen a full moon."

One or two of them were inclined to argue about the matter and to say the moon had not been full before. But as night succeeded night on their descent in search of the Rure Valley, there could no longer be any doubt. Something had happened to the moon. It remained always full.

The second change concerned the night itself. Once they began their descent it increased in length by one hour each day so that the days rapidly grew shorter and the nights longer. Two days after King Bjorn had first mentioned the moon, it became quite clear to all of them that the universe around them was in the grip of a cataclysmic change. That night at their supper feast, when King Bjorn asked Mab what he thought, the old man rose to his feet as though he were in a daze. John's eyes, like those of the rest of the company, were fixed on him. Slowly Mab began to speak in a soft sing-song voice.

"And when the ruler of darkness reigns,
 the days shall be painted with gloom.
And the light of the stars shall slowly increase
 as a shadow crosses the moon.
For then shall the tower of Mystery wax great
 and an odor of death shall blow
'Til the sword shall be free in the bearer's hand
 and the tower shall sink below."

His words fell like a spell on the company as they stared at him, their faces softly painted with firefly light. Queen Bjornsluv was the first to speak. "What does it mean?" she asked softly. But Mab's eyes were glazed and again he repeated his strange prophecy.

There was a deep rumbling in Oso's throat. "The tower," he growled. "Same as in swamp. Thin white tower. You saw."

"Yes. And the stench," John muttered. "That must be the odor of death."

Mab sat down with a sigh and King Bjorn addressed him. "What does it mean when you say, ' *'til the sword shall be free in the bearer's hand*'?" he asked.

Mab was frowning. "The words come to me," he said slowly. "I feel them rising and then they come—if I let them. I do not always know what they mean. A seer is only a mouthpiece. Probably Oso is right. The tower in the swamp is the tower of the Mystery. Doubtless the growing length of the night and the fact that the moon remains full is because of powerful emanations from the tower in the swamp. Until the tower is swallowed into the depths of the earth, things will get worse."

"And what about the sword being free in the bearer's hand?" Bjorn insisted, looking hard at John.

Mab also turned and looked at him. "Draw the sword from your scabbard," he said.

"Why?" John asked.

"Because I command you to," Mab replied.

John felt sick. He knew what the prophecy meant. The sword was not free. He could not draw it. "I don't want to," he muttered. "I don't see why I should just because you say so."

There was a heavy silence. John could see that every eye was on him. Slowly Mab said, "I see. You refuse to try because you have found that you can't. The sword is no longer free. You need to drink the wine of free pardon." His voice was gentle, but John dropped his burning face and shook his head.

After that there was a noticeable lessening of respect in the company for John. The members of the rebel group still called him "my lord," or "your lordship," but John would sometimes catch a smirk on their faces as they did so. Yet as the company descended into the Rure Valley and as the days rapidly shortened and the nights lengthened, he continued to mingle with the rebel group.

Day by day his unhappiness grew. He hardly ever spoke to Mab. At night he would pretend to be tired and fall asleep, waiting until Mab himself was asleep and then getting up to stare in misery through the window of whatever Gaal tree Mab had managed to find. For they were now above the tree line, and trees were nonexistent except, curiously, for one solitary tree in each place where they camped. John was never sure whether the trees were different trees or whether the same tree had transplanted itself ahead of them to await their arrival.

But three days later as they entered the upper Rure Valley, they encountered trees again, and the farther they descended the denser and more magnificent the forest became. They followed a pathway that wound along the side of a steep slope. As they looked in the direction of the river, now hidden by the trees, the land fell sharply away beneath towering eucalyptus which along with giant ferns sliced the soft green light into monstrous and awesome shapes, creating space sculptures dappled with faint sunlight.

Apart from the ferns there was no undergrowth. Bracken arched over the pathway and the palmlike fronds of the giant ferns sprouted luxuriously around them. Soaring eucalyptus columns rose awesomely to the green roof far above them, dominating and dwarfing everything else.

"Forest fires keep the undergrowth cleared," Mab said. "The trees survive it. Mind you, they look black and dead until the spring when they simply sprout green again." And as John looked he saw that there were no lower branches. Huge trunks rose sheer and naked until they burst into green fountains of light.

Somehow that day John had become separated from the rebel group and had found himself lagging behind the company with Mab. He ducked beneath a half-fallen tree that arched over the path like a low, lichen-draped portal, and turned to help the old man do the same.

"Thank you, John," Mab said. He clung to John's hand as he straightened himself. John looked up into the lined and wrinkled face. He suddenly remembered the night on which the old man had three times tumbled from the sky into the forest glade, and as he did so his heart softened and he smiled to himself.

"Why do you not let me help you?" Mab asked him, still holding his hand.

"You mean drink the wine?" John asked.

Mab nodded.

"I don't know," John said. "I just can't—yes, I think that's the way it really is. I just can't face the stuff. I'm sorry."

He pulled his hand away from Mab's and turned to resume his way along the path. The sounds of the rest of the company had been swallowed by the vast forest. They were quite alone.

"It's all very well for you," he said as they resumed their way. "You're a magician, a wizard. You can do magic. I've just—it's all just sort of *happened* to me . . ."

He paused, uncertain of himself and a little ashamed.

"I am neither a magician nor a wizard," Mab's deep voice sounded behind him. John was startled.

"But you are. I mean you must be. You do magic."

"Not magic, Sword Bearer. *Miracles.*"

"What's the difference?"

For several minutes they pursued their way in silence. Then Mab spoke again.

"I know they call me a magician," he said. "Magician, sorcerer, wizard. But I am none of these. For several hundred years I have refused to become one. And in a few minutes I shall refuse for the last time. I am a prophet—a seer. And a seer I will always be."

A deep gully sliced the hillside just ahead of them, and as they scrambled down into it to the stream that had wounded the hillside, they found themselves in a dell. Its slopes were clothed with feathery ferns and wildflowers. The branches of stunted trees were draped with hanging moss. The stream fell among huge boulders in musical waterfalls from pool to reflective pool with water so clear that every detail of sand, stones and darting trout delighted John's eyes.

Steppingstones crossed the stream, and above the steppingstones lay a small pool, deep enough to swim in. Beyond the pool was a massive, moss-covered boulder over whose shoulder the water fell in a shimmering scarf. Mab stared at the boulder fixedly.

"That's where he lives," he murmured.

"Who? You mean in that rock?"

Mab nodded. "He who calls himself the chief sorcerer Qhahdrun. You will see him in a moment. He comes to make me his final offer and to bully me with his final threat."

John stared at the boulder. Qhahdrun. The very sound chilled his blood for some reason. Qhahdrun. Was he *inside* the boulder? Would a door open in it? There was no sign of an opening. Then in the space on the side of the boulder opposite the waterfall a man appeared. He was tall, as tall as Mab himself, but there the similarity ended.

For whereas Mab was bearded and wrinkled, the stranger was clean-shaven, smooth and bald. His lips were thin and his nose delicately chiseled, the nostrils widening or closing from time to time. From an elaborate gold filigree round his neck, white satin fell in folds over his shoulders to his feet.

John's impressions were confused. In part the strange being made him think of a tall, elaborate candle. But the eyes were awesome, compelling, and he shrank behind Mab to shield himself from them. The sorcerer reminded him also of something or someone else. In vain he searched his memory for an answer. Where had he encountered something like this before?

"I am Qhahdrun, lord of the Qadar!" The words burned in the space between them.

"And I am Mab, servant of the Changer."

"Kneel before me, Mab. You are a servant, so kneel." The proud head tilted back and the nostrils flared. Mab's reply was almost gentle.

"Qhahdrun, I bow to none but the Changer."

The sorcerer's arms shot skyward, and from his hands a wall of flame swept toward them, but from Mab's staff blue lightning flashed, cutting the flames and dispersing them. Qhahdrun's face settled itself into contempt.

"I am Qhahdrun. My power is my own power. I do not shelter behind the power of others. I am a sorcerer. I have studied hidden things. The secrets of the universe are mine. I have mastered them." He paused for a moment, then continued. "Your power is not yours. Join us, O Mab. Become a true sorcerer."

"You know what my answer will be, Qhahdrun. I am a seer,

not a sorcerer." Mab's voice was weary and flat. His face was sad and his shoulders rounded. "My power is great. Greater, as you have observed, than your own. Yet you are right. It is not mine but the Changer's. I use it only to accomplish his bidding."

"And it is his bidding to bring the Regents," Qhahdrun spat. "And when the Regents come, you will die."

"When the Regents come *and when the Sword Bearer has killed the Goblin Prince,* then I will die."

John felt Qhahdrun's eyes burning through his skin. "The Sword Bearer cannot use the sword. He is no servant of the Changer. He will come to us and you will not be able to stop him. And you will die. The Changer will discard you whether the Regents come or not and whether the Goblin Prince lives or dies. Only as a sorcerer can you live on. Look at me, Mab! Do I age? Does death creep through my members? I am immortal, Mab! Bow to me! You alone have defied me! I will give you power *for yourself alone!* Bow to me and live! Look at my followers! Do they look as if they are dying?"

John gasped with fear. For the dell was suddenly crowded with men and women robed in deathly white, crying, "Come to us, Mab! Join our ranks! We are free! We have our own power! It belongs to us! We know the deep secrets of power!"

But Mab straightened his shoulders and raised his staff high. "It is enough!" he cried. "It is the last time! Never will I do as you say! Avaunt! Avaunt! In the name of the Changer, avaunt!"

Terrible blue light blotted out the whole scene for several seconds. Then as the light faded, they were once again alone. With a sigh Mab picked his way across the steppingstones and scrambled up the far side of the dell. John followed him. In less than a minute they had resumed their way along the path through the forested mountainside.

For a long time neither of them spoke. But at last John could bear it no longer. "Who were they?" he asked.

"Sorcerers, wizards, magicians—call them what you will,"

Mab replied. "They were brought here from other worlds by the Changer when this world first began. But they chose to serve themselves. You heard what Qhahdrun said. They want their own power. They want magic. And the Changer will have no truck with magic."

"But you do magic!" John said, bewildered.

"No, Sword Bearer. It is true that I have power from the Changer. So have Aguila and Oso. But the power is his power, not ours. It is to be used in his service. Magic is stolen power. The power that Qhahdrun has is magical power. It was stolen by the Mystery of Abomination when he rebelled against the Changer. Qhahdrun really thinks it belongs to him. But one day it will be taken from him. For at the last all power will go back to the Changer from whence it first came."

There was silence, and for a while they walked without speaking. "The Qadar," Mab said at length. "Qhahdrun rules them. I suppose they will be on our trail sooner or later." But John was not listening. Darkness began to fall and Mab increased his pace, anxious to reach the company ahead of them. John was thinking of Mab's death and wondering how to talk about it. But it seemed that Mab might have been able to read his thoughts.

"Yes, I will die," he said. "After all, everyone dies in the end. And I have lived long, very long. But if I'm honest I do not wish to die. I wish to see him fulfill his promise of a son to me first.

"I serve the Changer, yet he rewards me with death, and though his plans will be fulfilled, the longings of my own heart will not. I shall die without seeing what I had hoped and longed to see."

"What—er—what is it you want to see?" John asked, only half listening to the old man. But Mab only sighed. "He could take the longing away. That way too I could die content," he said. "Yet year by year my longing increases. And all he promises me is death."

14

The Coming of the Copper Moon

In some ways their journey down the Rure Valley was easier than the first part of their journey, and in other ways it was much more difficult. It was easier because they were now going downhill. It was more difficult because day by day the nights grew longer and the period of daylight shorter. Soon the company found that they rose by the light of a full moon, traveled into brief daylight and made camp long after the sun had set, again under a full moon.

But three nights after Mab's encounter with Qahdrun, a change came over the moon. They had left the eucalyptuses behind and were pitching camp in an open space above the river, surrounded by tall pines. King Bjorn was the first to notice it.

"Look!" he cried. "An eclipse of the moon is beginning!"

Work on pitching camp ceased. John lay on his back to avoid the crick in his neck as he watched a curved shadow steal slowly across the silver face. In an hour or so the moon was covered. All that remained was a dead moon, faintly glowing a dull copper shade.

"The shadow will pass after a while," King Bjorn said. "I saw it happen in my youth." But the shadow did not pass. The eclipse remained fixed. The stars shone a little more brightly, and Mab repeated his strange prophecy.

"And when the ruler of darkness reigns,
    the days shall be painted with gloom.
And the light of the stars shall slowly increase
    as a shadow crosses the moon.
For then shall the tower of Mystery wax great
    and an odor of death shall blow
'Til the sword shall be free in the bearer's hand
    and the tower shall sink below."

That night their sleep was troubled, and they woke frequently, hot and feverish. When they rose, the darkness was deeper and the camp was filled with drifting smoke that bore an odor of death. John drank greedily from a stone jar of water, his eyes smarting from the smoke. "I'm hot!" he said. "What's happened?" But Mab only shook his head.

It was too dark to proceed with their journey, for the eclipsed moon and the stars were now blotted out by smoke. Anxiously they waited for the three hours of daylight.

But the daylight never came. Instead, a terrifying orb, bearing the face of the Lord Lunacy, burst into the sky and shone for three hours, peering down at them through the dirty yellow haze.

The ground was warm and here and there cracks appeared, exuding blue-black bitumen. At first they were alarmed, but at least the bitumen provided them with a means of making torches. They spent the day preparing these with rushes from the river, anticipating that most of their journey now would have to be in darkness. Mab pursed his lips and talked constantly about forest fires.

The foul stench not only made their eyes smart but sickened them so that for the first day they ate nothing. They had no idea where the stench came from, though they noticed that the river water had become warm, and that multitudes of dead fish floated on their sides to feed growing numbers of vultures and crows. They now boiled all their water. But it still tasted foul. "The smell in the air doesn't smell like *fish*," John said to Mab. "It's more like the smell of the swamp."

The following day there were only two hours of light from the strange orb, the next day only one. Thereafter they journeyed through darkness, a lurid company with flickering torches, weaving single file through wreaths of smoke among tall pines. They watched the ground carefully. Cracks would open up, disgorging boiling bitumen. One of the horses plunged its forelegs into the stuff and screamed with pain. They had to kill it.

Every night, or rather every suppertime, for it was night the whole time now, Aguila and her eagles came with the same table and freshly prepared food and drink for the weary company. Without the nightly feast it is doubtful whether they could have continued. The faces of the Matmon were pale and gaunt, and their movements heavy with weariness.

Yet as they ate at the long table their strength would revive, and as many of them drank of the wine of free pardon, the only wine most now drank, light would shine from their eyes again, and smiles paint their faces. Soon the songs would begin again, and after a while the rhythm would get into their arms and legs, and they would be upon the table, dancing.

One night as firefly music refreshed their ears and firefly light scattered gentle beauty over them, Mab stiffened.

"What is it?" King Bjorn asked. Bjornsluv and Vixenia also stared at him.

"Hsst!" the prophet said.

John listened carefully. Then far above them and strangely discordant with the firefly music, he heard it. Faint as the screech was, it chilled him. It came again. And again.

"Qadar!" Mab muttered darkly. "Qhahdrun rules them. Doubtless he now plans to use them to destroy the company. They fly the night skies. I would have thought that with all this smoke they could never see us. But they are looking."

Bjorn's face paled and John could see that his hands were trembling. "Qadar!" he breathed softly, "O Mi-ka-ya. What have we brought on ourselves?"

"What danger is there right now?" Queen Bjornsluv asked.

"Very little," the old man answered. "Their eyes cannot penetrate either the branches or the leaves of trees. Moreover the canopy of fireflies affords us protection. They can see neither them nor us. But I fear that when we journey on by torchlight they will see light and come upon us. We can no longer travel in safety."

"*No longer?*" Vixenia's voice was contemptuous. "What safety have we enjoyed so far?"

"What are Qadar?" John asked.

"Scourers of the night skies," Mab replied grimly. "Swifter than thought and deadly in rage. Nothing can stand against them. Earth creatures tremble when they fly."

Their faces were grave that night and their thoughts troubled. But after much discussion it was decided that their only option was to proceed with caution. The pine trees would provide good cover. They would use only one torch which King Bjorn's torchbearer would carry at the head of the column. They would proceed slowly and in single file, keeping close rank and cautioning one another as they came to any bituminous cracks. Anytime they heard a Qadar the torch would instantly be put out.

Their progress was slow but for two days their plan worked well. No one fell into the cracks and they lost no more horses. Only once did they hear the distant shrieking of a Qadar, and on hearing it they extinguished the torch and sheltered beneath the pine trees. Within an hour they had resumed their way again, moving cautiously but continuously toward their goal.

But on the following day the whole company was nearly wiped out. They came across a lake of boiling pitch, about a hundred yards in diameter. Acrid fumes rose from it, threatening to choke them. Yet their path clung to the borders of the lake. The thickets were so dense that they could not push through them to give the pitch lake a wide berth. Coughing and spluttering they stumbled hurriedly around it, their faces and legs burning with the heat of the pitch.

On the far side of the lake there was a clearing, and the torch bearer waited until they had all gathered away from the edge of the lake and had been accounted for. In their preoccupation with what they were doing they failed to hear the telltale shrieks until it was too late, until in fact a piercing and terrifying screech awoke them to their peril. Hovering over the lake of boiling bitumen was the shadowy figure of a Qadar.

In spite of the heat John shivered with terror. Vaguely he was conscious that the rest of the company were as still as painted shadows. The torch bearer stood transfixed, his torch sputtering and flickering, but still held high. Yet the light revealed little of the Qadar beyond an ominous silhouette shrouded in the vapors that rose from the boiling lake. To John it seemed as though a tall figure stood upright on the back of what might have been a gigantic bat. The only clear features were the burning red eyes of the rider that seemed to penetrate his soul. Two more screeches pierced the darkness, and two more terrible shadows hovered behind the first. Six red eyes now stared at John.

His right hand was inside his tunic and he felt the stone resting in the pocket. Hardly knowing why he did so, he slipped it over his head, and as he did so it seemed as if his head cleared. "Put out the torch!" he cried.

The torch bearer did not move.

"The torch!" John screamed. "Put it out!"

It was as though his body had come alive. In an instant he was beside the torch bearer and snatched the torch from his hand. The Qadar were beginning to glide slowly toward them from the lake. John ran to the edge of the pitch and, with all his strength, flung the torch toward the red eyes.

Instantly the lake exploded. With a terrifying roar the vapors above it caught fire, rushed up in a column of flame a hundred feet high. John was hurtled head over heels backward. The members of the company were flung to the ground by the explosion and scorched by searing heat. Instinctively they crawled in terror into the woods beyond, sheltering behind pine trees and staring from a safe distance at the blazing light that illuminated the forest, wondering all the while what had happened to the Qadar.

They never found out. Mab thought they must have perished in the explosion. Otherwise, he argued, the Qadar would have continued to search for them. "Qadar never leave a quarry until the quarry is dead," he said emphatically. "Therefore they must be dead themselves."

Slowly King Bjorn and Mab mustered the frightened company.

There was no need for torches now, for the column of fire lit the region for acres around. By some miracle no one had been seriously injured. Generally hair and many beards had been scorched and skins superficially burned; even John suffered only bruises. And in the darkness no one had observed the effects of the stone, which John had removed again during the general confusion.

Because the danger of a forest fire was now great, it was decided that they would travel by river.

"It is not without risk," Mab said. "But there may be no more Qadars to contend with. Should there be a forest fire, the safest place will be on water. And two days on the water should take us into Lake Nachash."

So the next three days were spent at the water's edge constructing rafts and tending to minor injuries and burns. They posted a watch for the Qadar, but there was no further sign of them. They also posted a watch as they slept because of Mab's fear of fire. And during the second night fire did indeed begin to sweep up the hillside and in the direction from which they had come. But it posed no threat to their safety.

So on the fourth day following the explosion they set out, a small flotilla of rafts, poling their way down toward Lake Nachash. It was a strange journey. Sometimes the drifting smoke hid even the banks of the river. At other times it would clear to reveal the outlines of the hills alight with a dozen lines of flame that in the distance looked like living fireworms writhing slowly up the mountainsides.

They never grew accustomed to the foul stench which attached itself to their skin and clothing, and mingled with the smell of bitumen. Washing themselves in the river only made matters worse.

But in many ways river travel was better than picking their way through the forest. They no longer had to beware of the ground splitting at their feet to disgorge boiling bitumen. Moreover when the smoke cleared, they would see on the riverbank the leering faces of goblins, watching their progress from among the branches of the trees.

At first John found them very frightening, but eventually he bolstered his courage by making faces at them and sticking out his tongue. Mab laughed when he caught him doing it toward the end of their second day's journey. "They're servants of your friend, the Goblin Prince," he said. "They number in the thousands. But unlike him, they are terrified of water. Here we are safe. But I shall not feel too safe when we camp, as we must, on the shores of Lake Nachash."

John looked at him anxiously, and Mab continued, "They are easy enough to deal with in small numbers, but they know no fear, and a concerted attack from them would be disastrous."

John stared again at the leering faces. They seemed to crowd every tree on the riverbank. Thousands? His fears returned with renewed force. He had not thought about the possibility of encountering the goblins around the campsite.

"How far now, wizard?" King Bjorn asked Mab.

Mab smiled, "No wizard am I, but a seer," he said, "and as a good seer I predict that Lake Nachash will lie a mile and a half beyond the next bend. There we shall have to camp. And there we shall have to determine how to handle the followers of the Goblin Prince."

John's heart sank. They could be drifting into a trap. The goblins were obviously waiting for them. It was crazy to think of going ashore and making camp. "Mab," he said hesitantly. "*Must* we make camp? Won't it be dangerous?"

Mab's face was grave. "Dangerous it may be," he said, "but to drift into the lake could be even more dangerous."

15

The Hideous Head

They camped that night on the shore of Lake Nachash. The goblins were nowhere to be seen. With the coming of Aguila and the fireflies, peace reigned among the company. But there were no songs and dancing that night.

Instead plans were laid. Mab and King Bjorn agreed that the disappearance of the goblins meant they were gathering reinforcements and organizing for an attack. "Which also means," Mab said, "that they will attack in overwhelming numbers. We will have little hope of throwing them off. But they're unlikely to come for some hours, and we may be on our way again before they do. We must post sentries, sleep on the shore itself, and be ready to board the rafts, cast off and leave at a moment's notice."

"Why don't we leave now?" John asked.

"We need paddles, Sword Bearer," King Bjorn replied. "We cannot pole rafts across a deep lake. It will take a good deal of the night to carve paddles."

"What's more," Mab added, "we must first find out whether the forces of the Mystery are back on the island, and whether the lake is patrolled. As soon as we've enough paddles, one raft will go ahead to scout."

They felt the tension again as the table was removed and the comforting canopy of fireflies left them. Instead of sleeping on the beach, Mab and John retired to a Gaal tree ten yards from the shoreline. Mab's last words as they retired were, "If anything happens, don't wait for me. Don't wait for anyone or anything. Make for the rafts!"

John found his bed uncomfortable. He itched and wriggled. At times he tossed the covers aside because he was hot, only to shiver five minutes later and pull them back across him. Whenever he closed his eyes he would see hideous goblin faces. And whenever he opened his eyes they felt as though they had been rubbed with sandpaper.

His mind went back over the strange events that had occurred since his thirteenth birthday. He found himself imagining a walk along Ellor Street with old Mr. Leadbetter, the lamplighter. But soon the memory of how he discovered his dead grandmother came back, and so he pushed it out of his mind.

He tried to do the same with the memory of Old Nick, but that was more difficult. Who was Old Nick? *What* was Old Nick? How could he inhabit two worlds and be the same person? Would he, John, really kill him? He thought of his useless sword and was filled with humiliation and bitterness. Everything that had happened in the strange country of Anthropos had been unsatisfactory—his capture by Bildreth and Gutreth, the strange experience in the cave, the trial in the glade, the horrible murder of Vixenia's mate and cubs, his own refusal to drink the wine of free pardon. Finally there was his failure to attack Nicholas Slapfoot in the cave and his discovery of the uselessness of his sword.

He could almost taste bitterness in his mouth. "Sword

Bearer," he muttered in disgust. He had so wanted to impress the Matmon who had witnessed the humiliation of his trial. He had wanted to prove he had power—like Mab.

His feelings about Mab had been changing and growing. Something about the old man powerfully attracted John, though he still resented his humiliating need to be with him constantly. Yet now as he listened to the old man's quiet breathing, he knew that he did indeed like him. Mab was one of the nicest things that had ever happened to him, apart from the Changer. Or *was* that just a dream?

Restlessness refused to leave him, and he slid his feet over the side of the bed and laced up his sandals. He knew now how to open the door of a Gaal tree. He would go outside for a while until he felt more sleepy.

The night air was clear at last. The dead copper moon stared down at him. A few yards away a group of Matmon were working, some preparing suitable sections of a tree they had felled for carving and others carving the needed paddles. He began to move toward them but changed his mind. They might insist that he return to the Gaal tree.

Instead he moved slowly into the trees. Almost at once a pair of steel-strong arms wrapped themselves round him, pinning his own arms to his side.

"So we meet again, Sword Bearer! What good fortune!"

That voice! Didn't he know it? The speaker went on, "I thought I would have to catch you in the middle of our attack. But you came, yourself, into my waiting arms." The arms around him had the strength of iron.

"Bildreth!" John was shocked and enraged.

"Bildreth, no less, my lord! And this time you are going to become the servant of the rightful ruler of Anthropos!"

John raised his leg to kick at the Matmon's shins, but Bildreth was too quick, tripping him from behind and flinging him forcefully to the ground where he lay winded. He tried to cry out, but he could not draw in any breath. He caught a glimpse of

Bildreth's silhouette, one arm raised and holding a club. The club descended with appalling rapidity. John felt no pain. Felt nothing at all. He was unconscious for the next three days.

At first he was only aware of a terrible pounding in his head. He opened his eyes but shut them at once as an extra wave of pain flooded his skull. Blackness again engulfed him and several more hours passed before he awoke.

This time the pounding in his head was almost gone. For a few moments he lay still, aware that he was warm and comfortable. He moved his fingers, feeling soft silky material. He had no recollection of what had happened and opened his eyes, expecting to find himself in bed in a Gaal tree.

He was certainly in bed, or at least on a couch, but he was not in a Gaal tree. He was in a very large and circular room with a high, frescoed ceiling and walls of intricately carved paneling. He lay on a canopied couch. Beside him on a low table was a flagon of wine and a bowl of fruit. A richly patterned carpet covered the floor. Opposite him a solitary window opened into the darkness. He lay back and stared at the ceiling thirty feet above him. Slowly as he lay wondering, the memory of Bildreth came back. But where was this? What had happened to him? It was not long before he found out.

"You are in the Tower of Darkest Night." A disembodied, musical voice was speaking. "From this tower I send out my powers to control the movements of the planets until such time as I bring this planet under my personal sway."

A white opulent presence filtered through the floor. And as it did so, there arose a terrible throbbing pain in John's shoulder. Yet John watched, fascinated as the mist rose in a cloud of luminous white, boiling gently and filling three-quarters of the large room. Soft lights flickered from deep within it, greens, yellows and an occasional flicker of fiery red.

The cloud grew denser and more solid. John had always been able to see shapes and faces in clouds, but this was different. It was indeed assuming a shape, the shape of a human head, a massive human head facing John. A film of skin spread over it, like the cooling surface of wax.

Blank, colorless eyes stared blindly down at him over a massive nose. As the nostrils opened up, John was horrified to realize they were big enough to climb into. The lips, on a level with the couch, were thick, wide enough if they opened to swallow John, the couch and the table all at once. Instinctively John shrank back, pressing his free hand over his shoulder in an effort to lessen his pain. The chin seemed to be lower than the floor which seemed to have disappeared.

The eyes suddenly opened to reveal bright and luminously yellow orbs, staring down at him. John gasped. He was looking into the hideous and beautiful face of the Lord Lunacy. It was like a death mask come to life.

The lips opened like theater curtains to reveal ascending teeth and the vast cavern of a mouth. Foulness enveloped him as the music continued, "I'm so glad we are together again. Welcome home!"

John said nothing. His mind was empty. The Lord Lunacy continued, "Let me go over our last conversation. You are evil—you remember?"

John found himself nodding. Yes, of course he was evil. The throbbing pain in his shoulder grew strangely pleasurable. His fear began to leave him, or at least to be transformed into pleasing excitement. He felt a little giddy.

"You are beginning again to feel the power of evil within you."

"Yes."

"It is good, is it not?"

"Yes. Yes, it is." The words jerked mechanically from his lips.

"And you are to be the ruler of Anthropos."

"I am?"

"Yes. You are to go to the Island of Geburah, the island on the lake, in readiness for the coming of the Regents. The Sword

155

Bearer is to be king. That is the real plan—my plan."

John stared at the mouth as the curtains of the lips fell once again. A surge of wild excitement exploded inside him. A *king!* He was to become a king! But how would it happen?

"How can I be a king?"

"You will drink the wine on the table beside you. When you do so, you will be filled with the dark powers that I have placed in the wine."

That was strange, John thought. First there was the wine of free pardon. Now this wine. But it was as though the Lord Lunacy had read his thoughts. The yellow eyes seemed to envelop him.

"You will never drink the wine of free pardon."

"I won't? Why not?"

"Because Mab the seer is dead. He was killed three days ago in the goblin attack while you were on your way here. Most of the Matmon were killed too. Only the king and queen escaped with your friend Folly the donkey and Vixenia. I told the goblins I wanted them to live a little longer."

For a brief moment John was appalled. *Mab dead!* Mab? He felt dizzy and faint.

"You didn't really care for him. You just thought you did." The Lord Lunacy was reading his thoughts. John shuddered.

"You thought you liked him. But deep in your heart you hated him. You are evil, you know."

"Yes, of course. I'd forgotten." The dismay drained out of him. A cold strength grew within. He felt no sorrow, only a fierce and exultant pride.

"And when you meet the Regents on the island, you will give them some of my wine. They will rule for you—but only for a short time. You are to be king."

"What is going to happen to them?"

"They are to become my servants and yours. This will be necessary if you are to rule."

"But I will be a king?"

"Yes." And then a pause. "There is a price, of course."

"A price? How much? I don't have any money."

"No. But you have something else. You have your father, don't you?"

"No. I mean, yes. You said he was a drunk and that he didn't want me."

"Then give me the ring and the locket around your neck!"

Something was wrong. John could feel it. But what was it? He didn't really want the ring and the locket anymore. So why was he hesitating? After all, what were the bits of gold worth in comparison with becoming a king? A *king!* He was to become a king! His hand strayed inside his tunic before he could stop it to close round the gold chain that rested in the pocket there.

"Let me put it on, just for a moment," he found himself saying.

"Just for a moment," the musical voice replied tolerantly, "and then you will give it up forever."

John slipped the chain round his neck and instantly all was changed. The giant head was no longer that of the Lord Lunacy but the head of a great red dragon with nostrils spurting smoke on either side. John had become invisible. For around his neck without realizing what he was doing, he had placed the chain bearing the magic stone he had found in Old Nick's cave.

He knew immediately that he had been lied to and that he had been believing lies. All that he had been told now seemed cheap and hollow. A king? What absurdity would he believe next? Hate Mab? He had *not* been pretending about Mab. He liked Mab. Indeed he loved him—and was filled with rage and despair at the thought of his death.

"I hate you!" he screamed at the dragon's awful head. "I hate you, and I will never give you my ring and locket. I don't care whether the Changer exists or not. I don't want to be a king, and I'll never serve *you!*"

There was a roar of rage as the mouth of the dragon opened

wide. Flames shot from its nostrils and John ducked beneath the stream of the flame on his left to get out of the dragon's way. He was just in time, for the head jerked forward and the jaws snapped together, consuming the couch on which he had been lying.

He stood to one side of the head with his back to the wall, shaking with uncontrollable rage and fear. He knew it could not see him. So for several seconds he stood perfectly still, making no sound. The head sank downward and disappeared. The carpeted floor became solid again. He was alone.

He wanted to remove the stone from his neck, for now that the excitement was over he was appallingly aware of his failures and guilt. He knew the Lord Lunacy had lied to him. But he knew that some of the lies were only half lies. For he was evil. How evil? He didn't know. He didn't want to know.

He realized that the feelings of shame and guilt would leave him if he removed the stone. But if he removed the stone he would become visible again. And if he became visible the Lord Lunacy would return. He had no choice. For the time being he must put up with the unpleasantness. He slid down onto his haunches and buried his face in his knees with a groan of despair.

16

The Cup in the Tower

Crouched invisibly against the wall, he lost all track of time. When he finally tried to stand, he was too stiff and cramped to move easily. He stumbled across the wide room to the window and peered out. His head spun giddily. In the dim light of the dead moon he could see the surface of the swamp about two hundred feet beneath him. Smooth walls fell sheer from the window.

In books people escaped by tying their bedsheets together. But since the dragon had swallowed the couch, he had no sheets to tie. In any case there was nothing to tie them to. As for the carpet, it was heavy and circular, not the kind of thing you could tie knots in.

He looked round the room. *There was no door.* How did he get in? Through the window? He looked out again and this time, in spite of his mood, he snickered. If only he were a beautiful maiden with lots of hair . . .

Smoke was rising from the swamp again. Idly he watched as it swirled slowly, creeping in a rising tide up the tower wall. Soon it stretched like a sea, glowing dimly under the feeble stars as it rose and rose. For an hour or more he watched until it came right under the window. And there it seemed to stay, inviting him to plunge into it and swim.

Indeed he felt a wild desire to do so. He little knew that the smoke was there for that very reason, to lure him to his death. Had he removed the stone from round his neck, he would not have seen smoke but the sparkling sea and an illusory boat. As it was, he was pulled by an enormous urge to fling himself through the window. With a pounding heart he drew back. The window spelled danger. He must get far from it.

Wearily he made his way to the middle of the room. The carpet was pleasantly soft. He stretched himself on it, cupping his invisible chin on invisible hands and staring at its intricate pattern. By and by his head grew heavy and he rolled onto his side, using one arm as a cushion for his head.

"Thank the Changer! I've made contact with you! I've been ill with grief!"

John sat up, startled. He was no longer invisible. Mab was standing in front of him and he flung himself at the old man.

"Mab! He said you were dead!"

"Dead? Goodness no! We were all close to it at times, but we're fine now. Mind the wine!"

"The wine?"

Mab was holding a silver cup above his head out of John's way.

"It's the wine of free pardon for you to drink. When you wake up it will be beside you."

"When I wake up?"

"You're dreaming now. We both are."

"Oh. You mean it's one of *those* dreams?"

"Yes. I've never been able to transfer anything in them before, but I think this time . . . Anyway look out for the wine

when you wake up."

"Oh, Mab, I'm so glad to see you. You really are alive?"

"Alive and well and on the island."

"Did the goblins attack?"

"They certainly did. It was all over very quickly. We got out fast."

"Is everyone all right?"

Mab took a deep breath. "Two of the sentries were killed. Five more Matmon were wounded, but they're doing well." He smiled. Your friend Folly, king of donkeys, used his hoofs very effectively on our foes!"

He smiled down at John. "And now we must get out of here."

"In a dream?"

Mab shook his head. "That wouldn't work."

"Then how, Mab? How?"

"Sit down," Mab said.

They sat and looked at each other. Mab was smiling. "The Sword Bearer has yet to make the tower sink into the swamp."

John stared.

"Remember my prophecy? Listen:

'For then shall the tower of the Mystery wax great
    and an odor of death shall blow
'Til the sword shall be free in the bearer's hand
  and the tower shall sink below.' "

"Yes, but—but I can't make it sink."

"That depends."

"On what?"

"You can drink the wine of free pardon, John. And if you do, not only will your sword be free but the tower will sink."

There was a long pause. John's lips were trembling so he bit them. "I think I'd like to," he said eventually.

"Listen," Mab replied. "You won't wake for three or four hours. By then I will have the coracle under the window of the chamber where you're imprisoned. I shall not call to avoid detection. Moreover you will not see me because the smoke and mist will still be present. Drink the wine. And as the tower sinks, your window will eventually reach the level of the swamp. At that point you climb out and I shall be waiting for you."

"And what if you're not there?"

"Then I shall have perished. And you will perish too. But I shall be there. I fully intend to be."

The vision faded and he was alone and fast asleep.

John remembered his dream the moment he woke. His eyes were closed and he feared to open them. Would he find the cup of wine there? Had Mab's plan worked?

Fearfully he looked around. To his joy he saw a silver flagon beside him. He sat up, reached for it and raised it slowly. It was heavy. The wine inside was dark, and as he stared at it he remembered the night when he had spat it out, had thrown the wine in Mab's face and then flung the cup away.

What had it tasted like? He could not remember. It was not the taste that had bothered him. But what was it?

He raised the flagon to his lips and tasted. Powerful emotions tugged at his chest. He breathed deeply and tilted his head back, gulping the contents of the flagon greedily. The wine tingled in his mouth and throat. A warm fire flooded his body. He lay back, letting the flagon tumble onto the carpet. His shame and guilt at first seemed to be crushing him, but as the fires inside him burned on he knew he was being set free. Tears flowed from his eyes, and he let them flow. His arms and legs were shaking. The shame and guilt were evaporating, leaving in their place a huge contentment that swept over him in waves of fire and light. He closed his eyes and let his whole body tremble.

It was a wonderful trembling. He wanted it to go on forever. He felt as though all his fears and angers and bitternesses were being shaken out of his bones. Something powerful was happening to him, powerful but gentle. "Changer—where are you? Changer! Changer!" He hardly knew why he was saying the words, yet they erupted from deep within him. The floor beneath him began to vibrate.

He opened his eyes and saw to his joy that the room was filled with luminous blue vapor. Gentle thunder began to rumble around him and the words the thunder formed were, "Get to your feet and pull out your sword, Sword Bearer!"

John cried, "Changer, O Changer! You came back!" He sat up, stood up and seized the hilt of his sword. As he pulled, the sword shot out, pulsing its own powerful blue light.

"I never left you!" the thunder rumbled. "I have pursued you day and night."

John lowered the sword. "I thought . . . I thought you might not be real."

A thunderous roar rocked the tower, a roar that was infinitely more terrible that the dragon's roar. The roar eventually subsided into laughter, echoing through the universe before it sank into an earthquaking chuckle.

"Now," said the Changer, as the tower's shaking subsided. "Raise your sword and in my name, in the name of the Changer, bid this tower sink beneath the swamp forever."

The luminescent blue began to fade.

"Don't go away!" John cried in fear.

But the light was gone, and a small and gentle voice said, "I never go away. And if you go away, you will find me waiting for you, wherever you choose to flee. You cannot escape me."

John was still trembling. Nonetheless he raised his sword, still vibrant with blue light, saying, "In the name of the Changer I bid the Tower of Darkest Night sink beneath the swamp forever."

But nothing seemed to happen. The room was empty now and he was alone. "Are you there, Changer?" he asked nervously. But there was no reply. Again he bade the tower sink. And still nothing happened. So he said the words a third time. But this time he shouted and stamped his foot. And still, so far as he could tell, nothing seemed to be happening.

Dismayed, he sheathed his sword and hurried to the window.

But there was nothing to be seen. The foul fog hid everything. Was the tower sinking? Slowly and silently perhaps? How would he ever know?

He moved back into the middle of the chamber. Perhaps he should draw his sword again and repeat the words a fourth time. Maybe he had said them wrong. He gripped the hilt of his sword and opened his mouth. But then another doubt occurred to him. If the tower was sinking and he was not at the window, then he would go down into the depths of the swamp with it.

He hurried back and perched on the ledge, peering down anxiously. He pulled the sword from its hilt again and raised it. "In the name of the Changer," he began. The mist was clearing, and dimly he perceived a shadow of something rising swiftly toward his window. "In the name of the Changer," he repeated.

"Sword Bearer, *leap now!*" came Mab's ringing cry. John lost his balance and tumbled, sword in hand. His ribs hit the side of the coracle in which Mab was waiting while his sword tumbled to the bottom of the boat. He never saw the pinnacle of the tower disappear nor heard the gentle soughing of the swamp that slid over it.

He could perceive Mab's shadow in the dimness as the old man peered over the side of the coracle. "Sword Bearer, where are you?" The voice was agonized.

"I'm here, Mab, *here!*"

Mab swung and looked into the boat.

"Where? Are you in the boat or beside it?"

"Mab, I'm here!"

Mab stared. "What witchery is this?" he said at length, groping toward John, his hand stretched out.

"Mab, what's the matter? Can't you see? I'm *here!*" He grasped Mab's hands. Only when he saw that his own hands were invisible did he realize what had happened. He snatched his hands free and pulled the stone from around his neck.

"I'm sorry, Mab, I forgot. I'd put the stone on to hide from the Lord Lunacy, and then I forgot I was wearing it because in the dream I was visible. I didn't mean to startle you."

But Mab's arms were around him, holding him against his thin old frame, rocking slowly back and forth saying, "I nearly lost you! Praise the Changer! You're safe."

But then he seemed to recollect where they were. "We must get out of here," he said. "You can explain later. The tower may have sunk. But the Mystery of Abomination is still about. The sooner we leave the swamp, the better. Put your sword back in its sheath."

He raised his staff and it, like the sword, pulsed with blue light. The light grew stronger and separated from the staff, whirling and condensing slowly as it settled on the surface of the swamp. Mab stared, transfixed. A shape was being molded before their eyes.

"A pigeon!" Mab cried. And sure enough, a beautiful blue-gray pigeon stood before them.

Mab's voice was awed. "They say it was a pigeon that brought Anthropos out of chaos as it brooded over the abyss," he murmured.

"I think it wants us to follow it," John said as the pigeon opened its wings, slowly hovering in a most unpigeonlike manner over the swamp and moving toward the treacherous maze of waterways that covered it.

Several times John began eagerly to talk, but Mab silenced him. For half an hour neither of them spoke.

Then John said, "The moon. Look at the moon!" But Mab's eyes were on the miracle of the beautiful and luminous blue-gray bird that led them.

The mist had largely cleared. "What about the moon?" he asked, staring at the pigeon.

"You can see it now. The eclipse is passing! You can see light coming out from one side!"

The eclipse was passing with astonishing speed. The moon

seemed almost to eject itself from its coppery shadow. Silver light fell around them. Their channel was now wide and clear. Ahead of them they could see the lake and the path of moonlight leading to the island.

Mab slowly stood. "The pigeon has left us," he said slowly. "But our way is now clear."

He turned to look back at the swamp. "And the power of the tower is no more," he said quietly. "Yet the game is far from over. Indeed the worst danger may still be ahead of us. But at least we shall begin to have daylight again."

17

The Sword of Geburah

Mab raised his paddle and paused, staring at the eastern end of the lake. Drops from the paddle caught sparkles of moonlight as they fell. "Notice anything?" he asked John.

John stared. "I see light on the horizon," he said eventually.

Mab nodded. "I think we're watching the dawn. You made the tower sink, Sword Bearer, and now the planets are ordered again."

"But I didn't think it was sinking. The Changer came, and he told me the words to say. But when I said them, nothing happened. At least I couldn't feel anything happening and . . ."

"Something certainly was happening!"

"I know. But I could *feel* nothing. I thought it hadn't worked."

Mab slowly shook his head. "I could see the window of what I knew was your chamber descending swiftly into the swamp. When I called to you I was afraid you would be trapped. But I'm curious about the stone that was around your neck. There is only one stone that has such powers, and I thought it was in Qhahdrun's possession. Let me see it."

John handed to him the chain and the strange blue stone. Even in the moonlight it glowed with cobalt fire, lighting up the wrinkles in the old seer's face. "It is the Mashal Stone," he said slowly. "I last saw it four hundred years ago. Where did you find it?"

"In the Goblin Prince's cave."

"Does he know it is gone?"

"I don't know. It was just lying on a sort of ledge. I used it to get away."

The old seer looked at him curiously. "We never talked about what happened in the cave, did we?" he said thoughtfully.

The sky in the east continued to lighten. A wisp of cloud was slowly being sketched in pink against the gray background. The horizon was now hard and distinct. But John was not thinking of the dawn.

"Mab," he said, "who is the Lord Lunacy?"

"He is one of the forms that the Mystery of Abomination takes on."

Quickly John described his experiences in the tower. "His head nearly filled that room I was in, but when I put the chain round my neck, it turned into a dragon's head."

Mab raised his eyebrows. "That could well fit the prophecies. A dragon is to approach the Regents—"

"Who are the Regents, Mab?"

"The Regents are to be the true rulers in Anthropos, ruling by decree of the Changer, until Gaal comes."

To John the whole thing seemed impossibly complicated. And one thing still bothered him.

"What happened to the Lord Lunacy when the tower sank?"

"I doubt that anything happened to him. His power in Anthropos has been curtailed. He can no longer control the courses of the planets. But I suspect we shall see a lot more of him before the Regents arrive. He wants to challenge the

Changer, and he seems to think he can best do that by securing the loyalty of the Regents."

John stared at him, troubled. "Is he stronger than the Changer?" he asked at length.

Mab smiled and shook his head. "He is nothing but a pawn held between the Changer's forefingers and thumb."

"Then why doesn't the Changer just get rid of him?"

Mab waited so long before replying that John felt uncomfortable. When at last he spoke, his voice was heavy. "Sometimes, Sword Bearer, I wish I understood the ways of the Changer. But my mind has yet to penetrate them. Often he does things that make little sense to me, and his silences wound me. I suppose he owes none of us an explanation of his ways. I serve him, and I will serve none other for he has been gracious to me. But I find him hard to understand."

John felt uneasy. "But will the Regents be okay?"

Mab nodded. "Yes. We needn't be anxious about them. One thing you can count on with the Changer is his word. He never breaks it. It always comes to pass." He hesitated. "At least almost always . . ." And again he dipped his paddle in the water. The look on his face was full of pain so that John was uncomfortable asking more.

Yet in a little while Mab continued, talking slowly more to himself than to John. "Did he really promise me a son? Or did I just dream it? In any case it is folly to think of a son now. Of what use would I be to one if I am to die so soon?" He paused again before continuing. "Yet the longing refuses to leave me."

By now light had crept across the whole sky. Silently John watched a large orange sun lift itself through the haze into the eastern sky. From time to time a gull's call echoed eerily across the water, but beyond that the only sound was the wash of water around Mab's paddle and a gurgling around the coracle. There was no breeze. The lake was calm.

John sighed and Mab looked up at him. The gloom on the old man's face subsided, and a look of concern took its place.

"These have been difficult days for you," he said slowly.

John nodded, "I was thinking about my father."

"Your father?"

John sighed again. "I don't know where he is. He's a drunk. At least that's what the Lord Lunacy said. But you can't really trust what he says. He even had me confused about what I felt and believe myself. But he says my dad doesn't want me."

"I find that hard to believe. All men want to have sons."

John said nothing. He trailed a hand in the water and noted that it was cool. "I wish I knew," he said softly, "—about my father, I mean."

"What about your mother?"

"She's dead. I never knew her. My granma looked after me, but she died too. They were going to put me in an orphanage, but I ran away. Then the Changer brought me here."

Mab stopped paddling and stared at him. He semed about to move forward and touch John, but changed his mind and continued to stare.

John's face was lit by the dull orange sun as it emerged over the horizon, magnified by the haze on the lake. Somehow it cheered and comforted him.

"I'm sorry," Mab said at length. "Perhaps you can make use of me—for the time being anyway. I could hardly be a father— but if you could use a great, great, great—I'm not sure how many greats—grandfather, then I'd like to step into the role."

But John never heard him. He was staring at the sun, wondering whether it was going to shine brightly again. Mab slowly resumed his paddling, and for another fifteen minutes they paddled in silence as the sun shook off the shackles of the earth.

John's attention eventually shifted to the island. As they drew nearer he was almost sure he could see figures crowded along the cliff top. "They must be watching for us," he said.

Mab smiled and said, "Yes. They're waiting to welcome us."

The nearer they drew the clearer the figures became, and

soon they could see the towering figure of Oso among the crowd of Matmon. Bjorn and Bjornsluv were there, and John was delighted to see Folly, who would run behind the watchers to peer at them, first from one side of the crowd, then from the other. Even Vixenia's small outline was visible.

"Isn't it dangerous for them to be so near the edge of the cliff?" John asked anxiously.

"It is a little," Mab replied, "but the Matmon seem to have no fear of heights."

Suddenly the sound of Folly's braying rolled across the water to them, and immediately, as if Folly had given a signal, a roar of cheering broke from the throats of the watchers. Wonder stole across John's face. "Why are they cheering?" he asked. "They make it seem like we're royalty."

For a moment Mab said nothing. When he did speak, there was something in his tone that John could not interpret. "The night has gone," he said. "Both the earth and the moon were released last night. The fires in the forest are dying out. The tower is buried forever and its power broken—all because the Sword Bearer sent it to its doom!"

"That's not true," John said, flushing. "I mean it was you who got the wine there. It's nice of you to say that, but it's you they must be cheering. Think of all the risks you took. You rescued me!"

The cheering had become rhythmical, beating on their ears with a strange insistence. Soon they were able to distinguish the words, "The sword! The sword! The Sword Bearer's sword!"

Shame and joy boiled tumultuously together in John's chest. He rose shakily to his feet and drew the sword from its sheath. At once he was almost blinded by a piercing, pulsating blue light. He closed his eyes tightly, but his eyelids could not shut it out. Trembling he held the sword above his head. And as he did so the tower on the island became alive with light so that an arc of piercing blue flamed across the water between the tower and the sword.

He never knew where the words came from. They rolled through his chest and throat before he could stop them. They echoed mightily against the cliffs as he cried, "The Sword of Gaal and the Sword of Geburah! The Sword of Gaal and the Sword of Geburah!"

18

The Building
of the Castle

They spent two years on the island, building a castle around the mysterious tower. In fact the island became an island fortress since for the most part the castle wall followed the line of the cliff. Bjorn said, "Castles are things we understand. This one will be impregnable. When the Regents come no evil power will be able to reach them here."

During their first days on the island, in the flush of their triumph over the evil tower, they were by no means sure that a castle was needed. Two things made the Matmon change their minds. "You can't get rid of the Mystery of Abomination that easily," Mab assured them. "He never forgives. He never forgets. One setback will only make him more determined."

More powerful than Mab's words was the column of night remaining over the swamp. No matter how clear the day or how brightly the sun shone, a black emptiness rose straight up from the swamp. Its appearance was hard to describe. As John put

it, "It's not as if something black was there, but as if everything else had been taken away and only darkness left." Indeed most times it looked as if the fabric of the universe had split, enabling them to look through an opening into a terrifying void beyond. Yet on calm days, when the lake became a mirror, a shaft of reflected blackness plunged deep below the lake, a gargantuan maw, eager to devour.

At first they thought the gap might close. But as one day followed another they came to realize that it was there to stay. Their battle was not over.

Now when Matmon think of danger they think also of castles. They can build with unearthly industry, skill and speed, constructing in a month what men take a year to build. From a quarry on the southern shore of the island they hewed stone. Aguila and her cohorts brought giant eucalyptus trees from distant mountain forests. The island became the scene of noisy and feverish activity.

Mab took little part in the activities. He was convinced that castle walls would prove useless against their own and the Regents' danger. "Remember," he told Vixenia and King Bjorn, "we have come here to welcome the arrival of the Regents and to celebrate their coming. We are not here to *protect* them. That is the Changer's business, not ours."

Bjorn nodded. "Yes, and celebrate we will, for they are coming to reign over us in the name of Mi-ka-ya, and their reign will be a reign of peace and prosperity. But we must take precautions. They are not here yet. And our enemies are powerful."

Mab preferred to spend part of his time on mysterious journeys he told no one about. Otherwise he was teaching John about the powers of the Changer or else about how to fish in the lake from a coracle. John had never learned to fish, and enjoyed the experience thoroughly.

John relished times on the lake with Mab. Gradually he forgot Mab's great age and began to feel as though the old man were his grandfather. Yet a curious restraint held him from talking anymore about his past, and he was relieved that Mab never sought to question him. He felt ashamed about his parents, indeed they had never really seemed real to him, and now they seemed less real than ever. But the ring and the locket were a part of him, and from long habit he took pains to go on concealing them, however precious they might be.

As they fished Mab would from time to time glance at the partly completed walls. "They work with skill. The castle will be a great one," he told John. "It could keep armies of Matmon out. But it will be of little value in facing our own particular danger. Stone fortresses cannot keep out evil."

On one occasion as they talked together about the Changer the topic of John's door came up, the door through which he had entered the land. "You saw it again," Mab said, "and if I am not mistaken, you saw it from the outside. That could be important."

John frowned. "I'm trying to think," he murmured. "It was when Gutreth and Bildreth first captured me. There was a number on the door—345. And the door was gray, like it had been painted. I've no idea what it was made of. Not wood. I'm sure it wasn't wood. Metal maybe."

Mab frowned. "345?" he repeated. "It sounds significant. But why? There's something about the number . . ." He continued to frown, shaking his head now and then. Several times after that they returned to the topic. But Mab was unable to make anything of the mysterious number.

They would also talk of the tower and of the mysterious Garden Room where the Regents lived. "I don't see how you can have a *garden* inside a tower," John said.

But Mab only replied, "I know you pretended not to be surprised, but you did see the large rooms inside the Gaal trees. So why not a garden in a tower?"

The Matmon were not the only workers. In addition to lumber, Aguila and her eagles brought immense supplies of stores which had to be organized and taken care of. Aguila did more despite her continual pain and discomfort from her encounter with Old Nick. Yet she worked without complaint. Throughout their time on the island, as each evening fell she brought their nightly feast. Just as their weariness had been melted away during the difficult days of their journey, so now on the island their limbs were strengthened and their spirits lifted. Every night their voices rang with songs and their bodies swayed as they danced with abandon under the stars.

Mab never joined the dances. Always he would turn and stare at the gap in the stars over the swamp, wondering when evil would break through it again and what would happen when it did. John, whose heart was now much lighter than it had once been, would laugh and dance until he was too tired to go on. But when the dances were over he would sit and think about Grandma Wilson and brood, sometimes tearfully, over the problem of his missing father. Yet as time passed he did this less and less.

The Matmon seemed to thrive on the hardest of labor. They sang as they worked. When they were not singing they would laugh and talk without ever slowing their pace. Sometimes John would watch them, and at other times he would engage in incomprehensible exchanges with Folly.

The tower and the Scunning Stones remained objects of wonder for the Matmon. They would stare entranced at the tower for minutes at a time, touching the masonry, examining the joints of the stones and shaking their heads at the marvel of workmanship that so greatly exceeded their own.

To them too the mystery of the Garden Room was a constantly recurring theme. They would look up at the upper windows, wondering whether the Regents would one day look out from them. They began to call the structure the Tower of Geburah, sensing a mysterious connection between it and John's sword. Still later they began to refer to the island as the Island of Geburah.

The Scunning Stones sadly became the scene of a tragedy. There were still a number of the Matmon who had never drunk of the wine of free pardon. These rebels, as they were called, worked well on the walls. But they tended to prefer their own company, and their leader continued to be the Matmon prince, Goldson. John had long since ceased to spend time with them. So he felt uneasy when one day he found three or four of them laughing with Goldson around the Scunning Stones.

The energy that pulsated from the stones had convinced most of the company of the truth of Mab's account of them. But Goldson laughed at the notion of their being dangerous. "They're safe enough," he said. "If there are such beings as Regents, *they* will be in no danger. They will sit on them and look very powerful. And we will be impressed because we've all been led to believe there *is* danger."

For a moment it looked as though he was about to sit on one of the stones himself, but one of his followers was quicker, leaping on to the seat of one of the stones with a merry shout.

But his merriment lasted only a moment. A surge of energy seemed to envelop him and his clothing burst into flames. The small group around the stones stood transfixed in horror as the unfortunate being screamed with pain and terror. Then he shuddered convulsively and grew scorched and blackened. A moment later his flaming corpse tumbled sickeningly at their feet. No one ever again doubted the power of the stones, and many weeks passed before John could get the picture of the horrible event out of his mind.

One thing that helped him was the arrival of a pig and a dog that had swum companionably together to the island, making their way into the tunnel below the tower. They told a tale of the cruelty and enchantment of a sorcerer whom they had displeased. The dog had been made to shiver and to itch, unable ever to be warm or to relax. And the pig had been put into an enchanted sleep.

They were never able to explain how they escaped from the

enchantment, but they declared that Nicholas the Goblin Prince was hunting them. He would bind the same spells on them again if ever he were to catch them. Everyone seemed to like the pair. They called the dog Itch, and the pig they called Grunt. The two spent a good deal of time on the wharf in the tunnel below the tower, watching for any sign of the Goblin Prince, so certain were they that he would attempt to visit the island by that way. Their best chance of escape, they thought, lay in spotting him before he spotted them.

Tabby was the only other pet on the island. She had been a kitten when Bjornsluv had found her alone in the woods on the last part of their journey. But Tabby soon proved to be a one-woman (or rather a one-Matmon) cat and rarely was found far from Bjornsluv.

It became clear long before the end of the first year that their original fears about the columm of darkness were unjustified. By the end of the year the column had narrowed to half its original width. Everyone had their own idea about what was happening, but nobody suggested that they stop building. Many of the Matmon felt that the Mystery of Abomination was deciding to leave as it observed the progress they were making on the castle walls. Mab's suggestion was more frightening. He thought that the opening had come because wicked powers had torn the skies apart to let in more evil from the outer darkness. It was now slowly closing because the evil had come through.

For another year the building continued, while the opening into the outer darkness narrowed to a crack until it finally disappeared. The company in the castle made a huge celebration. Everyone except Mab and John (who tended to adopt Mab's point of view) believed they had a double cause for celebration—the successful completion of the buildings and the final retreat of the Mystery of Abomination. But before long their joy gave place to fear.

It started with Itch and Grunt. On the day that the castle was completed everyone except the dog and the pig toured the castle walls and inspected the great rooms and halls of the castle itself. There was a keep, a large square tower that rose from the cliffs on the north side of the island, a little to the east of the Tower of Geburah. There Bjorn and Bjornsluv had their chambers above the royal rooms reserved for the coming Regents, whose home the castle would become.

A large banqueting hall and ballroom filled a low building connecting the keep with a building in which were the kitchens, sculleries and servants' quarters. Stables and workshops were to the east in yet another low building. It was decided that they would continue to exercise and to breed the horses until things were more settled and stables could be built on shore.

A new excitement seized them all, and they were filled with wonder as they inspected the work of their own hands. Itch and Grunt did not share the general enthusiasm, however. They spent the day on the rocky wharf beneath the tower, vigilant for any sign of the Demon Prince. Normally they would have joined the diners at the evening feast. Though their table manners lacked the finesse of King Bjorn and Queen Bjornsluv, there was a certain piggish dignity with which Grunt delicately pushed his nose around his food and a positive elegance about the way Itch handled bones on a silver platter. But at the hour of feasting they failed to appear.

Oso went in search of them, knowing where they would be. He returned holding two sorry specimens, one in each of his gigantic paws. Itch shivered pathetically and scratched himself constantly. And Grunt, who had been a merry and mischievous sort of pig was drowsy and bad tempered. "They are bewitched," Vixenia cried as she looked at them.

"Then that must mean . . ." Bjornsluv hesitated.

"It must mean that the Goblin Prince has been around," her husband muttered grimly.

"And that all their vigilance was in vain," Mab added.

The incident dampened everyone's spirit and cast an air of gloom on what had begun as an enthusiastic celebration. But when a week passed without further incidents, the matter was almost forgotten. Unfortunately it could not be forgotten altogether for every day they had to encounter the misery of Itch and the somnolent stupidity of Grunt.

The next thing that happened at first raised no suspicions. It was only weeks later that anyone realized its strange significance. Bjornsluv lost Tabby. The young cat simply disappeared. The only conclusion they could come to was that she must have fallen from the walls and drowned though everyone agreed the explanation sounded unlikely.

Another cat, however, came on the scene, a very large and self-assured cat. No one seemed to know exactly how or from whence it had arrived, and everybody assumed that "they" (meaning Bjorn, Bjornsluv, Vixenia, Mab and John) knew. But "they" were too concerned with other matters to worry about a stray cat, even a large and self-assured stray.

The cat never walked. Rather, it *modeled*, modeled its sleek black coat for the benefit of anyone who wished to admire. It held its white head with sophisticated disdain on the end of its long black neck and waved its white-tipped tail sedately in the manner of a bored conductor. Everyone detested it—everyone except Folly, who became protective of the creature. They called it Poison because of its sarcastic remarks. John wanted to name it The Perpetual Sneer.

But John, Vixenia and the Matmon royal pair were worried. Mab had had a dream and pronounced a prophecy. "The Mystery of Abomination is coming," he told them. "It will come during the night of the full moon to spread madness and death among those who expose themselves to the night air. And there are some who will not heed our warning and will do so."

Thus was ushered in the final phase of their struggle against the Mystery. For on the night of the full moon, a cloud of impenetrable blackness rose over the swamp and stole across the lake to envelop the island fortress. Everyone remained inside the castle, fearing to expose themselves to the night air—

everyone, that is, except for the followers of Prince Goldson. For though the prince himself had been obliged at Bjorn's insistence to remain in the royal chambers with Bjorn, Bjornsluv and Rathson, his followers who had not drunk of the wine of free pardon defied Mab's warning.

The remainder sat inside the building, oppressed with dismay and dread that their troubles seemed far from over. No one had realized that the rebel group was outside until against the background of the velvet silence they heard cries of pain and fear followed almost immediately by insane laughter.

The laughter was the worst. It was the laughter of mad Matmon, doomed by stubborn folly. "We go to join the Mystery!" one of them screamed in merriment.

Mab's wrinkled face was wretched as he listened. "The *fools,*" he breathed, "the wretched, heedless fools! They will fling themselves into the lake from the castle walls. And then the Changer alone knows what will happen to them."

King Bjorn's stubborn face was set in rage. "We shall fight back," he said. "Our former master shall not win so easily. We have a castle, and the Regents soon will join us. He will never master us!"

19

The Fight
in the Cave

The awful oppression passed soon after midnight. A full moon shone clear again. They searched the castle grounds for the rebel Matmon but found no trace. Though they stared long and hard at the dark waters below the castle walls, the lake kept its own secrets and told them nothing. The Matmon were never seen again.

Since nobody was in a mood for sleep, Bjorn called for a counsel of war. No one had any suggestions as to how they might combat the Mystery, who according to Mab would return any time there was a full moon. Indeed the only glimmer of hope came from Mab himself.

"I do not know how we can oppose the Abomination," he said slowly. "I only know that the stone in Vixenia's ear is what the ancients called a proseo comai stone—pross stone was the term they commonly used." He paused.

Vixie nodded. "My grandmother called them pross stones."

"At the beginning of time it is said that the Changer built a mountain of such stones," the seer continued, "and with the breath of his mighty winds he blew them far and wide like floating bubbles through all universes and all ages so that whoever might wish to call on him for mercy and aid could do so. In my journeys from the island I have been searching for more, but I have found none."

"There is the one in my ear," Vixenia said quietly.

Mab ignored her. "I have hesitated—for too long now—to return again to the swamp. But I am sure I could find some there. With pross stones we may be able to do something. I could set out at daybreak and be back the next day."

"If you survive," Bjorn added grimly. "No, wizard (or prophet, as you insist on calling yourself), we need you too much to take the risk."

For several minutes they argued, but in the end Mab had his way. But Vixenia was staring at the prophet. "It worked before," she said slowly. "You came when I poured my longing through it. Why don't we secure your safety with the one in my ear? My grandmother told me that whenever a grave need arose I was to tear one of them from my ears and pour my longing into its heart."

She paused and the circle of creatures watched her intently. "I was in despair when I used the first one and I am in despair still. I have seen the death, the darkness, the bitterness, the fear that is spreading among you all. Sir wizard, may I not use it to plead for your safety?"

"After all, there would be no harm in trying to invoke its silly magic, would there?" Poison purred gently. John stared at the cat and hated it. "It might, of course, confirm that old fables are nothing more than . . . old fables. But in that case poor, dear Vixie would merely have gained a bloody ear and lost a worthless bauble."

"—that had been in her family for generations," brayed Folly. "More haste gathers no moss, Poison dear. I mean, too many cooks live in glass houses, and all that, if you follow my meaning. You do, don't you?"

Mab raised his hand for quiet.

"The stone belongs to Vixenia, and no one will tell her what she is to do with it. One stone in any case may be of little use. We may need several, and rumor has it that some lie among the bushes in the swamps, feared by the goblins who dare not touch them. I shall seek some there, but much as I appreciate your offer, Vixenia . . ."

"There is great danger in the swamps," Bjorn said, shaking his head slowly. "If protection is offered do not venture there without it, sir wizard!"

The prophet was standing, a deep frown on his face. Finally he shook his head. "I suspect the goblins there are more afraid of me than I of them. As for the Mystery of Abomination I suppose I will have to take my chances. And my staff is not without its powers."

The vixen had risen and was standing before him, inclining to him the ear with the moonlit stone. "Tear it out," she said in a low voice.

A stillness gripped the group. The seer shook his head. "No, Vixenia. I cannot."

"Do it!" Her voice was low and urgent. "Do it before my longing fails me!"

He stared at her, horrified, but she stood rigid, waiting. "Do it!" she repeated, almost angrily. "Do it at once or it will be too late!"

The seer tore it from her ear and laid it between her feet. Though her voice was low they could all hear her, "Protect him! Bring him back to us! Save us from the Evil One!"

Mab did not leave at dawn the next day, for by dawn it was clear that he was a sick man. Fever had him in its grip. His skin burned, his face was flushed, and as day succeeded day flesh fell from his bones and he grew weaker. Even though Bjornsluv was highly skilled in medicine, Mab would let no one attend him but John, instructing the boy how to mix the herbs he took for a remedy. The fever broke on the eighteenth day, and it took him eight more days to regain his strength.

At dawn, two days before the full moon, he left in the coracle. They watched him from the parapets until the coracle was too small to see. And for the rest of the day and part of the next no one could think of anything but Mab's safety.

The following afternoon John was sitting beside Vixenia, puzzling over the previous forty-eight hours when Folly approached them. The donkey knelt before John, trembling.

"He's coming," he announced.

"Who is coming?"

"The wizard. Mab. I saw his little boat. But it's still a long way off, and a bird in the hand is worth half a loaf of bread. I hope you understand."

He sighed and went on his way, but Vixenia had sprung to her feet. "Quickly," she said. "Let us see if it truly is he!"

They ran up stone steps to the top of the castle wall, crossed to the parapets and stared out across the lake. A hundred yards away they saw a tiny coracle dancing on the waves in the afternoon sunlight. The seer paddled it wearily toward them.

"He's making for the tunnel," Vixenia said. "I prayed that Mika-ya would give him success. I hope he has reaped a harvest of pross stones. I little knew their power. We need more of them."

For several minutes they watched as the prophet approached. "What a gorgeous view," said John, staring at the water a hundred and fifty feet below them. For two years he had only grown to love the island more. Once or twice he waved, but Mab seemed unaware of them. At last Vixie turned from the parapet. "Come," she said, "we must be there to meet him."

Folly trotted toward them again as they crossed the grass-covered courtyard and made for a large stone archway to the left of the Tower of Geburah. As if from nowhere Poison appeared, rubbing her head and neck along John's leg, as though she had known him all her life. He was startled at her size. Her head was almost level with his knee.

Folly talked endlessly, braying from time to time. "How fortunate we are to have you with us, er, Sword Bearer John, *Sir* John, that is. Or ought I to have said Lord John? Your highness will pardon my failing memory. I know you told me which it was . . ."

"*King* John," said Poison. "And his majesty does not suffer fools gladly."

"No, just *John*," John said, irritated both by Folly's chatter and by Poison's incessant rubbing which made him stumble a couple of times as he hurried to keep up with Vixenia. He was too polite to tell either of them to quit. Instead he said, "There's Itch and Grunt lying in the grass."

He glanced at them curiously as the little party passed them, the pig slumbering contentedly in the sun, the dog scratching endlessly beside it. He wondered whether pross stones cured spells.

"Your majesty will, I am sure, . . ." Folly began.

John tripped over Poison and fell heavily. As he scrambled to his feet his face was red and he was inwardly furious with both Folly and Poison. He hurried after Vixenia and caught up to her as she passed beneath the archway. Beyond it broad steps curved down into the rock to emerge on a rocky platform beside the water. Several boats of various sizes were tied to iron rings in the rock. Dim red light illuminated both the cavern and a tunnel beyond it.

Folly clip-clopped behind John to stand on his left while Poison inserted herself in front of him, rubbing herself hard along his knees and purring contentedly. He felt an insane urge to kick her into the water but merely bit his lip in irritation wishing she would go away. Vixenia remained standing, tensely watching the tunnel from John's right.

Silence fell around them. Even Poison's purring died away. The placid water reflected the curved rock roof above their heads. On their left the tunnel opening looked like a perfect circle, its arch reflected flawlessly in the almost invisible water. An occasional drop of water would plop musically from the rock above onto the surface of the water below, breaking it into ripples. No one spoke. Only the drips broke the silence.

Poison's rubbing bothered John increasingly. In spite of his curiosity he stepped back a little to get away from her. She followed him complacently and continued to rub herself against his knees. "You'll hear him in a few seconds," she purred gently.

"How do you know?" John whispered.

"My ears are sharper than yours, and I can hear him already," she purred back.

Vixenia's ears had flicked forward as she half turned in the direction of the tunnel, and a moment later John could hear the distant sound of the splashing of a paddle as it echoed faintly from the tunnel. Poison ceased to rub, but to John's annoyance she curled herself contentedly over his feet, her head still raised, watching the tunnel opening. Four pairs of eyes stared at the dim circle as the rhythmic paddle splashes drew closer.

Finally John saw him. For a moment he was nothing more than a dim shadow, crouched and kneeling in the coracle. But as it emerged from the tunnel they could see him more clearly. Across the water, which broke into a hundred waving fragments of red and black, he called, "Hail, Vixenia! Hail, John! Hail, Folly! Hail, Poison!"

"Did you find any stones?" Vixenia barked in her eagerness.

The seer drew his dripping paddle inboard and rose gingerly to his feet, pointing as he did so to a small leather bag slung over his shoulder. "Four of them!" he said. "I had a fifth which was plucked from my hands by invisible fingers, but the four are safe."

A throbbing pain arose in John's shoulder. Then it seemed to him that one of his nightmares began to happen all over again. Just as the hands had come over the backyard door of the Smith's house in his dream in Pendleton, so now the fingers of a man's hand gripped the stern of the coracle while the fist of a second hand, a fist carrying a vicious iron hook, hung on beside it. Was John the only one to notice? The pain in his shoulder became excruciating.

"Behind you! Look behind you!" he cried. But the seer stared at him uncomprehendingly.

Two bare white arms attached to the hands began rocking the craft as a man's head and shoulders appeared between them. Pins and needles stabbed John's body. "Nicholas Slapfoot!" he screamed, for it was indeed the Goblin Prince. "Old Nick! Look out! He's climbing into the boat behind you!"

Vixenia had seen him by this time too. "It is the goblin!" she cried. "It is the Goblin Prince and he is behind you!"

Nicholas Slapfoot heaved himself in one swift smooth motion over the stern. Eagerly he grabbed at the leather pouch containing the pross stones. As Mab swung round, the coracle, already rocking, lurched and he fell. John had the sensation that the whole cave was turning. His heart was beating wildly. How in the world had Old Nick got there?

By now the drifting coracle was less than a yard from them. "Sword Bearer! Draw your sword and save him!" Vixenia called to John.

Poison hissed. "Stay where you are, majesty! Folly, now let us see your boasted courage at work! Into the coracle with you! Defend the magician!"

Folly brayed loudly and leaped wildly forward. But he leaped too far. His forelegs landed in the water beyond the boat while his hind hoofs caught the far side of it, rocking the coracle and Slapfoot more wildly than ever. Folly disappeared into the dark water with a huge splash.

Then John did kick Poison, as well as you can kick anything that is already sitting on your feet. Two years had added to his height and weight, and terrified or not, he plucked the sword from its scabbard. He never noticed the blue light that throbbed from its blade but jumped immediately for the coracle.

By a miracle he landed in it without either turning it over completely or putting at least one foot through the leather. Feet widely spaced and sword held high, he stood rocking unsteadily and breathing heavily, face to face with Nicholas Slapfoot. Old Nick's arms were raised high above his head. In what seemed to John like slow motion, the goblin swung the iron hook up intending to bring it down on John's skull. "I said I'd get you, young John," he spat at the boy, his black eyes flaming hatred.

But John was quicker. Ignoring the agonizing pain in his shoulder, he swung his sword in an arc at the hand that held the hook, and before he knew what had happened the blade had sliced through Old Nick's wrist with a sickening crunch. The hand fell into the water, slowly releasing its useless weapon as it did so.

With a scream of pain and rage the creature leaped at him. But from behind John came the sharp crack of blue lightning that struck the Goblin Prince in the chest with power, hurtling him into the water. John turned to see the prophet standing behind him, his staff held high.

"Did you do that?" he asked breathlessly.

Mab nodded. "Look over there!" He pointed with the staff.

John looked and saw the head of Nicholas Slapfoot rise above the waving black and red surface. He waved his mutilated stump at John and screamed again. "I'm coming back for you, young John. I'm coming back!"

Again the blue lightning streaked from the prophet's staff, and again the Goblin Prince disappeared beneath the water. They waited a full minute, but there was no further sign. "He will not return for a little while," Mab said with grim assurance.

John's knees gave way and he sat down in the coracle. "I think I'm going to be sick," he said. He was still gripping the pulsating sword, but his body was shaking. Gently the wizard pulled him to his feet. The coracle was bumping against the wharf. "Come," he said, "you'll feel better presently."

Vixenia was staring at them both. "The bag of stones," she said. "What happened to it?"

The strap around Mab's shoulder had been broken and the leather pouch no longer hung from it. Vixenia peered into the coracle. "There," she said, "—down beside that rib . . ."

John stepped shakily onto the wharf as Mab reached for the bag and tossed it on the wharf. Three perfectly round stones that glimmered like opals scattered across the rocky surface. The seer collected them carefully and replaced them in the bag, but continued to grope around the wharf for the fourth.

John sat down and Poison leaned her heavy body against him. "You are a tremendous swordsman," she purred. "But look at that idiot, Folly!"

John looked. He had forgotten all about the donkey, who had swum to the far side of the tiny cavern and was scrabbling with his forehoofs on the rock wall opposite. "He-haw, he-haw! Oh, dear, dear, dear, dear! Help! Help! Where there's a will, there's no way out! Oh, what a fool I am! A fool and his money will both likewise perish—oh dear, as a fool I will die! Help! Help! Where *has* everyone gone?"

John scrambled to his feet, suddenly ashamed both of his weakness and his previous irritation with Folly. "Over this way!" he shouted. "Turn around, Folly! Turn the other way! You can get out over here!"

He had to repeat his instructions several times, but at last the bewildered donkey turned and swam toward them. Vixenia had her eyes fixed on the bottom of the coracle, and Mab was still groping on the wharf for the missing stone. "Perhaps it has lodged itself somewhere in your robe," she suggested. But all his further searches produced no result.

"Five, then four, then three," Vixie muttered endlessly. "Perhaps that was the meaning of the numbers on the door to Mi-ka-ya."

Meanwhile Folly was scrambling frantically out of the cold water and onto the wharf.

For a moment Folly stood shivering, saying, "Thankyou, oh thankyou, thankyou, Lord John—King John—Sir John. Oh, that I had such wisdom! A word fitly spoken is like a pearl in the snout of swine!" Then he shook himself like a dog, dousing John and Poison with cold water. John gasped and the cat, to his immense relief, leaped away hissing and spitting at the donkey and arching her great back.

The seer took hold of John's elbow again. "Well, we have three of them," he said quietly. "Let us be on our way."

John still felt sick. "What about his hand?" he asked guiltily. "Will it get better?"

The seer smiled. "First blood?" he asked. "Have no fear about what you did. He has power to regrow that hand. He will live to attempt your life again."

They turned to make their way up the wide stairway. Into John's mind flashed the memory of a crowbar that had flown toward him to crash against the wall of the scrapyard. It had not really occurred to him at that time that Old Nick had been trying to kill him. But he could see it now. "He . . . he doesn't seem to like me very much," he said.

They had emerged into the sunlight again. "You'd better clean your sword," Mab said. John stared at the naked blade in horror.

"The green stuff, . . ." he murmured. Oily green fluid was dripping from it.

"Goblin blood," Vixenia and Mab said simultaneously.

"Just plunge it into the ground, and it will come up clean. Here let me show you." The prophet pulled the sword from John's hand and stabbed it down into the turf as far as the hilt, and then pulled it up again. It emerged shining brilliantly, and John replaced it cautiously into the scabbard.

Mab placed his hands on John's shoulders and looked searchingly into his eyes. "You may not like the idea very

193

much," he said, "but remember—one day with that same sword you will *kill* the Goblin Prince. He is the source of every evil within you. He is the prince of fear and doubt. In killing him you will know freedom."

20

Descent of the Four Winds

As darkness fell they held a council meeting on the grass lawn of the courtyard. The moon would rise an hour after midnight. If any action were to be taken to defend the castle it would have to be taken before the moon appeared.

Tension gripped the company. News of the pross stones and of the attack by the Goblin Prince had spread rapidly among them. Even Grunt was half awake. And though Itch shivered, he seemed too excited to remember to scratch. Bjorn and Bjornsluv sat on their dark oak chairs whispering solemnly to each other. Bjorn's beard rested on his lap.

The Matmon sat around them on the softly cushioned turf. John was happy to be again with the seer, grateful that the old man had survived both the fever and his perilous journey. He gave John the reassuring feeling of security that only someone who knows what he is doing can give. Vixenia, in spite of her courage, had never given him that feeling.

He wondered what Oso and Aguila were thinking. They watched Mab and Vixenia through curious eyes. Rathson snuggled against his grandmother's chair. The dim light could not conceal the glitter of a gold chain round his neck, a gold chain that was smaller and thinner but of the same pattern as the one worn by his grandfather King Bjorn.

John stared at the chain unthinkingly for several moments. Then, like being knocked on the head with a soccer ball, it hit him that not only was this the chain Rathson and Goldson quarreled about endlessly in his dreams, but this was the first time John had actually seen Rathson wear it. For two years John had put the dream out of his mind, but seeing the chain around Rathson's neck awakened his fears again. Did dreams come true? Was a murder going to take place? Was there something he could do to stop it? Was he supposed to? Or was the whole thing nonsense?

Folly had settled next to Rathson. Poison sat scornful and erect nearby. Only Goldson was missing. Vixenia, who as the founder of the company was to preside over the meeting, was waiting for him before she opened it. When Goldson finally arrived he pushed himself haughtily between Rathson and Queen Bjornsluv. John stared with fear and dislike at his cruel face. He often marveled that Goldson had not, like his followers, exposed himself to the Mystery and died with them.

The sun had left a few of its delicate colors to linger in the western sky, but very slowly it was drawing them below the horizon. Numa the north star, sovereign of the night sky, shed her rays imperiously down on the island. But the quiet beauty of the evening did nothing to alleviate the tensions in the group.

Vixenia began to talk as soon as Rathson and Goldson were settled. "Your majesties, fellow members of the company: welcome. Some of us once questioned the value of John the Sword Bearer to our cause. Yet as all of you know, his valiant action this day saved three of the pross stones and possibly the life of

Mab the seer. He also wounded the Goblin Prince, the same Goblin Prince who killed my mate and cubs. I believe the Goblin Prince must be that invisible presence whose slapping feet haunt the wharf below the castle from time to time. He is known to John by the name of Nicholas Slapfoot. What you may not know is that this Nicholas Slapfoot, invisible haunter and Goblin Prince, tried to kill John in a previous encounter."

She turned to John and laid a delicate paw on his knee, crying, "I hereby name you *John-of-the-Swift-Sword!*"

There were murmurs of approval and John blushed and wriggled uncomfortably. Itch was heard to murmur, "Yes. The goblin who makes himself invisible! It was he who touched me!"

Bjorn, without rising from his seat, gave John a very different look from the kind he had given him two years before at his trial in the forest glade. Embarrassed, John was not sure how to behave. Hoping he was doing the right thing, he scrambled to his feet, bowed awkwardly to Vixenia and said in a nervous, unsteady voice, "Thank you, Vixenia, and thank you all." Then he sat down again.

Vixenia continued. "Mab the seer's courage has brought us three stones, proseo comai stones as he calls them. As you know, tonight the moon will be full. And that being so, the Mystery of Abomination may return. I wish to know your counsel about how best the power of the stones may be used. But first I have asked the seer to explain the nature of the pross stones."

Mab, shivering a little for the evening became cooler, remained sitting. He looked frail, hugging his velvet robe about him for warmth. The sky was by now curtained with its own dark velvet, and through it shy stars peeped one by one. Only the barest trace of rose lingered on the horizon.

Mab cleared his throat. "The stones themselves have no power," he said, pausing a moment to catch his breath. "They can put us in touch with the power of the Changer. We are encouraged to express our distresses to him by means of them. His power is capable of anything. But there are some things he will change and others he will not."

"If the stones have no power," Vixenia replied quickly, "what power brought you back safely?"

"The power of the Changer," the seer replied.

"And what is the power that comes from your staff?" she asked.

"It is the power of the Changer."

"But is it not you who use the power?" She seemed to be coaching the seer for the benefit of all of them.

"That is true," the seer said slowly. "I raise my staff when the Changer instructs me to. And when I raise it his power does its work."

"And if you were to raise it when he did not instruct you to? Have you never done that?"

Mab hesitated. "Yes, I confess I have used my staff in ways he never instructed me to. Sorcerers and magicians do so all the time. To them the power itself is important. Yet for nearly seven hundred years whenever I have used the Changer's power wrongly, however great the demonstration of power may have been, it brought no lasting good. I once breached a castle wall with it, but the castle was never taken. I dried an unfordable river with it, but the army was defeated after crossing it. My staff was given me to accomplish the Changer's purposes, and only when it is so used does lasting good come. You will find the same is true of the proseo comai stones."

Vixenia stared at him. She did not seem to care for his answer. "We will see," was all she said. Then turning to the rest of the circle she asked, "In what ways can we stop the Mystery? What can be done tonight? Time is passing."

Folly scrambled awkwardly to his shaky feet. "I have been— I know you all think I'm foolish and you are right—but I have been thinking . . ."

"Thinking? What, *you*? You can't. You never have," Poison

mewed venomously, her voice like squealing chalk on a black-board. Her tone changed, and she hissed, "You're nothing but a fool!"

". . . about clouds." Folly was trembling as he often did, but he had not even paused during Poison's interruption. Words exploded from him in bursts like bullets from a machine gun. "The Mystery of Abom—er, of Abom—er, the Mystery of Anticipation—please don't laugh" (a titter floated lightly over the group) "—he who laughs last bring joy to his mother's apron strings—but as I was saying, the Mystery approached us in the form of a cloud. And I thought, that is, I *remembered* that clouds are blown by wind—"

Again came the sound like squealing chalk, "Oh, the intelligence!"

"Go on, Folly!" Vixenia said encouragingly.

"Well, I thought that if we could arrange a wind to blow it back—a powerful wind, a really strong wind, then . . . It's just an idea. I mean, it's an ill wind that blows things to kingdom come." He paused. "Perhaps it's a stupid idea after all. I just thought . . ." Suddenly the machine-gun bursts of words were over. He hung his head and flopped down in clumsy embarrassment, muttering, "Shouldn't have opened my silly mouth."

Goldson hooted derision, but Vixenia persisted. "Where would the strong wind come from?"

"From the stone!" Folly brayed eagerly. "You could ask Mika-ya to arrange four winds to blow permanently away from the island, one from the north, another from the south, another from the east and one from the west. It's an ill wind . . . no, I've said that already. Then the Mystery couldn't approach us from any direction. I know it sounds silly. But where there's a will there's a silver lining!"

There was a pause. Then Poison said, "No clouds, no rain. No rain, no water. Do we want to live on a desert island?"

A long and heated discussion followed about rainwater, the height of rain clouds compared with the height of the cloud of the Mystery, about lake water, wells, pumps and other technical matters. Folly took little part in it. He was staring at the ground muttering, "Why am I so stupid? Rain? I never thought of rain clouds. Oh, dear. It never rains but the cows come home."

But the idea of the winds gained ground steadily, until Rathson said, "How about fire? Fire burns evil things. Fire purifies. Why can't we have some sort of magic fire that springs up from the water whenever something evil approaches?"

"The Goblin Prince swims *under* the water," Goldson sneered.

"Then we could have a curtain of fire going both above and below the water every time evil approached," his cousin countered.

"And boil all the fish in the lake?"

It was too dark to see the flush of anger on Rathson's face as he muttered, "*Magic* fire doesn't have to boil anything." And once more a discussion broke out. It was clear that the magical possibilities of the pross stones aroused excitement and new hope in the little company.

King Bjorn was convinced that iron was the key to their safety. "For weeks we have been building an iron gate to protect the entrance to the tunnel from the lake," he said. "We now have it suspended in a slotted recess above the entrance from the lake. Everyone knows that iron repels evil. We could leave it down to block the entrance only to be raised by magic words known just to us."

Vixenia was not convinced. "The darkness does not come through the tunnel, your majesty," she said.

"Possibly not, my dear Vixie," he replied. "But the only true entrance, the magic entrance to the tower, is the one at the head of the narrow staircase leading up from the wharf. We did not build that staircase. It was built by the word of Mi-ka-ya. If we can protect the entrance from the lake, no evil will ever enter the tower."

To John all the suggestions sounded exciting—winds to blow

from every quarter of the island, walls of fire to rise above and descend below the water, an iron gate that only the right magic words would raise. But as the discussion grew ever more complex and agitated and confused, he found it hard to follow. The arguments seemed endless. Eventually he tired of them.

By now the sky was a velvet black. No longer shy, the stars shone with startling brilliance, stars he could not recognize, stars clearer and brighter than any he had ever known, hovering in silent, effortless formation above him. But there was as yet no sign of the moon.

Vixenia's voice rose above the rest, "It lacks but an hour to moonrise. You have mentioned three principle plans, and each has something to commend it. Mab the seer has written the name of each on pieces of parchment and King Bjorn has sealed each parchment with his seal. I shall choose one parchment and whichever is chosen will be the plan we request from Mi-ka-ya tonight." Her voice sounded tight and strained.

Mab rose unsteadily to his feet. John could not see his face, but there was something about him that seemed troubled. "I do not wish to discourage you," he said. "The Changer may grant you your request, or he may not. But even if he does, it is far from certain that we will be safe. Remember what I told you about my staff. There have been times when its power has worked, but the power did no good. Sometimes it even caused harm. We may inflict on the island useless powers that will act unpredictably for generations yet to come. Strange tales will surround the powers, but they will achieve little of true value."

Vixenia rarely quarreled with anyone, but clearly she had set her heart on using the powers of the stones. She sounded angry. "Does Mi-ka-ya not want us all to be protected?" she cried.

"Beware that you speak not ill of the Changer!" The seer's voice was quiet but it trembled with anger. "The Changer cares. He cares greatly. But our little minds cannot conceive the greatness of his plans. Have any of you thought to ask him what they are? Or do you think he has gone on a journey, leaving you all to do his thinking for him?" He sat down angrily.

"The parchments!" Vixenia barked.

Rathson brought the three from Bjorn. Carefully she selected one with her two paws. "Unroll it!" she ordered John.

Unhappy at the quarrel, he obeyed reluctantly. Rathson held a smoking torch in his hand and by its light John read aloud three solitary words: "The four winds." A thrill of excitement ran through the group.

"A pross stone, please!" Vixie said to the magician.

"As you wish," he responded quietly.

Once more, as she had done of the previous night, Vixenia crouched over the stone as it glowed pale and shimmering between her forepaws. John could not hear all her words, but clearly her mind and will were focused on it as she muttered fervently. Occasionally he caught phrases like, "Heed, oh, heed my yearning!" or, "Let them blow for thousands upon thousands of years."

Stars had paled as the moon prepared to rise. There was no breath of wind. A minute passed. Then another. Then several more and still no wind.

"I think I can hear wind," John said at length, "but it sounds far away. You know if winds are blowing *away* from the island we won't necessarily feel them *on* the island." But he was talking to himself. Everyone else was watching Vixenia.

He ran to the steps leading up to the wall and stared out across the water. There was a steady rushing sound as though air was swooping down from above and then crossing the water. "There *is* a wind!" he shouted back to them. "On this side there's a strong wind blowing out! Come and look! You can see it better from here! It doesn't sound that loud but the waves are rising. You can see them in the moonlight." The moon was crossing the horizon, and by its soft light he could just discern waves scurrying shoreward across the water.

The winds were blowing. And as the party toured the castle

walls they discovered that they were blowing from each of the island's four sides. The pross stone had worked. Only Poison and Mab seemed not to care. Mab stood beside John. "Can wind stop the Mystery?" he asked himself aloud.

"But isn't it the Changer's wind?" John answered excitedly.

The seer looked down at him. "But is it the Changer's plan?" he asked. "And if it isn't, will it do any good?"

They gathered on the south wall to gaze in the direction of the swamp. Would the darkness come again in spite of the wind? Or would it be buffeted and driven back?

John stared till his eyes grew sore. At first he felt a strange combination of excitement and fear. "I didn't see the cloud when it came before," he said. But Mab was lost in reverie. The look on his ancient face forbade questions.

Slowly the moon rose higher. Cataracts of air thundered awesomely from the skies, driving an army of black waves to assault the far shore. As John leaned against the parapet the rushing thunder penetrated his brain, making him drowsy. How long he remained there he could not say. Eventually his head began to nod sleepily.

He was startled awake by Mab's voice, "It has arisen, and it approaches us."

"It's not a cloud. It's a *nothing!*" John's eyes widened as he saw what appeared to be the effects of an invisible giant eraser wiping the stars from the blackboard of the sky. At first he wondered whether a space was again opening into outer darkness, but he quickly rejected the idea. As the blackness moved he got the feeling that everything was about to be wiped clean, that all of them, even the island and the castle walls, were as insubstantial as chalk drawings.

"Numa still exists. She is hidden, not destroyed," Mab said quietly. "The Mystery is not a nothing, and the winds are not holding it back. We must get out of the night air if we value our safety."

Ever afterward the winds would blow from the island from

time to time. They became known as Vixenia's Winds. But Vixenia's use of the proseo comai stone had failed. The winds had not deterred the Mystery in the least. Panic spread among the group. They stumbled hastily down the steps from the castle wall and streamed toward the buildings.

What horror awaited them now?

21

Goldcoffin

They rushed into a large stone-flagged room at the base of the castle keep. A dark wooden table beside a blazing log fire bore fruits, cheeses, nuts, milk and sparkling water. But the sight failed to cheer them. John and Mab picked at the nuts from time to time. Mostly they strolled to and fro waiting until the danger was over, hoping they would be safe as long as they kept out of the night air.

Some of them shivered in spite of the fire. Deep disappointment at the failure of the winds was reflected on many faces. Murmurs of conversation would rise only to fall into silence. Folly huddled alone in a dark corner sighing and shaking his head disconsolately. Vixenia paced endlessly backward and forward across the floor. Only Poison, purring contentedly, sat before the fire.

Then when moonlight and starlight could no longer be perceived through the diamond-paned windows a blanket of gloom settled over them all. The Matmon king and queen with their grandson Rathson and his cousin Goldson retired to their quarters through a door at the back. The rest lapsed into complete silence.

John fiddled absent-mindedly with the chain around his neck, then jumped as he realized what he was doing. The chain! Rathson had been wearing a chain. In his dream it had been a chain that they had fought over. Was Rathson's murder what the Abomination wanted tonight?

The darkness outside grew yet more ominous. He had to tell someone. But whom?

Determination seized him. He hurried up two flights of stairs and rapped on the door of the Matmon royal quarters. The voice of Bjorn sounded from within, "Come in! Come in!"

He entered a large room of dark shadows and flickering firelight. Its walls were lined with black oak, its tiled floor littered with rugs.

"Hail, John-of-the-Swift-Sword!" The booming voice of Bjorn, who was seated on a wooden throne beside an open fireplace, was almost drowned by crackling, roaring, spitting logs whose flames leaped up a wide chimney. Firelight danced on the Matmon king's rugged features so that his nose, his forehead and his beard shone over his wrinkles and the deep hollows of his eyes.

John stood still, uncertain whether to advance or not.

"You see my fire?" the king cried. "I know not whether it drives away the darkness from the marshes or the darker fears from my heart. But come and sit beside me. If darkness and cold crawl round your heart as they crawl round mine, sit on my footstool and let heat and light singe your skin! The winds—a thousand curses on all donkeys—have failed us. Perhaps fire will succeed where wind has failed. And if fire fails, there will always be iron. Come, John-of-the-Swift-Sword, come and be warmed!"

Normally John would have been delighted by such a welcome. But he was too troubled by his fears to enjoy blazing logs. He advanced slowly to sit on the stool beside the king, staring at the flames and wondering how to begin.

"You are troubled, I see, by the Mystery. Take your mind off it. It will pass. Look at the flames in front of you. See how they swirl and laugh! Let your heart leap with them!" He paused, then muttered softly, "Would that my own heart could do so."

For several moments neither of them spoke, both staring at the flames and avoiding each other's eyes. Finally Bjorn, his voice again subdued said, "Perhaps there is more on your mind than the Abomination. Perhaps there is something you fear. What is it, you who come from Mi-ka-ya?"

"It's . . . I don't know. I'm not sure. I'm afraid of what might happen. It's to do with my dreams."

"Your dreams? What of your dreams?"

"I used to have the same dream again and again. It was about Rathson and Goldson. I dreamed about them before I met them."

John continued to stare at the fire. His back was cold and his face was burning, but he could not bring himself to look at the king. He sensed rather than saw a swift movement as the king turned to face him more directly, but he continued to stare into the fire. Then with a rush his words came.

"I saw Rathson's chain tonight. That's what scared me."

"Scared you? Why should the chain I gave him scare you? It is his right. He is the oldest son of my first-born. The kingdom is to be his when I die."

"That's what they fought about—with their swords. Goldson wanted the chain. It happened the same way each time I dreamed it. It was at night, and there was this ghost creature all in white—I'm sure it was meant to be the Lord Lunacy— laughing at them."

He took a deep breath and determined not to stop until he had told the whole horror. "They were between the edge of a cliff and a high wall. Every time I dreamed it, Goldson screamed, 'I'll kill you for it. It's going to be mine!' And he did. Every time I dreamed it. He killed Rathson and snatched the chain from round his neck. I should have told you before . . ."

"Child, your imagination is running away with you!" Something in Bjorn's voice warned John to be silent. Bjorn's heavy breathing could be heard against the roar and crackle of the fire. After a moment he continued. "He is my pride. My heir. Today is his hundredth birthday, and in honor of it I gave him the chain which is his birthright. He is still a boy—though married and with little ones of his own—*but he will rule and rule well.*"

Again he lapsed into silence. Then more gently, "You must not think such things. Dreams are dreams. Reality is reality. Speak no more of dreams. Rathson has been with me since his father died. There was something about the child that lifted my spirits whenever I saw him. I love his boldness, and he has a wisdom beyond his years.

"Think of the idea he came up with tonight. His suggestion about the fire was excellent. He was quite right. Fire purges. Fire purifies and burns away evil. We will see what this Mystery can do once flames leap up around the island."

He paused again before resuming more slowly. "I am aware that my nephew is jealous. But that is nothing. It will resolve itself in time."

John turned to stare at the old king. His craggy features had grown older and careworn. Bjorn spoke so softly that John could scarcely hear him. "When will they come? When will the Regents come? I am three hundred and seven years old, yet still I wait. Will I see their emergence from the tower? Is our vixen leader right? Is the seer? Or will I die before they come?"

He turned to look at John. "Think no more of your dreams, John-of-the-Swift-Sword. You did well to tell me of them, but they are dreams and nothing more than dreams. Prince Rathson is my heart's delight."

His face changed again in the firelight, once more suffused

with strength and confidence. Fire kindled in his eyes, and as John looked at them his resolve to pursue the matter of Rathson's murder seemed to melt away. How could he tell the old king that his hopes might be doomed? Yet what ought he to do?

"May I—I don't want to be rude, your majesty—but may I go now?" He had to do something. Time might be running out.

"Of course you may, John the Sword Bearer, John-of-the-Swift-Sword. But come back again that we may speak more together, for there is much I would love to tell you of our ways and customs, of our hopes and our dreams."

John Wilson rose, bowed to the Matmon king and left. As he closed the door behind him he found he was trembling with panic. How real was the danger? How much time was left? He descended the staircase and re-entered the stone-flagged room.

For several moments he stood with his back to the door of the royal chamber, unaware of what was around him in his growing terror of things he might not be able to control.

"Are you ill, John-the-Omen?" It was Mab's voice that brought him to his senses. "Is it the darkness that disturbs you, or are you in pain?" Mab's thin hands were gripping John's arms and the seer was looking hard into his face. Briefly John told him what had taken place in the royal chamber and of his fears for Rathson.

"You see, in my dream he was always wearing that gold chain, the one he wore tonight. When I came here first there was no gold chain. But tonight he had it on. It was the first time he wore it."

"So you fear he will be killed tonight."

"I don't know. It's just a feeling. The dreams were so vivid. It always seemed as though I was actually there watching and that I wanted them to stop, but I couldn't do anything. It feels that way now."

For a moment the seer continued to stare into John's face. Then he released his arms, took a deep breath and said, "It would be foolish to take no action. We might act in vain. But not to act should the danger be real would be to let the Mystery work its will. Come with me!"

When Mab rapped at the door of the royal chamber John heard again the voice of Bjorn bidding them enter. When they entered Bjorn was no longer alone. Bjornsluv was bending over him.

"With your majesties' permission," Mab said as he strode toward them. John followed reluctantly. They paused and stood several paces from the throne.

"It is about the boy's dream, I suppose." Bjorn's voice had hardened. "I advised him to forget it, but I see he has sought an ally. Dreams are folly, and magicians should know that."

"I am no magician but a seer—and seers know no such thing. As for the boy, he sought no ally. I bade him tell me what ailed him, for he came from this chamber like one about to die. He was sick with the grip of an evil that will take place if we do not take steps to prevent it. Tell me, your majesty, Queen Bjornsluv," here he bowed to the queen, "are you not yourself in terror even now of some peril in which your grandson stands?"

The Matmon king sprang to his feet. "Are you all in collusion? Have you been plotting together to turn me against my nephew Goldson? I know he has faults—"

"Sit down, I say! Be not so foolish!"

John jumped at the queen's unaccustomedly shrill voice.

"What know I of dreams, this boy's or any other's? What know I now? What are you hiding from me, husband? What dreams has the boy had? Do they bear on the safety of our grandson?"

Bjorn sank slowly back into his seat. His shoulders slumped. His face had again grown old. His lightning flash of anger had vanished without a trace. "It cannot be true," he muttered. "It cannot, *cannot* be true."

For several seconds no one spoke. Then Mab said, "It *need* not be true. Where are your nephew and your grandson now?"

Bjornsluv answered him, "I had come to tell his majesty that only tonight I discovered that Goldson has been talking of communing with the Mystery and inviting Rathson to join him."

"And where are they both now?"

"They were commanded to be in their rooms until the darkness had passed."

"And are they there, majesty? Are they in their chambers now?"

Wearily Bjorn rose to his feet and walked across the chamber to two doors a few feet apart. Without knocking he flung back the first to reveal a small bedchamber lit by a flickering torch. "Goldson! *Goldson!*"

He strode into the room and emerged shaken and pale. At the second door, the door of his grandson's chamber he knocked. There was no reply. Opening the door he strode into the chamber as he had done into Goldson's. Again he emerged, trembling. "They are not there, and the windows are open in both rooms."

His face was now an iron mask of resolution. He clapped his hands sharply together and from yet another door a servant entered the chamber. "My cloak and my sword! Hurry!"

All thoughts of ceremony and propriety were forgotten. Mab and John hurried from the chamber and within seconds were out of the keep. The torches they carried threw light for only a few feet, so thick was the darkness. It reminded John of Pendleton fog. One or two of the more venturesome members of the company, sensing something amiss, followed John and Mab from the keep. Soon a small crowd, including Vixenia, Folly, Poison, John, Mab, Bjorn and Bjornsluv were hurrying to a point on the castle wall John thought he recognized from his dream that was at the southwestern end of the island. It overlooked a narrow strip of turf between the foot of the castle wall and the cliff top.

No one ever forgot what they saw there. A ghostly white glow illuminated the scene. As John looked at the source of the light he saw the ghostly Lord Lunacy looking like a corpse—a living corpse. He heard Vixenia gasp, "An angel of light!" But to John the "angel," however beautiful he may have appeared, was glowing with the whiteness of death.

"It is no angel. It is the Lord of Lunacy, one of the forms assumed by the Mystery," Mab muttered.

The Lord Lunacy watched in contemptuous silence at the furious battle Rathson and Goldson were fighting with their short swords on the turf below them. "Desist!" Rathson gasped, struggling to fend off his cousin's onslaught. "Speak with . . . our king . . . if you must . . . but cease, cease this . . . senseless bitterness . . . over a gold bauble!"

But Goldson only pressed him the harder. Rathson tried to shield himself without hurting his cousin. So great was the fury with which they battled that it seemed inevitable that both would be cut to pieces. A sudden shriek from Goldson chilled his blood. "I will kill you! I will kill you! Give it to me, or I will kill you!"

A rope ladder led from the wall to the turf below, and before anyone could stop him Bjorn was scrambling down. The seer acted quickly. "Avaunt, proud spirit! Avaunt and begone! In the name of the Changeless One, get thee hence!"

The creature turned to face Mab. Then raising his long white arm and pointing at King Bjorn he said, "Take care, little magician! I may not harm you, but him I can destroy." His voice was chill with menace.

Mab raised his staff and as he did so several things happened so quickly that John could never be sure afterward which of them happened first. It seemed that almost simultaneously a bolt of blue lightning shot from the prophet's staff toward Lord Lunacy and a broad ray of blackness sped from the finger of the ghost to strike the Matmon king, hurling him to the turf.

But no sooner had the ray left the creature's finger than the bolt of blue light passed through it and it disappeared. With it went everything of the Mystery of Abomination. Only the clear light of the moon remained.

No one moved. No one that is, except for Rathson and Goldson, and they for only a brief second. They were too close to each other for anyone to see clearly what happened. There was a swift movement, then a grunt, then the soft thud of a body falling on the turf. And as they watched helplessly, Goldson, with a yell of delight, tore the gold chain from around Rathson's neck. The rest of them remained transfixed.

Then with a laugh Goldson flung his sword aside and ran to the cliff top shouting, "Gold, I will have gold! I go to join the Mystery. Now I shall live forever and hoard more gold than any being who has ever lived."

He leaped over the cliff and vanished from sight. In the stillness that followed, a voice from the skies cried, "Henceforth shall his name be Goldcoffin! He will live many ages in a castle beneath the Northern Mountains, surrounded by a lake of death, surfeited with the dead things he has chosen."

At first they moved slowly as though they were waking from a dream. But soon Mab, John, Bjornsluv and several of the Matmon servants were clambering down the ladder. Even before they reached the bottom, the old king had staggered to his feet and was stumbling across to where his grandson's body lay. Rathson was dead. Bjorn and Bjornsluv wailed softly over his body while the rest of the company watched in silence. Gently the seer took John by the arm and urged him to go to bed.

22

Folly's Comfort

They buried Rathson the next day inside the castle walls. The Matmon king and queen bore themselves with dignity, weeping silently, but holding their heads high. John's feelings were confused. One part of him was overwhelmed with grief at the thought of what Bjorn and Bjornsluv were suffering. But another part of him was anxious and guilty.

Why had he not acted sooner? Why had he not spoken to the old king as soon as the council meeting was over? He had clearly seen the hostility of Goldson (or of Goldcoffin, as everyone was now calling him) toward Rathson. Why had he not spoken up as soon as he had seen the glittering chain of gold on Rathson's neck? Was it his fault that Rathson had died?

He talked the matter over with Mab after the funeral, but their conversation left him unsatisfied. Mab felt that it was silly for John to blame himself. Mab was more concerned about the royal succession than about Bjorn's grief. "He has great grandsons to carry on his line," Mab told John. "Rathson has three children of his own. Many of the Matmon people still live in the Northern hills because of the danger here. Rathson would not allow his wife to come to the island." But John could not forget the glow in the king's eyes as he had spoken of Rathson the night before nor the soft moaning in the moonlight.

"Couldn't you bring him to life again—like you did with Aguila?" John asked.

The seer shook his head. "I don't often do things like that. And when I do, I know beforehand that it will happen. I *see* it. That's why I'm called a seer. In the case of Rathson, I saw nothing."

John even approached Bjorn, his lip quivering and his voice shaking as he said the only things he could think of. "I'm so sorry. It was my fault. I should have told you sooner."

Wordlessly Bjorn had gathered him into his strong arms and held him. "No," he said at length. "I should have listened to you as soon as you told me. Something in my heart said that you were a messenger from Mi-ka-ya, but I did not want to listen. The fault is mine, and I have paid dearly for my stubbornness."

John marveled at the softness of the Matmon's beard as he clutched John tightly, breathing heavily. He found himself weeping. But he was thinking not of Bjorn nor of Rathson. Or if he was thinking of them, he was thinking more of Grandma Wilson and of a funeral two years before that he never had a chance to attend.

When Bjorn eventually let him go, John made his way to a lonely spot on the castle wall, sat in a corner of the parapet overlooking the lake and wept, quietly at first, but in the end brokenly. He wept until he was exhausted, letting his sobbing subside slowly and his thoughts wander wherever they wanted to. His own world and his own past were with him again. He thought of Salford Grammar School, of his friends there and of his former foes on Ellor Street. He thought of the Smiths and of Nicholas Slapfoot. But most of all he thought of Grandma Wilson and of nestling against her long black skirt as he snuggled on the floor night by night in front of their fireplace where she read "The Phoenix and the Carpet" to him.

Slowly his sobs subsided and his breathing grew quieter, punctuated only by an occasional sigh. It was late in the afternoon. He had not eaten all day, but he felt no hunger. He pulled the chain over his head and opened the gold locket to examine its contents for the thousandth time, staring at the Great War soldier. (He called World War I the Great War because, of course, he knew nothing of World War II.) Then he felt a soft nose touching his knees.

"I would not intrude on your grief, King John—"

"Not King John, Folly, just John."

"I would not intrude on your grief, Just John—"

John snickered. He was about to say, "Not *just* John, just John," but Folly was already launched on a speech.

"Weeping may endure for a night, but better is a dry morsel with quiet . . . at least I *think* that's how it goes. I am foolish to suppose that I can offer comfort to one so infinitely wiser than myself, but it is my understanding, Just John, that you blame yourself for the tragedy that befell our company last night when all the time it is I who am to blame."

John was startled enough to forget his private sorrows.

"You? How could you be to blame?"

"The winds, Just John, the winds. What a stupid idea they were! How could winds blow evil away? Had I but kept my folly to myself (fine speech is not becoming to a fool—better to meet a she-bear robbed of her cubs than a fool in his folly) the Abomination might never have come. What a fool I am! What a fool, what a fool!" His face took on a woebegone expression. He placed his head on the ground and moaned.

Then John, who a few moments before felt he had no feelings left inside him, smiled. "Yes, Folly, you are—for so am I. And you're the nicest fool I ever met."

He hopped down from his seat, stroked the despondent donkey's neck and continued to laugh in soft, unsteady little spurts.

"I've never met anyone like you, Folly!" Folly lifted his head and brayed a little uncertainly.

"It is said that weeping may endure for a night but that's where flies go in the winter time . . . or am I repeating myself?"

John laughed heartily, and warmth began to kindle inside him. Folly studied him carefully for a few moments. Then he said, "You have dropped your chain, Just John. You have also dropped two gold ornaments that were attached to it."

At first John did not hear what the donkey said. His thoughts had wandered again. But eventually, after Folly had repeated himself several times, the words penetrated.

"Oh, yes. Sorry, Folly. I was thinking of something else. It's my ring and my locket. Let me show you."

John picked his treasures from the stone pavement on the castle wall and opened the locket, which Folly studied carefully. He displayed a great deal of interest in the photograph. "It appears to be the head of an adult male of your own species," he said eventually.

"Yes. It's a soldier. A soldier from the Great War. It *might* be a picture of my father."

"But he is small. Very small. In fact one could say that he is tiny. The head, now, is infinitely smaller than your own. I did not know that your species could be as small as that. You yourself are much larger. Could so tiny a father produce a son of your size?"

"But it's just a photograph," John said. "It's not a real human being."

"Well, I didn't want to sound offensive, especially if the father in question should be *your* father, but I did, yes, I must confess I *did* think he was rather . . . er, *flat* and . . . er, *strangely colored* and *thin*."

John smiled. "Folly, a picture is only a picture. It's not a real person. It's just to help you think what the person is really like."

Folly nodded. "The Matmon paint life-size pictures with all the proper colors. They too are flat, but I think I understand.

Oh, my feeble brain! I am supposed to look at your father's picture and with my brain, which is a very small brain, I must make the picture larger and fatter and more colored. Then what I see is the real human."

"Yes, that's the idea."

Folly nodded solemnly. "He who walks with wise men becomes wise. Wisdom will yet become an adornment round my neck." He looked at the picture again. "But why did they cut his body in two? Surely they did not have to kill him to make the picture?"

John stared.

"The picture is of the top half of a male. What did they do with the bottom half?"

The remark touched something in John that made him laugh helplessly. At length he said, "The bottom half was still there. Nobody took it away. They just didn't take a picture of the rest of him. Oh Folly, how can I ever explain it to you?"

But Folly was frowning in deep concentration. "So I enlarge the male father. I fatten it in my mind. I color it, and I invent all the parts I cannot see. Oh, how little I know! Wisdom has yet to become an adornment round my neck. Thank you, Just John, for explaining these mysteries to me."

John placed his arm round Folly's neck. He began to tell him about life in Pendleton, about Salford Grammar School. He told him things he had told no one else, not even Mab, about the ring and the locket and the strange mystery of the parents he had never met, of his longing to find his father and of his terrible thirteenth birthday. Over two years of dammed-up pain were slowly released.

The explanation was long and complicated, for it required involved discussions of things that Folly could not understand at first. But John felt relief in talking, and the explanations cemented a relationship between them. Folly *wanted* to understand, and he seemed to have the same comforting effect on John that the Changer himself had had.

"It was my thirteenth birthday," John explained slowly. "My granma was going to tell me all about the ring and the locket. But I never found out. She was dead when I got home."

"How terrible, Just John. How very terrible! What did you do?"

"Well, I didn't really think she was dead. At least I did and I didn't. But I called the Smiths (they're the folk who lived next door) and they helped me."

"But they were going to put you into this orn-a-fage . . ."

"Orphanage."

"Yes, that's what I said, wasn't it?"

"But I had to get away . . ."

"And to think that in the midst of your personal troubles you thought about us and came to help us!"

"Well, it wasn't exactly like that . . ."

"Perhaps not, but we will never cease to be grateful. How kind you are! How very generous and how kind!"

John knew he was not particularly kind or generous. It had been the Changer who had rescued him and had redirected his course. But how could he explain that to Folly? The afternoon sun was descending and he felt sleepy. He was leaning against Folly, feeling strangely at peace. He closed his eyes. Slowly his head slipped forward and his breathing deepened.

The sun set and darkness fell, but Folly never moved. Nor did John feel the thin and wasted arms of the seer who struggled to lift him when he eventually found them both. Mab carried him laboriously to John's chamber, there to tuck him gently between soft sheets.

23
Journey into Pain

King Bjorn's sorrow was turned into rage against his former master, the Mystery of Abomination. And his rage resulted in an outpouring of energy. Within two days he was feverishly at work on his scheme for the iron portcullis guarding the entrance to the tunnel. The remaining work on it was quickly finished. And immediately he got Vixenia to use a proseo comai stone to create a spell so the portcullis would only be raised when certain magical words were used.

Mab was indignant. He had made it plain that he would have no part in "misusing pross stones." And it was not by any means clear whether the "magic" had worked. The portcullis was certainly locked in place. It was in fact impossible to raise. The magic words they had chosen were a total failure. Mab watched their futile efforts to raise it. Though he said nothing, his view was well known. This may be why Bjorn made it clear that in *his* view they had achieved at least a partial success. "After all," he said, "we want to protect the tower. And with the iron of the portcullis rigidly in place we shall."

Bjorn called a meeting. Vixenia, Mab, Poison and John were the only ones who came. Bjornsluv was still too full of grief to attend. No one knew who invited Poison. King Bjorn was surprised to see her, but said nothing, supposing that Mab or John had brought her. He had called the meeting, Bjorn explained, to consider what the Mystery might do next and what steps could be taken to protect themselves and the Regents.

Mab's face was weary. He had never really recovered from his illness, and though he still held himself erect, his movements were slow and labored. "Let us be clear about one thing," he said slowly. "We are here to welcome the Regents, not to protect them. What happens in the tower is the Changer's business, not ours."

"You have confidence surely in the strength of the portcullis," King Bjorn observed.

"My confidence is in the wisdom of the Changer. We have yet to see whether the portcullis affords any protection. You will remember that the winds did not protect us. Besides, they do not blow constantly anyway.

"But we *must* be concerned about our own danger. It is all too real. We can leave the tower to the Changer. But we must prepare to defend ourselves from attacks. They are certain to come."

John fully expected Bjorn to defend the portcullis, but to his surprise the king's only comment was, "And what form might those attacks take?"

"I only wish I knew," Mab said. "The Mystery is malicious and unforgiving. It will attack us out of spite for destroying his tower. I am surprised that it has so far done so little. I know that to your majesty it has brought great pain and suffering—a suffering in which we share. But we must not suppose that it has finished."

Bjorn's face was dark. "Who will rid us of this great evil?"

"The Sword Bearer will—at least for a period of time. Once the Goblin Prince is dead, the Mystery's power will wane for several hundred years. The Qadar and their riders wll be banished to the caves of Aphela. The Goblins will not be seen for centuries and likewise the power of the sorcerers. But in the meantime our enemy is both unbelievably powerful and extremely spiteful. I can think of but one way in which we can anticipate its moves."

"And what is that?" Vixenia asked, her brush wrapped daintily around her tiny feet.

"The goblins always seem to know what the Mystery intends. For some reason, they and their prince play a key role in all that is happening. The goblins must meet somewhere in the swamp the night before the full moon. It might be possible— I do not say easy—but it might be possible to learn something by attending their meeting."

Bjorn shook his head. "It would be extremely dangerous even if it were possible. But how could it be done? How in that treacherous maze could you even find the goblins?"

"My staff may help. But the Sword Bearer has an infallible way. He simply walks into his own pain." Mab reminded them about the meaning of the pain in John's shoulder.

John began to feel his heart beat. What adventure awaited him now? He did not like the thought of going in whatever direction increased his pain in order to find the goblins. Yet interest quickened as everyone realized the possibilities John's painful shoulder had.

"Does it trouble you at all now?" Vixenia asked.

John shook his head. "I hardly ever feel it. Only when I'm near the Goblin Prince . . . or the Lord Lunacy. Perhaps just faintly now and then. I can feel it a tiny bit now, but it's nothing."

Mab looked at him keenly, glanced at Poison, but said nothing.

King Bjorn cleared his throat. "Suppose you find your way to this assembly of goblins with their prince. How do you propose to be present without being detected?"

"Again, the Sword Bearer has an answer. Show them the Mashal Stone, John."

For two years John had carried the Mashal Stone in an inner pocket without ever using it. His restraint had a reason. Soon after their arrival on the island John had, in fun, again made himself invisible to Mab. But Mab had been indignant and had urged him to secrecy and to use the stone only for a valid reason. "Our enemies must never find out that we have recovered the stone," he said.

There were expressions of admiration at the beauty of the stone which all of them were invited to handle. "Now," Mab said to John as he dangled the stone from its chain, "sit close to me with your arm against mine."

John did so. Mab whipped the thin chain around both their arms. Instantly they disappeared. Poison hissed while Bjorn and Vixenia both leaped to their feet. "Powers of Mi-ka-ya!" the Matmon cried. "Where have they gone?"

But John was preoccupied with his own astonishment. He was staring at Poison, or at least at the place where Poison had been. What he saw was Tabby, Bjornsluv's missing cat, with an impish goblin seated on her back.

Quickly Mab unwound the chain from around their arms and handed the pendant back to John, making them instantly visible. Mab had seen what John had. Ignoring cries of astonishment from Bjorn and Vixenia, he raised his staff above his head, looked hard at Poison and cried, "Avaunt, evil thing! Begone in the name of the Changer!"

"The cat is *shrinking*," Vixenia breathed.

It was true. Not only so, but its silhouette remained painted on the air like a ghostly thing, as the cat inside the silhouette grew smaller. Its color was changing too. Within seconds there were more cries of astonishment as the normal-sized Tabby appeared inside what looked like the ghost of Poison. Then slowly the ghostly creature turned and stalked across the floor and through the wall while Tabby rose and rubbed herself affectionately against Bjorn's legs.

He picked her up, resumed his seat and petted her on his lap. He was shaking his head. "This is a morning full of surprises," he said.

"Could you do that for Itch and Grunt too?" Vixenia asked.

Mab nodded. But King Bjorn was more concerned with the mission to the goblins, and for some minutes the discussion centered around the possibilities that invisibility held. It was agreed that an attempt should be made to learn the plans of the Mystery and that in view of Mab's growing weakness, John should accompany him on his mission. But Bjorn was filled with concern. "Take great care," he said. "Much depends on your safe return." He looked at Tabby, now asleep on his lap. "What was it that left her?"

"A goblin, of sorts," Mab replied.

"And where did it go?"

Dismay filled the seer's face. "I was a fool not to think of it," he said slowly. "Doubtless it has gone to its master, the Goblin Prince, bearing tidings of our counsels. They will know all too soon both that we have the Mashal Stone and what we intend."

There was a dismayed silence. Mab shrugged his shoulders wearily. "Since we have no alternative we shall still have to go. It would help a little if we could have the remaining proseo comai stone . . . in case of difficulties."

Vixenia quickly left the room returning a moment later to give it to Mab. "Take it," she said. "I realize now that perhaps I should have let you be in charge of them all along. After all, you risked your life to get them, and you know better than we how they are meant to work."

On the morning of the eve of the full moon John and Mab rose early and made for the coracle by the wharf in the cave below the tower. "How are we going to get out of the tunnel with the portcullis stuck in place?" John asked.

Mab smiled. "I didn't want to embarrass the king by asking that question. I'm sure he is aware of the problem. He must be pretty worried if he is awake, wondering whether we will in fact get out. There's no way to lower a boat from the walls. At least it would be very difficult."

But Bjorn was already at the wharf awaiting them. "What, then, are you going to do?" he said, as soon as he saw Mab. "I could get some of my followers to lower you from the parapets—but the method is not without peril."

Mab shook his head. "I don't think there will be any need," he said. "The powers of the Changer are infinitely greater than the power of a magic spell—especially of a spell that only half works!"

He raised his staff, and facing the inner entrance to the tunnel, cried, "Open! Open in the name of the Changer!"

It was impossible for them to see the portcullis from where they stood, but from the tunnel came hollow, rumbling, rattling sounds as the metal gate was raised. Bjorn shook his head in wonder. "Will you be able to close it again?" Mab nodded.

"Seer, I begin to see what you have been trying to tell us about the difference between magic and the power of the Changer. Certainly the Changer's power seems to be greater."

"All power comes from him."

They climbed into the waiting coracle and John, by now an expert in handling the small boat, began to paddle it gently toward the opening. Bjorn's face clouded again. "May Mi-ka-ya protect you!" he cried. "Take great care. My heart quakes with fear at the peril of your mission. We shall await your return with great longing."

Mab had chosen the early morning because he knew that goblins were the least watchful and the most careless around sunrise. "When dawn breaks they grow sleepy," he told John. "By sunrise most of them slumber."

The lake was calm. (As Mab had pointed out, the strange

winds that came to protect the island not only failed to protect it, but did not blow constantly.) Halfway across Mab instructed John to put the Mashal Stone around his neck. "You can stop paddling," he said. "There is a wind behind us blowing us to shore. Use your paddle occasionally if you must to keep it headed toward the solitary tree at the edge of the swamp."

John looked puzzled. "If anyone does observe us," Mab said, "I want them to see a drifting coracle, not one containing two people that is paddled by an expert. I shall lie on the floor of the coracle, and you, of course, will be invisible. Then if they spot us, though they will probably come down to examine the coracle, they will be less suspicious at finding it empty."

The day was, however, totally uneventful. If goblins spotted them they gave no sign of it. And once the coracle lay resting against the shore in the shade of the tree the day became distinctly boring. They took turns keeping watch, Mab standing and leaning against the tree trunk, and John, when it was his turn, climbing onto a high bough of the tree. Whoever was on watch wore the Mashal Stone.

The minutes crawled by, taking an eternity to turn themselves into hours. It was hot. Flies buzzed round them continually, and eventually on his time off, John fell asleep in the bottom of the coracle. He woke as darkness fell, ashamed to realize that Mab had stood watch for several hours.

They set out two hours before midnight, Mab wearing the Mashal Stone, invisibly paddling along the channels of the swamp while John lay on the bottom of the coracle. "Let me know when you feel the pain," Mab instructed him.

"I can feel it now."

"Badly?"

"No, but it's slowly getting worse."

"Good. That means we're going in the right direction."

From the bottom of the coracle John could see nothing except an almost full moon, veiled partly by the foul vapors arising from the swamp. He could hear Mab breathing heavily, and wished he had let him paddle. For a while they continued in silence.

"Mab, I think the pain's beginning to subside."

There was a pause. "We passed the entrance to another channel a hundred yards back," Mab said thoughtfully. "Let's try it."

It is not easy to concentrate on pain or to tell whether it is getting better or worse. For a while John was uncertain. Then he said, "That's better, I think."

"*Better?*"

"I mean better because the pain's getting worse again. We must be on track."

"How bad is it?"

"Oh, not bad. Not bad at all—yet."

They continued in silence for several minutes, the coracle moving slowly and silently across the wierd landscape, with no visible means of propulsion. At last John said, "Hey, it's beginning to jump a bit!"

"Your shoulder?"

"Yes!"

"And I can see why!" Mab whispered.

"What d'you mean?"

"We're coming to a goblin sentry. Keep down. He looks *very* surprised."

John tensed, forgetting his pain which was still relatively slight. The coracle drifted for several seconds, then lurched gently as it grounded. John could hear footsteps approaching. A moment later a shadow bent over the coracle. He found himself staring into the face of a goblin sentry.

It is hard to say who was the more surprised. But they were given no time to enjoy the sensation. John had only the most fleeting impression of a three-eyed, two-nosed, pointy-eared visage before a heavy blow made the head jerk convulsively. The goblin lurched sideways and struck the side of the coracle as it fell.

John scrambled to his knees. "What happened?" he asked,

staring over the side and looking for the goblin.

"I killed him with the edge of the paddle," Mab said as he pushed off and resumed his paddling.

"How d'you know he's dead? I don't see any sign of him."

"He dissolved. They all do when they die . . . into a sort of green oily muck. Lie down again. How's your pain?"

John lay down and focused his attention on his shoulder again. "It's hard to say. It's not jumping anymore. I think it's about the same."

They proceeded in the same manner for about an hour and a half, during the course of which the invisible Mab dispatched four more sentries. The pain had grown steadily and by now was hard to bear. It drove all thoughts from John's mind but the consciousness of the pain itself.

"There are hordes of them," Mab whispered to him. "I can see where they're heading. There are droves, swarms, and they seem to be taking absolutely no notice of us."

John felt the coracle ground in the mud. Mab whispered, "Don't move. We'll just wait here until they're settled in their gathering. I can see where they are congregating from here."

For several minutes John lay on the floor of the coracle wishing the pain would go away. Then he heard Mab say, "Time to go. They've settled now. We must join them. I think your Nicholas Slapfoot has arrived."

24

Tragedy in the
Amphitheater

They got out of the coracle together to stand on a path in the wet and misty moonlight. For a brief instant you might have seen them standing there, Mab still taller by a head, his white hair and beard flowing over the upper part of his velvet gown. Moonlight could not conceal the weariness on his haggard face nor the dullness of the pain on John's. They stood holding their wrists in front of them so that Mab could loop the chain that bore the Mashal Stone around them.

Instantly the landscape, such as it was, was wiped clean of the pair. You would only have seen an abandoned coracle, resting at the side of a narrow, muddy channel in a barren swamp. Here and there a naked tree bore silent witness to better days in the past. Bubbles the size of soccer balls would ooze their way up in the vile mud to burst wetly, releasing a foul stench.

The path ahead of them was almost as invisible as themselves. Mab proceeded cautiously, testing each step with his staff. They no longer needed the pain in John's shoulder to guide them for from a mound ahead of them came the faint hubbub of many voices. But needed or not, the pain refused to subside.

In time they ascended the rise, reassured to find firmer footing but cautious because they knew that over the lip of the mound they would encounter the gathering of the goblins. The sounds from the crowd were now more powerful. As they topped the hill the hubbub suddenly subsided. Mab froze and John lurched against him.

They were looking down into an amphitheater filled with a sea of goblins of all shapes and sizes. The silence had arisen out of their fear of Nicholas Slapfoot, the Goblin Prince, who had ascended a dais in the center of the stage. With the aid of the Mashal Stone they saw the shark that John had seen in the cave.

The shark was addressing the crowd. "Can you hear what he's saying?" Mab asked, after a few moments.

"Not really. Something about the glory of darkness." He paused. "He's saying something now about goblin power—what's that?"

Mab did not reply. "Let's move cautiously among the goblins," he said after a moment. "We might be able to hear better lower down."

The crowd thinned round the edges and it was possible for them to worm their way silently and invisibly among the scattered goblins to a position where they could sit and hear the Goblin Prince more clearly. The goblins stared at him, entranced by the wild music of his speech and terrified by images Nicholas Slapfoot conjured up with an ability that gripped John in spite of his pain. "I never knew he could speak like that—and those *pictures!*" he whispered to Mab. Not only was the oratory awesome, but luridly colored images imprinted themselves magically in the air above the shark's head as the speech proceeded.

"This is how he keeps them in his grip of fear. He controls them by terror."

For more than an hour the Goblin Prince's frenzy continued to mount, as the weight of terror on the goblin multitude grew and grew. John's shoulder throbbed with every word Slapfoot spoke. He longed for the speech to end. Eventually a note of malice crept into the speaker's voice, "And we will show them as follows th' Changer, Mi-ka-ya, 'ow we treat deserters of th' true cause. Five 'undred years ago you sowed efel spawn in th' lake bed. Tomorrow th' efel spawn will ripen, and efel spawn by th' million will arise to destroy 'em and capture th' Sword Bearer . . ."

"Efel spawn?" John whispered. "What is he talking about?"

"Say no more," whispered Mab. "That is all we need to know. We must lose no time."

He pulled John to his feet, but at that moment a goblin could be seen hobbling across the dais toward Nicholas Slapfoot.

"I can't see properly," John whispered, "but it looks a bit like the creature that was on Tabby's back."

In that case we must move with extra speed," Mab hissed.

Quietly, yet as quickly as they could, they picked their way through the crowd. The speech had been interrupted. A hush filled the amphitheater. The chain that bound their wrists together was loosened, and in their hurry it slipped from them and fell to the ground. At once they were visible in the moonlight.

John turned, dived for the Mashal Stone and scrambled to his feet.

"Quickly!" Mab hissed, stretching his hand to receive it.

"They've come among us!" Nicholas Slapfoot's voice rang over the amphitheater. "Th' Sword Bearer and th' magician—they're 'ere, right 'ere somewhere! Smell 'em out and capture 'em!"

Nicholas Slapfoot had not yet seen them, but the nearby goblins had. Yet they seemed to be transfixed with terror.

"Now—your wrist! Give me your wrist!" Mab cried.

John extended his left wrist alongside Mab's right, but at that moment a spear plunged deeply into the old man's back and he fell heavily against John.

A groan burst from him, and for a moment he struggled for breath. Then, enunciating carefully, he breathed, "It is mortal, *mortal*, John! I know it! Hold me up!"

John's arms were about him, sustaining him. Clumsily with his left hand the old man flung the chain that bore the Mashal Stone around the boy's neck, immediately making him invisible. To his horror John saw the point of the spear had emerged from the old seer's chest near his right shoulder. The nearby goblins remained immobile. One or two had risen to their feet, but still fear paralyzed them, fear made worse by the sudden appearance of both of them and now the disappearance of John.

Twenty yards away on their left the figure of a Matmon, the Matmon who had thrown the spear, was hurrying toward them.

"Bildreth!" John gasped. He could clearly see the triumphant leer on the Matmon's twisted face. Suddenly he saw the hopelessness of their situation. The pain in his shoulder made it almost impossible to hold up the old seer.

"Go!" Mab gasped. "Do what I say! *You must leave me! The news must get through to Geburah or they will perish! Now, go!*"

"What news, Mab?"

Bildreth had halved the distance between them, and the voice of Nicholas Slapfoot now rang out, "Thur 'e is! Seize 'im! Seize 'im!"

"Tell them *efel spawn*," Mab breathed in a hoarse whisper. "They will know what to do. Now *go*! And here . . . " he thrust his staff at John, " . . . this must not fall into goblin hands!"

"But I can't leave you here like this. *I can't do it.* Please, Mab. I want to be with you!"

Rage convulsed the old man's features. He no longer had voice or breath but he mouthed words and John read them

clearly on his lips, "Fool! Fool! Go!" They were his last words. Suddenly the light of intelligence left his face. His head fell onto John's shoulder.

John laid him on the ground face down, shuddering at the sight of the spear. A sob convulsed him. He began to back away, hardly noticing that now the goblins were moving toward Mab. Bildreth, who by now had reached them, plucked his spear from Mab's back. In rage, and still invisible, John raised the staff high and clubbed the Matmon to the ground with a single blow.

From behind, startled goblins bumped into him as they began to crowd around Mab, and with another sob John turned to make his way out of the amphitheater. Once he topped the rise he turned to stare in the direction of Mab but saw nothing but a mass of agitated goblins.

25

Efel Spawn

John had never known a sense of desolation like the one that
filled him as he made his way down from the amphitheater.
The occasional sob that burst from deep inside him had nothing to do with his shoulder pain or with self-pity. The emptiness
within him was larger than himself. It was larger than the universe.

He had no difficulty in finding the coracle. Laying Mab's
staff in the bottom of it he pushed off, clambered aboard and
mechanically picked up the paddle. But instead of paddling he
let the boat drift.

Mab had said his wound was *mortal*. Mortal. The word ob-
sessed him. He supposed it had to do with death. Well, Mab was
dead all right. He had not realized how much the old seer
meant to him. Their relationship had begun stormily but had
become a thing of joy. He thought of the many times they had
fished together, laughed together. He owed his life to Mab.

Mab's intervention had prevented his beheading. Mab had saved him from death in the swamp, from the hatred of Nicholas Slapfoot in the cave below the tower. Mab had rescued him from the Mystery's clutches.

Yet his loss was of Mab himself. Even if Mab had not done any of these things, yet he would still be as dear. Mab had filled the space inside him, the space that was larger than himself and that now lay empty and desolate again.

The staff between his feet began to glow, slowly turning itself into a line of living blue fire. And from the burning rod a flaming blue pigeon emerged, to rise and hover ahead of the boat.

He knew what he was meant to do, but for several moments he refused to move. Why should he follow the pigeon if Mab was dead? But then the old man's words sounded clearly in his memory, "*The news must get through to Geburah or they will perish!* . . . Tell them *efel spawn*. They will know what to do."

He followed the beautiful bird wearily. He had no sense of urgency, only a need to do what Mab had said. And as it had done on the previous occasion, the pigeon led him through the maze of drifting channels to the wide outlet that opened into the lake. Then, as before, it disappeared.

He remembered their previous escape from the swamp and Mab's bewilderment over his invisibility. And remembering, he removed the Mashal Stone from round his neck, careless now about whether he was seen or not. The same pathway of the moon's reflection led across the wild water to the tiny silhouette of the island fortress.

What was efel spawn? The words were disquieting, hinting at evil and at perils that were the uglier for being vague and uncertain. He looked again at the island. As he repeated the strange words to himself a sense of urgency began to take hold. Vixenia's Winds had arisen and were blowing strongly. But the pain in his shoulder was gone. He dug his paddle purposefully into the water and the coracle seemed to gather itself together to do battle with them. Forward he surged into the darkness.

The urgency of the situation had gripped him thoroughly. He reached the island just before sun up. The winds had tossed him about angrily. He was wet and tired. One of the sentries watched him idly, but there was obviously no one waiting for him. Carefully he directed the coracle to the tunnel entrance and stared at the mass of ironwork. Hesitantly he picked up the seer's staff and, still seated, raised it above his head, crying in a shaky voice, "Open! In the name of Mab's Changer, open!"

The gate shuddered and rattled, but it did not rise. His words had had some effect but not enough. He tried again in a louder, firmer voice. But the response was the same. A third time he shouted, but still the gate only rattled.

From the clear skies above came a low peal of thunder, a low growling thunder that asked, "Of *whose* Changer?"

Perspiration broke over John's face. In little more than a whisper, but with growing delight, he said, "Open, portcullis! Open in the name of *my* Changer!" At once the gate rose, and the tunnel entrance was open.

News quickly got around that John had arrived and just as quickly that Mab was dead. But John said nothing about the efel spawn. Bjorn sent a message requesting John to join him for breakfast. When he arrived in the king's paneled chambers he found Bjorn, Bjornsluv and Vixenia waiting for him. Their faces were grave, and none of them did more than play with the food on their plates.

He described all that had happened, some things a little tearfully. Their faces registered horror and dismay when he described Mab's death. "We shall miss him grievously," Bjornsluv groaned, shaking her head.

But the moment the words *efel spawn* left his lips his hosts reacted violently. "Cursed, cursed efel spawn," Vixenia cried.

Bjornsluv said, "I thought it could never happen again. Surely once was enough."

"What is efel spawn?" John asked.

"Efel spawn hatch after five hundred years," the king explained. "It is the spawn of Efilish, the Spirit of the South. The goblins also sowed it in a lake beyond the Northern Mountains—horrible, most, most horrible!" He shook his head but said no more.

"Mab said you would know what to do."

Bjorn nodded. "Fire," he said. "We shall have to build fires in the courtyard. Everyone must be out in the open air. And torches. We must prepare a supply of them. But how long can we hold out? If the battle should continue as long as last time . . ."

"What do they look like?"

"Efel spawn are like eels. There will probably be an endless multitude of them," he sighed and did not speak for several seconds. "They are blind and are drawn by the heat of our bodies. Mild heat excites and attracts them. Strong heat kills them. At least that is what we think. There are other explanations that we prefer not to believe."

"But if they're in the lake . . ."

"They won't stay in the lake. They crawl—all two or three shining black yards of them—moving slowly, but swarming cliffs and walls. They will come over the parapets. We think they can sense our warmth from the bottom of the lake. Mercifully they are active only at night. If we survive, we can sleep by day."

"Why the fires and the torches?"

"They try to come from behind. They are very skillful in getting behind and deadly when they succeed in doing so. Therefore we stand in circles with our backs to the fires. The torches are our weapons. One touch from a torch kills."

John was awed more by the tones of Bjorn's voice and the looks of horror on Bjornsluv's face than by what was said. After a while he asked, "What exactly do they do?"

This time Bjornsluv replied. "Spawn of evil!" she cried angrily. "Their poisoned bites fill the minds of those who are weak with hellish lusts that drive them mad. Murder and hate set them apart from their fellows! And those who are strong and resist the evil grow sick in body and often die." She shook herself. Then a haunted look replaced the look of anger. "But it is the overwhelming mass of them that appalls. You kill one and ten take its place. You kill ten, but a thousand are writhing behind them."

They spent the next few hours piling wood for burning and making sure there would be a good supply of torches. Timber left over from building the castle was dry. Soon they had built four huge piles all ready to light. Round each bonfire twenty or so Matmon would station themselves.

Sunset found them on the parapets, staring at the water. A full moon had risen in the late afternoon. No one knew when to expect the efel spawn to rise. Slowly darkness fell. Vixenia's Winds were no longer blowing and the water was almost calm. "Better so," Bjorn said, "for we shall more easily be able to see them."

He stared at the lake for several minutes before continuing. The sun had set and darkness was deepening as he said, "When they attack they look like a rising tide of black sea coming to wash everything away and drown it. Sometimes I have thought they are driven by blind instinct, but there are times when I think that a malevolent mind controls them, inhabiting them and turning them all into the cells of its own vast body. When I think like that my blood curdles, for I do not see *them*, I see *It*."

They continued to watch until the dark sky was governed by a clear full moon. The moon's reflection became a wide fragmented circle.

And then they saw it. It was as though there was a general stirring of the lake water. Then suddenly the whole lake was boiling. "The efel spawn have risen!" Bjorn called out. "Light the fires and station yourselves round them! They will be over the parapets within minutes!"

The dry wood kindled quickly. In two minutes eager yellow

flames were licking and leaping among the timbers which crackled and roared in protest. The fires had been prepared at the eastern end of the long courtyard so as to be farthest from the buildings. The Matmon formed four circles, one round each fire, all of them facing outward so that the fire would protect their backs from efel spawn. Their eyes were fixed on the surrounding parapets, watching for the first sign of the black wave of terror.

They all saw it at the same time. An audible gasp could be heard above the crackling of the fires. It was as though shimmering black paint was being poured over the length of the walls as a million efel spawn slithered slowly down them. They descended in a turbulent sheet, covering the walls as they descended. Then on the ground they became an undulating sea, encircling the Matmon who waited with lighted torches and pounding hearts, watching the approaching tide.

The watchers around the fires were now on islands of grass surrounded by a heaving black sea that glittered under the moon. And the islands were growing smaller. The black tide was rising and swallowing them. Soon they could see the individual efel spawn, the blind shapeless heads gleaming now in the firelight and rising to probe the space around them, searching for the feel of body warmth. John could see now that they were not really black but a very dark green.

"Keep your stations! Do not move away from the fires!" Bjorn called out.

For John the tension was unbearable. He wanted to dash forward and thrust his flaming torch in among the disgusting tide. But he resisted the impulse and waited. The last minute seemed to stretch itself into eternity. There were now hundreds of efel spawn just beyond the reach of their torches. They could sense the heat of the flames, but seemed also to know that living flesh was there.

A second wave slid over the bodies of the leaders and a third wave over them. The next second they were slithering toward his feet. He thrust at them fiercely with his torch. To his surprise, several instantly inflated like balloons, burst and were gone. And as more came he repeated the process. From all sides he could hear the sounds of bursting efel spawn mingling with the crackling fires and the excited cries of the Matmon.

It was terrifying but exhilarating. There was the constant surging forward of blind ranks of waving heads, the thrust of torches among them and swelling balloons that vanished like gigantic exploding soap bubbles. Always there was the fear that one might get through and bite. Again and again John would spot a head thrusting at his leg. Several times there would be three or four at one moment just about to bite, and with one last-minute sweep of his torch he would save himself from death.

On and on they came. The work was hot and tiring. The heat of the flames behind them drove them out as it drove the efel spawn back. John was perspiring and panting, and his arm and back ached. But he could not stop. Once or twice out of the corner of his eye he caught sight of Vixenia, who in defiance of Bjorn's order would dart forward among the efel spawn. She held the torch between her jaws and danced with incredible dexterity among the writhing green bodies and the waving green heads, as her torch swept death through their ranks.

But John had no time to watch, for he needed to be constantly alert to avoid death himself. He grew thirsty and tired, but he could not stop. Each new wave of efel spawn swept forward without any pause. Yet it seemed to him that the ranks were thinning. When he glanced up at the walls he saw to his joy that they were no longer carpeted with the writhing creatures. Was the attack ending?

There was no leisure to stand and watch. Efel spawn were still lunging at his legs, and feverishly he resumed his work with his torch. There was a moment of peril when it burned low and extinguished. But he backed swiftly toward the flames, snatched a spare from where he had left it, lit it by thrusting it into the flames, and whirled round to face his attackers.

But it was clear by now that the pressure was less. Indeed twenty minutes later they were mopping up the remaining creatures. A wave of exultation swept through the ranks. As the last efel spawn were exploding John caught sight of Itch (whom Mab had delivered from his spell) rushing excitedly up and down the court with his torch in his mouth. From time to time he would drop it, bark eagerly and wag his tail as if challenging anyone to take it away. Then he would crouch low, growl, seize the torch, shake it, then run madly up and down again.

Bjorn called them to order. "We must not suppose this is the end," he said. "There are far more efel spawn in the lake than we have killed. You can be sure that another attack is coming, and I have a fear it may take another form. These attacks are not by blind instinct, but are the product of a cunning mind.

"Heap more wood on the fires. Make sure of your supplies of fresh torches. Drink plenty of water, and let us stand on our guard."

They had scarcely resumed their stations around the fires when the second attack began. Only the watchers on the south side of the fires could see plainly what was taking place. A dark shape was rising above the parapets along the south wall. It was roughly circular, flattened on the lower side and about ten feet in diameter. It moved over the wall, crushing the parapets as it did so, and slithered serpentlike down the wall and onto the courtyard.

"The monster of the lake!" cried a lone voice.

"It is no monster," Bjorn called. "The efel spawn have formed themselves like this! Stand at your posts! Remember, they cannot get too near the fire! Do not be lured from your positions beside the fire!"

John knew Bjorn was right. Yet it was hard not to think of the thing that writhed toward them as a lake monster. He remembered Bjorn's earlier words by the lake that a malevolent mind controls them.

John held his torch stiffly in front of his tense body, his eyes focused on the slowly undulating mass in front of him. Slowly he realized that he was not looking at *them*. He was looking at *It*. The efel spawn were now cells, a billion writhing moving cells, controlled by a mind that had drawn them to itself as clothing. And the mind was approaching them. The hair on the back of John's head began to rise. Terror of a kind he had never before felt gripped him. He was sure, though he did not know why, that its malice was directed toward him personally. Then he remembered the words of Nicholas Slapfoot, "Efel spawn will . . . capture th' Sword Bearer . . ." So he was right. Its malice *was* directed toward him. In fact *the monster was coming to get him!*

26

The Third
Pross Stone

Mab lay on his back in the mud. A goblin guard raised the
seer's head and poured fluid from a phial down his throat. A
moment later the old man shuddered and opened his eyes.

The goblin stared at him a moment and then said in a high-
pitched singsong voice, "Eet weell bee fine. Eet weel remain
leeveeng for torture."

The old man sighed softly. He might live for torture. But in
any case, he would not live long. He was deathly weak. Four
goblins stood around him. They were positioned at corners of
a rectangle looking not unlike four ghoulish bedposts, or perhaps like four waiting vultures anticipating a feast. "It is a
strange way to die," he thought. "Yet such must be the
Changer's plan. Perhaps he will tell me soon why he did not
suffer my name to be carried on."

His thoughts turned to John and his mission, and the hint

of a frown rested like a shadow on his face. "Will they survive?" he wondered. He shuddered. What if they didn't? John, he was sure, would get through. But then what? What of John himself when the efel spawn swarmed over the castle walls?

The dying man shuddered again. He tried in his mind to go over the precautions he had taken to protect John and himself. What had he done? Could anything have been done better? His staff now. But no, his staff would have been in the hands of the goblins had he not given it to John. But surely there was something else.

Then he remembered. The proseo comai stone. It was concealed within a pouch inside his right sleeve. Gently he fumbled for it with the fingers of his left hand, grasping it with growing excitement. But he lay perfectly still, not removing his hand from the sleeve, while he gripped the stone with his fingers.

His lips scarcely moved as he formed the words silently, "Let them be protected by fire! And for ten thousand years let walls of fire rise to remind any who approach the island that the Changer protects his own!" A wave of power momentarily filled his body, and he knew that all was well. Or he thought it was. There would be many hours before the efel spawn rose for it was still night.

How long had he been unconscious? The thought disturbed him. One of the goblins addressed him, its singsong voice disturbing his thoughts.

"Eet leeves, ees eet not?"

"Yes. I'm still alive. But not for long." The words were low and faint.

"Wee keep eet leeveeng."

"Why?"

"Eet weell bee tortured by Preenz Neecolas."

Mab could feel no pain. His body felt cold but quite comfortable. He concluded that it was incapable of feeling pain and so he was unafraid. He made no reply. The high-pitched voice

246

continued, "Wee keep eet alive to geev eet good news. The Sword Bearer, eet was feeeneeshed beeeeng danger. Efel spawn capture eet just now. Take to Preenz Neecolas. Eet weell see eet."

Dismay filled him. He knew it now. Twenty-four hours had passed while he was unconscious. Had he used the pross stone too late? So this was the torture he was to experience, the torture of witnessing John in the hands of the Goblin Prince. That would be torture indeed.

But no! It could not, *would not* happen! He was a seer. And that one prophecy had been given to him! He had *seen* it! *Seen* the Sword Bearer split the Goblin Prince in half! It had already happened in the eyes of the Changer!

John could see no details of the monster. Moonlight reflected on a shimmering dark green surface. Directed by a superior will it glided toward him more swiftly than the efel spawn. John wanted to shout, to tell everyone what was happening, but his throat was dry and his mouth was paralyzed. He tried to run, but his legs refused to move. Inside his body an ongoing scream was trapped unheard. The creature was upon him. Its head flattened and butted his legs. He fell forward onto a mass of writhing efel spawn cells.

Immediately he felt himself being raised, and as he lifted his head, he saw that he rode on the back of the creature. Strangely, none of the efel spawn had bitten him. Out of the corner of his eye he caught a glimpse of two neighboring Matmon who were striking the monster's head with their torches. The sight mobilized him. He raised his own torch and plunged it deeply down into the creature.

At once a dozen efel spawn cells ballooned up, thrusting him into the air. As they exploded, they tossed him over the side of the creature. He fell heavily and lay uninjured but stunned with the wind knocked out of him. But the life instinct was now strong in him. He struggled to his hands and knees. Galloping

hoofs approached him. Folly seized his belt with his teeth, lifted him and carried him to a place around Folly's own fire.

He dropped him there. John never heard him say, "Better late than dead. Or is it better red than never? Anyway it's not true. And now the efel spawn are at my back, and I am tempting fatality. Once bitten, never no more to roam. It is a far, far better thing I do than every day in every way—good-by, Just John." But John was still too shaken to realize what was happening.

It was only later that he learned of the titanic struggle between Aguila and the monster, of how she swept down from the skies with a shriek to burst through the middle of it, scattering the efel spawn cells by the flapping of her enormous wings, and of how, covered with efel spawn she yet managed to clear the castle walls before plunging to her death in the lake. What he did see later was Oso, sitting on the outer parapets and mourning her every day for a week.

How long he lay by the fire he did not know. But with his cheek resting against the hot stone, his faculties began to return. He saw he was beside a different fire and that once more a tide of efel spawn threatened his life. But he could do nothing. He lay on his stomach, struggling to rise, gasping, croaking and retching as he fought for breath. Two Matmon women on either side of him were battling to protect him with their torches.

Eventually he managed to get up and to breathe. Then, aching and dizzy, he groped for a torch, lit it and turned to fight. Folly was nowhere to be seen. But something was wrong. Now there seemed to be fire everywhere. Across the courtyard the whole sea of efel spawn was ballooning and exploding. There was heat in his face, heat every bit as intense as the heat at his back. Titanic walls of fire had surrounded the whole island.

"Leave your positions!" he heard Bjorn call. "Take shelter beneath the tower on the wharf."

There were soon no efel spawn to be seen. Brilliant light

from the fire walls illuminated the courtyard, and terrible heat scorched it. John limped as well as he could in terror of the inferno that surrounded the island. Was the island itself on fire? Was the water of the lake burning?

There was panic, jostling and confusion at the head of the steps that led down to the wharf. By some miracle no tragedy occurred and soon nearly eighty of them were crowded on the rocky wharf below the tower. All were weary, and all grateful for the coolness of the cavern and for their escape from the efel spawn. But what was the meaning of the fire? Had they been saved from one ordeal only to face a fiery death?

"Seven dead, including Folly and Aguila," Bjorn said as the hubbub settled. "Deeply we mourn their loss. They sold their lives dearly and we owe them much." But the immediate excitement blunted the significance of his words to all of them. Certainly John did not take them in. And since they had nothing else to do, most of them squatted on the stone surface of the wharf. Those nearest the water would stoop to scoop it into their hands to drink, and there was a regular shuffling as Matmon who had quenched their thirst made way for those who were still thirsty. In the cave all was stillness. No roar of fire could be heard, only the whispering echoes of their low voices.

Bjorn had gone to the top of the stairs to see what was happening. Soon he came down and called for silence. "Good tidings!" he said. "Or shall I say the tidings *seem* good. The fire has pulled back. It surrounds us on all sides, but at a distance of fifty yards from the walls. The heat can no longer be felt. Best of all, the water in the lake is free from efel spawn. The fire must have destroyed them!"

There was an outbreak of excitement and of confused cheering. Matmon crowded eagerly to the stairway to see for themselves. John found himself pushed and jostled along with them up the steps, across the courtyard and up more steps onto the walls.

It was an awesome, awesome sight. Across a stretch of blood-tinged, black water, a curtain of fire rose from the lake five hundred feet into the air and extended in a sweeping circle round the island. The flames undulated with stately majesty. They were not the flickering flames of a fireplace but flames that waved upward in ponderous sweeping movements as though offering homage to the feeble moon.

Spellbound they watched them for an hour while the curtain slowly extended and drew back from them. Then without warning, two hundred yards from the island, it disappeared in an instant. They rubbed their dazzled eyes and stared. The moon was again clear. Reflected moonlight glittered on the black waters. The efel spawn were no more.

John joined Vixenia and the king and queen in the royal chambers. "The fire," Vixenia said, "—it was like the fire we would have asked for with the third stone. Where could it have come from?"

"Rathson's idea was good. Would that he might have lived to see it work," Bjorn murmured.

"But our grandson is no longer with us," Bjornsluv answered. "Yet the fire came. From whence?"

"Surely not from the dead," the king said, looking startled.

John had no stomach to talk about the dead. Now that the excitement was over, a weight of oppression rested on him. Grief for Mab rose fresh within him, twisting his heart and burning his eyes. Folly too was dead, and he struggled to come to terms with the fact. "Well, we have a spare pross stone and nothing to do with it," he said bitterly.

"No," Vixenia observed slowly. "We have no more pross stones. Mab the seer took the last one with him. We have no more unless we should some day find the fourth one he dropped in the cave."

"The one he took did little good for him," Bjorn said.

John's heart was beating wildly.

"I'd forgotten about that. Yes, of course, he took it with him. You don't think . . . ? No, that's impossible. His head simply

251

flopped. . . . Oh, but was he really dead? What if . . ." Suddenly he rose to his feet. *"What if he's still alive and he used the stone? What if the fire walls came from him? What if he needs our help?* Oh, whatever can we do?"

There was a stunned pause. Suddenly John shouted, "His staff! I've got his staff in my room!" And without even excusing himself he turned and left them.

It took him less than a minute to reach his chamber. Seizing the staff in a shaking hand he cried, "In the name of the Changer, *my* Changer, take me to Mab!"

The staff vibrated gently in his hand and began to glow with blue light. Relief and joy surged in him. He half-laughed, half-sobbed. His arm began to glow, then his whole body. The room vanished. He was drifting among whirling stars and suns. Brilliant lights flashed past him as the drifting became a rushing and the rushing a hurtling. Then suddenly he was surrounded by pale blue haze.

Mab lay on a stretcher in front of him, his face pale, his eyes closed. Four goblins had been carrying the stretcher but had stopped and were staring at John. The blue glow shone from him. Suddenly he knew where he was. *The Old Way.* They were taking Mab somewhere. But where? He dared not pause.

With one fierce movement he bent over Mab and plunged his free arm under the old man's waist, drawing him to himself. Two of the goblins flung themselves on him. "In the name of the Changer," he cried, "take us back!" Again the whirling stars and planets and again the hurtling through space. But now there were four of them, John, Mab and two goblins.

They stumbled to the floor in a lighted room. Somehow John managed not to fall on Mab. One of the demons was trying to choke him, but he struggled to his feet. The second had dropped to the ground and now crouched in front of him, ready to leap at him. The staff was still in his hand, and as a flash of blue fire leaped from it the goblin disappeared in a cloud of smoke.

The flash had caused the goblin on his back to drop from him, and he swung round to face it. Like the second goblin it crouched to spring at him. John did not wait for the staff to act but swung it furiously at the creature's enormous skull, cracking it like an egg shell. It sank to the ground, melting into a slimy green patch.

As the blue light faded from their bodies, only then did John realize that he was in the royal chambers, and that Vixenia and the king and queen were staring both at Mab and at himself in amazement.

Bjornsluv fell on her knees by Mab, who lay on his back on the floor, unconscious. Noting his pallor and the stains of blood and of mud on his robe, she swiftly pulled it from his shoulders and was surprised to find skilled bandaging around his wounds. She placed her ear over his chest and after a moment said, "His lung was not pierced. There is hope." Then she straightened her back, rose to her feet and said, "I have herbs. Let us also get some of that wine of free pardon into him. Let him be placed in my bedchamber so that I may attend to him myself during the night. There is life in him yet, and we may need his services."

27

Battle of the Titans

No one in all Anthropos possessed medical skills like Bjorns-luv's, and she exerted them to the full to save Mab. The next day he opened his eyes, and when he saw her he said, "So you too are at it!"

"I too?"

"A goblin physician bound my wounds and gave me herbs to keep death at bay."

"Ah, yes. I wondered at the bandaging."

"Their skill was great . . ."

"But to what end? Why would they do you good?"

"They wished to keep me alive to let me see the Goblin Prince put the Sword Bearer to death. How came I here? I gather he is alive?"

"And well! He brought you here. And the perils that surrounded us were consumed by curtains of fire."

A look of warm delight swept over Mab's face. "That is good. It is very good. So I was in time after all! I had thought it was all in vain!"

He closed his eyes then and slept peacefully.

As day succeeded day he gained more strength, but as Bjornsluv herself admitted later, the presence of death never really departed from the room. Yet on the seventh day, Mab insisted that he rise from the couch in the queen's room. "I have dreamed of things that are to come," he said, "and I have somewhat more to do before I leave you all."

An hour or so later, assisted by John and Bjorn, he went into the courtyard. Vixenia and Bjornsluv accompanied them, and Oso lay down nearby to observe. It was late afternoon, and the courtyard was deserted. Seven stone markers now were arranged in a circle around the Scunning Stones, placed there in honor of those who had perished in the battle. John had wept over two that had places of special honor—the stones for Folly, king of donkeys, and Aguila, sovereign over the eagles—the two who had given their lives to rescue the Sword Bearer.

Mab sat on the well to rest. His face was gray, and his long white hair fell lifelessly over his shoulders. But his eyes burned with a strange urgency. "Doubtless you all feel that through the courage of John and myself, by the valor of Aguila and Folly, to say nothing of your planning and valiant fighting, you have all battled well against terribly superior odds. Is it not so?"

Bjorn nodded but said nothing. Mab continued, "I now intend to show you that the odds are different from what you think." He raised his staff high. "Show them, Changer! Show them what mortal eyes so rarely see!"

The staff vibrated, and blue light began to flash from it.

The scene around them faded. They seemed to stand on a plain, before a gate in a wall that almost reached the skies. And from the skies two seraphim descended, shining blue and tall as the walls themselves to stand as guards on either side of the gate. The earth shook as they reached the ground. Their faces and robes were molded in blue flame, while their voices were the thunderous notes of a vast pipe organ, as they cried, "See then, if you have eyes to see!"

It took John's breath away. Bjorn and Bjornsluv stood beside him, their faces white, their eyes wide and staring, while Oso crouched on the ground hiding his head beneath his forepaws. And as they watched, a legion of angelic beings, flaming blue and armed with swords and whips of light, descended with claps of thunder to take their places on either side of them. The ground was shaken into waves and ripples by their ponderous weight and solidity. John and the king and queen stumbled against one another and fell in a heap together.

"Stand then and see what the Changer is doing!" Mab cried from his perch on the well. "Behold what hereafter was hidden from you. Stand and see—so that after my death you will not forget!"

Still shaking, the members of the little group rose to their feet and stared.

"I have seen things no mortal eye should look upon," said the Matmon king. "I spoke foolish things with my mouth and I am ashamed."

The company huddled together, awed by the gigantic size of the wall and gate, overwhelmed by the flaming giants whose voices were the thunder of cataracts. But John looked around him to make sure there was nothing he missed. And as he did so he caught sight of another wonder.

"Look," he cried excitedly, "look at those clouds in the south! I bet we're in for a real storm. Gosh—I've never seen such clouds!"

Glowering dark brown and ominous, the clouds from the direction of the swamp were scrambling madly upward, boiling ever high to tower miles above the earth. They began to move slowly and menacingly toward the island. John had always enjoyed seeing shapes in clouds—heads and faces, animals and benign creatures of mythology. But now he found himself struggling *not* to see. For the shapes in the clouds were terrifyingly real.

"They're just clouds," he muttered fiercely to himself. "They're only water vapor. There aren't any *things* in the clouds. It's only a storm, an ordinary thunderstorm."

But his eyes refused to obey him. Horrified, he could not prevent himself from seeing a gargantuan black serpent whose coils wound and unwound in a slow orgy of desire. John shuddered and tried to turn away. But his eyes were trapped.

"They're clouds, only clouds!" He was repeating the words aloud now, his voice cracked and his throat dry.

One of the clouds was sprouting wings that covered a quarter of the copper sky. Between the wings a lion's head appeared. Limbs pushed outward and terrifying claws were thrust into space. "Oh no! A *griffin!*" The words that came from his throat seemed to belong to someone else.

One by one clouds boiled themselves into monstrous shapes. Imperious phoenixes looked down disdainfully on the island. From the center a sinuously writhing dragon emerged, breathing red fire and lashing the forests of the mainland into flames with his tail.

Jagged lightning flashed from the clouds. But it was lightning the like of which John had never seen. For there was no light in the lightning. Afterward John called the flashes *darking* or *darkening*, for they seemed like jagged cracks which split the sky to reveal the terror of blackness beyond it.

Hot stirrings of air began to scorch his face. His neck was aching, his head strained back. With the roar and rush of mighty winds, the flaming blue seraphim and the host of angelic beings rose to meet them, swelling as they rose to match the size of the dragon. Hot wind flung John on his back. He caught a glimpse of Bjorn lying on the ground across the body of Bjornsluv. He wondered if they were dead. Vixenia cowered on the ground beside Oso. Only Mab remained at ease, seated on the well, his ancient, wrinkled face alight with exultation.

Then John's head was split by a peal of thunder of a kind he had never heard before and would never hear again. Mab was hurled on the ground beside him as the flaming army engaged its foes. Flashes of red lightning blinded him so that he could no longer see what was happening. His body was tossed to and fro by hot wind and the terrifying shaking of the earth. His ears were deafened by screams, thunderclaps and roarings as the battle raged about him. Then with startling suddenness it ended.

He sat still. After several moments he struggled to his feet and looked up. The clouds, still dark and ominous, were clouds and nothing more, clouds that were hurrying away from the island in the direction of the swamp, shrinking as they went. Behind them in a glory of blue light the angelic hosts were driving them, lashing them with awesome whips of light. Soon they were lost from view.

One by one the members of the little company picked themselves up. King Bjorn and his queen were quite unharmed. The giant walls and gate could no longer be seen. The tower, the keep and the castle walls were in their accustomed places. They were once more surrounded by the familiar courtyard.

No one spoke. The vision had numbed their brains and stilled their tongues. The king and queen moved silently into the keep. Oso and Vixenia disappeared from view, and John and Mab were alone.

It was then that John noticed that something had changed. The double doors to the tower, which had been closed by magical powers since first the tower was spoken into being, were now standing widely ajar.

28

The Seven-Headed Dragon

The wrinkles on Mab's forehead gathered themselves into a frown. For several minutes he stared through the open doors at the tiled floor inside the tower.

"What can it mean?" he mused. "Surely something of great moment is about to take place. I saw nothing of this in my dreams. Or can it be that . . ." He paused and his frown deepened. "Can it be that something is direly amiss?"

With John's help he moved toward the doors. "Let us close them," he said. The doors were iron embossed and of solid oak. He leaned against the doorpost as John seized one of them and pushed. But it might just as well have been set in cement. It could not be shifted.

A shadow crossed Mab's face. "My own strength fails," he said quietly. "Would that I could assist you. But death claws at my bones."

John felt a stab of fear. He used his shoulder as a sort of battering ram, and then heaved with his back and his thighs, but his efforts were unavailing. "You're not dying," he panted fiercely. "It's the door. It just won't budge!"

Mab shook his head wonderingly. "Then something mysterious is afoot," he said. John creeped cautiously inside the tower, peering at the stone walls of an empty room that formed the ground floor. Its high ceiling was crisscrossed with massive beams. The stones that formed the glass-smooth walls were irregular in shape, fitting together like pieces of a jigsaw puzzle with only hairline cracks to show where one stone joined another.

Two diamond-paned windows admitted patterned shafts of afternoon sunlight on the floor. A stone stairway led up the left-hand wall to an opening in the ceiling. A second door which must have led down to the wharf was closed.

Mab followed John into the room and stared in wonder at the cunning marvel of the closely fitted stones. "No human hand put these together," he said softly.

"This place is prickling with magic," John replied.

"Yes," the seer breathed, "and the power you sense is putting life and strength into my bones! It is not magic. It is the Changer's power."

For several minutes they moved along the wall, fingering the smooth stones and trying in vain to feel the joints, commenting from time to time on the workmanship. Mab's body straightened. His step grew firmer as the minutes slipped by. Imperceptibly the room had grown slowly darker, until at last John said, "It must be getting late. It's nearly dark."

The seer turned and strolled to the window. "It is no natural darkness," he stated after a moment. "The Mystery of Abomination has changed its custom. Three weeks yet remain to full moon. Yet it is descending on the courtyard. This bodes ill for the cause."

Quickly John joined him. Darkness grew even blacker outside until they stared at unrelieved obscurity. "What now?" John muttered grimly. They did not have long to wait to find out.

A vertical line of light appeared like a crack in the blackness. Slowly it broadened to reveal the deadly pallor of the Lord of Lunacy. John stared at it with revulsion.

The white specter stood motionless for a full minute, its face creased by a frozen sneer. Slowly the skull began to split down the middle, and through the opening there poured out first smoke, then tongues of flame. A red snout thrust itself from inside the skull and a crowned dragon head emerged. Then six more heads erupted from the skull. As the pale body of the Lord Lunacy shriveled like a cast-off garment, a red and scaly dragon emerged to stand in seven-headed splendor in the court-yard.

The darkness was gone, and John gasped as many-hued flashes of late afternoon sunlight sparkled from the myriad jewels adorning the scales of the dragon's long and sinuous body. It coiled and uncoiled itself like the body of a snake, the tail lashing the ground in fury. And as it writhed and lashed, it grew, until it had stretched to sixty or seventy feet, the four scaly feet tearing the green turf with their cruel claws. Then the crowned heads squeezed themselves close to one another and the dragon moved purposefully toward the open door of the tower.

"It had only one head in the Tower of Darkness," John breathed. "At least I only saw one."

"Quick!" hissed Mab, seizing John by the arm, "Up the stairs! Large as it seems it can still enter the tower."

"Can you make it?" John asked. Yet even as he stared he could see that the old man was possessed with something like his old vigor. They quickly climbed the steps and emerged in a broad corridor that led them past an open door to another staircase. This too they climbed, to arrive at a second landing where another door lay open to an empty room. They waited and listened at the top of the stairway, stifling their breathlessness so that they could hear what was happening below.

First came the hideous sound of fire being breathed from seven pairs of nostrils. Then came the scraping of scales against the doorpost. John said, "Let's hide in the room and close the door. I'm sure it doesn't know we're here. Anyway it's too big to get through the door." But as they tried to close the door behind them it proved as stubborn and resistant as the main doors.

"The Garden Room!" the seer gasped, holding a trembling hand to his head. "It is our only hope."

John had no time to think for Mab pushed him toward the stairs. "Go quickly," he said. "I will follow." Afterward John marveled at the astonishing strength that emerged from the seer.

The third staircase angled to open on yet another corridor and a third open door. For a moment the sight of what lay beyond the door checked them, for it was as though on the other side no room existed. Instead an open hillside sloped down to a sunlit valley hundreds of feet below them.

"What . . ." John gasped.

But the seer pushed him through the doorway. They stumbled down the hillside to where a clump of bushes afforded a hiding place. Flinging themselves on the ground they lay behind the bushes and peered at the doorway from which they had emerged.

Its frame stood alone and unsupported. Behind it the hillside rose. Through it they could still see the corridor of an open room in the tower. Bewilderingly a blue sky arched the heavens above the door. The tower itself was nowhere to be seen.

They had little time to marvel at the mystery of the Garden Room and the magic of the doorway, for within seconds seven crowned dragon heads began to squeeze themselves through it. The long scaly body and tail followed, and rapidly the mighty creature was growing to an even greater length. Then it stretched its wings and swept voluptuously into the air.

"It's a flying four-legged snake with seven heads," John marveled. Slowly it circled to a great height. Then breathing fire it hurled itself toward the valley below. Relief settled over them. They were safe—for the moment at least.

But the seer's sense of urgency did not permit them to rest. "I know it is the Changer's business, but it can be up to no good," he told John grimly. "The Regents must be where the creature is headed. Come. We cannot fly but we must make what speed we can. Let us see what is afoot."

For two and a half hours they hurried stumblingly in the direction of the valley floor, the seer swaying drunkenly from time to time. Then their way was blocked by a dense copse. "Around—or through?" Mab panted. His face was gray and wet with perspiration. The strength he had gathered from the tower seemed to be leaving him. Then, with all the urgency of his being, he said, "We must go through. Follow me."

They plunged into a thicket and found their feet on a narrow path. A cool, green dimness wrapped them round, chilling their perspiration and relieving the aches in John's limbs. But scarcely had they proceeded a dozen yards when Mab seized John by the shoulder, pushed him into a bank of green ferns and staggered toward a streambed on the far side of the path. "Hide!" he breathed. "And lie still!"

By now John had grown accustomed to the prophet's sudden instructions, for the years in Anthropos had taught him trust. For a moment he lay still. Then, curious, he peered through the screen of ferns in which he lay.

A scraping sound caught his ear, the sound of a great mass being dragged along the ground toward him. He raised his head but could see nothing. The sound grew louder. "Whatever it is, it's *big*!" he thought. "And it sounds as if it's coming along the path."

The dragging, scraping sound continued, accompanied by the intermittent sound of broken twigs and branches, and the sound of thrashing and smashing. A spasm of fear closed round his heart. What was it? What kind of place was he in? What hidden dangers lurked here?

Fighting his rising panic, he raised himself further in an attempt to see the source of the noise. His heart contracted. Twenty-five yards away he saw a twisting coil of vivid red. The dragon! The seven-headed dragon! What was he to do?

He eased himself back further into the ferns, until his feet met something solid. Twisting his head round, he saw it was a tree, an eminently climbable tree that invited him to ascend. In his panic he scrambled madly. Then as he peered through the leaves, he saw it clearly.

But it wasn't the dragon. Or was it? Could another set of jeweled red scales exist besides those of the dragon? For clearly the writhing creature bore the dragon's scales, yet it had neither wings nor legs as it twisted, thrashed and dragged its way through the copse. Nor did it have seven heads, but only one.

On its belly it groveled and suddenly John knew. It *was* the dragon. Something had happened to it, something momentous. Then, to his horror, the serpent slowly coiled itself in rings, not ten yards down the path on which he had been pursuing.

Had it seen him? He was sure it could not have. Scarcely breathing, he watched it as it lay coiled, massive and immobile. What should he do? To cross the path to the streambed where Mab must still be lying would involve the risk of drawing the wrath of the snake on both of them. He would have to make a wide circuit to rejoin the prophet.

Scarcely breathing and moving with more caution than he had ever before exercised, he descended from his perch. He tiptoed through the ferns away from the path, testing each step. A twig cracked explosively under his left foot and he froze, straining his ears for a full minute. But the only sound was that of his own fevered breathing. He moved more deeply into the copse. When he judged he was far enough away, he began to make his circuit to rejoin Mab. Such at any rate was his intention. For half an hour he turned and twisted cautiously but with growing bewilderment. Something had gone wrong.

He did not find the path again. Nor did he find the stream. Dismayed, he tried to retrace his steps, but before long he knew he was hopelessly lost. His limbs were shaking and rivulets of sweat made his eyes smart. Suddenly, scarcely knowing why he did so, he murmured, "Changer—help me. I don't know what to do."

Ahead of him there seemed to be more light. He resumed his way forward and emerged a moment later into the most beautiful garden he had ever seen. But he had no time to enjoy the beauties of the place even if he had been disposed to do so. A blue mist came swirling from the ground, the same radiant mist that first had surrounded him in the cellar of the bookstore on Ellor Street. And once more his fears subsided and he drew in a deep breath of relief.

The two figures approaching him through the mist did not frighten him. Soon he was able to see them clearly, for they stood two yards away, staring at him gravely. Both were draped in regal robes of fur, and their heads were crowned with circlets of gold bearing stones of white fire. The man was the taller of the two and with his left arm he drew the woman to his side. The expression on their faces spoke both of pain and of gratitude. John smiled at them and they returned his smile.

A gentle thunder echoed above him. "John the Sword Bearer, I commend the Regents to your care. You will conduct them from the tower and bid the company yield to them the allegiance that is their due. Tell the company that from the loins of these their Regents will come the Victorious One, the Vanquisher of Death and Destroyer of the Mystery of Abomination. He will slay him in personal combat. Do you hear me, John-of-the-Swift-Sword?"

It was the voice of the Changer. And John said, "Yes, sir. Yes, sir. But . . . sir, . . . how do I get them out of the tower?"

Again the thunder rumbled. "The door to the Garden Room is behind you." And when John turned round, the doorway that

had three hours previously been a long way up the hill was indeed behind him. Another doubt occurred to him. "Sir . . . please, sir, I've lost Mab."

"He too is standing behind you." Relief flooded John. He turned again and saw Mab, a look of astonishment on his pale old face. He stood with his staff in hand beside the open door. John turned and moved toward him. But he paused and addressed the invisible Changer for the third time.

"Oh, and sir, please, sir . . ."

The thunder rumbled gently.

"You won't be angry, will you, sir?"

The silence that followed was unnerving, and John's words tumbled out of his mouth in haste. "Please, sir, you said something about you'd . . . I mean, you were going to tell me about my father?"

The thunder was laughing, and John laughed too, though rather nervously.

"Your father, John-of-the-Swift-Sword, is safe and sound. Tonight you are to return to the world you came from. And tonight you will also find your father. Now begone! You have a task to perform. See that you perform it well."

The mist rose with thunderous echoes of laughter, leaving a clear and shining pathway to the door. John turned to the Regents, his eyes alight with excitement. Then remembering a school play he once had taken part in, he bowed deeply, and with an aplomb that later amazed him said, "Your majesties will please follow me through the doorway."

29

Old Nick's Triumph

They walked solemnly along the corridors and down the stair-
cases of the tower. John led the way followed by the Regents
and then Mab. Once again the old man's strength had left him,
and he lagged behind the others, stumbling weakly. They had
already descended two of the stairways when the king spoke.

"Your name is John, I believe. John the Sword Bearer and
John-of-the-Swift-Sword," the Regent said.

"Yes, your majesty," John replied over his shoulder. "At least,
that's what they call me."

"You mean those are not your real names?" the lady Regent
asked.

"They call me John-of-the-Swift-Sword because this," John
touched his scabbard, "cut off the hand of Old Nick, the Goblin
Prince."

"I see," the lady murmured mischievously. "You yourself did

not cut the hand off. The sword cut it off. Was the sword in your hand at the time by any chance?"

John laughed. He was feeling at home with the Regents. "Yes, your majesty. I was holding the sword. But it, it sort of acted on its own . . ."

"Remarkable!" she replied.

John was about to explain that his real name was John Wilson, but at that moment the four emerged from the open door of the tower, which closed with a boom behind them. They saw that the whole company had gathered in a circle below the Stones of Scunning in the courtyard. Heads turned and startled faces surveyed them at the sound of the closing door. One by one they rose to their feet. Beyond the company, the Scunning Stones were radiating waves of light and power.

John strode boldly forward. The Regents were now walking side by side, but Mab, whose face was gray, sat quietly on the grass. The Matmon parted ranks to let them pass. King Bjorn and Queen Bjornsluv bowed low while the Regents walked unerringly to the Stones of Scunning and sat on them.

For a moment a pale blue glow penetrated both of them so that like the stones they seemed to radiate soft blue light. Then slowly the radiation subsided. A murmur of awe and delight swept the little company and a cheer rose which echoed from the castle wall. "It is the sign," Vixenia whispered. The stones had not harmed the Regents.

John turned to face the company, a little unnerved at the awe and the questioning looks on their faces. He saw Mab sitting on the grass and was dismayed at the exhaustion written on his face. He tried to remember what the Changer had told him, took a deep breath and said, "You can sit down if you like.' Then he cleared his throat carefully and took another deep breath as he searched for the proper words in his mind. The silence was unnerving.

"The Changer commended the Regents to my care," he said. "He told me to conduct them from the tower and bid you . . ."

he frowned slightly, trying to remember the exact words, ". . . and to bid you, er, yield to them the allegiance that is their due."

His heart was thumping. It was unnerving to be stared at. Were they staring at him or at the king and queen behind him? Suddenly it was as though he were back in school. He felt for his glasses and had both hands up to the side of his face before remembering that he didn't have glasses anymore. Somehow his hands felt extra large, and he wondered where to hide them. He put them behind his back. Embarrassed, he cleared his throat for the second time and took a third deep breath.

"The Changer told me to say that from the loins—I think that was the word—from their loins will come the Victorious One, the Vanquisher of Death and Destroyer of the Mystery of Abomination whom he will slay in personal combat."

Was there anything more? He couldn't think of anything. But everyone was still staring at him. What was he supposed to do now? He could feel his face reddening. Things had gone quite well up to that point, but now he felt lost and confused.

"That's all, I think," he concluded, feeling flustered. He strolled with embarrassed clumsiness, stumbling through the crowd to Mab, and sat down beside him. He hoped that somebody else would do something to break the awful tension.

The fur-robed man was already on his feet when John looked up. "We come to join you all in your struggle against the Mystery of Abomination," he said. "For the moment his attacks on you will cease. But he will begin his mischief again after a while for he hates the Changer.

"As for you, we know you. Only John-of-the-Swift-Sword and the seer . . ." He looked questioningly at Mab.

"Mab the seer, at your highness's service." Mab rose unsteadily, bowed slowly and sat down again.

"Only John and Mab were unknown to us. Vixenia we named and Bjorn and Bjornsluv likewise we named when the Changer brought them before us. They did not perceive us when that happened. We likewise named Oso and Tabby and many others." Another murmur of astonishment could be heard. "The Changer has bidden us to rule over you."

"We are willing to acknowledge your sovereignty, sire, for you alone have dared to sit on the Stones of Scunning and live. Yet this Changer is a mystery to us." King Bjorn had risen to his feet. His tone was respectful but his manner was troubled. "Your majesty speaks as one who knows him. Do you indeed know him?"

"As well as a man can know of the Changer," the king replied.

"And what is he, sire?"

"He is the Unmade Maker, the Beginner without Beginning, the Changer who cannot be changed. What more can I say?"

"But that tells us little, sire. Does he have other names? Is it true that he is the same as Mi-ka-ya?"

The king hesitated. "He doubtless has many names," he replied after a moment, "for certainly there are many sides to his character. He will tell us more of his names in time."

"Is he animal, sire?" Oso asked curiously.

"Animal—no, he is not an animal."

"A Matmon?" Bjornsluv asked.

"No, not a Matmon either."

"Is he then a man?" King Bjorn asked.

"Can a man make man?" the lady Regent asked. "No, the Changer is not a man. He is a *maker,* the maker of everything that ever was made, a maker made by nobody."

"What does he look like, your majesty?" Grunt inquired.

"Yes," Itch the dog barked eagerly, "can you describe him to us?"

A puzzled frown stole across the Regent's forehead. "I'm not sure whether I have actually seen him. He rides the winds," he said slowly. "We have heard his voice- like the thunder of a waterfall—but as for seeing him—can one *see* light? He is light, light that sees through a man yet makes him strong and joyful." Again he paused and then seemed to talk to himself. "Is he light or does he just dwell in light?"

No one spoke. Fear looked out from several pairs of eyes.

"We walked with him daily," the lady on the throne said after a moment, "until we failed to believe what he told us. Then we fled from his presence and hid. For we were confounded . . . Yet he clothed us in fur and appointed us to rule a kingdom. And together we will form that kingdom. His kingdom. From the midst of which will come the Victorious One."

The Regents smiled and stepped down from the Scunning Stones. Both of them sat on the grass among the Matmon, and suddenly smiles ran like spreading sunshine among them all. Fear and formality melted away. The questioning continued, but now there was laughter. The lady's sense of humor removed the last vestiges of stiffness, and before long the Regents had clearly become part of the strange family on the island.

Vixenia had slipped away, taking with her Matmon servants to prepare a feast to welcome the two Regents. "We must air the royal chambers for them," she told herself.

The open-air discussion continued, but John's thoughts had wandered. The talk about the Changer set him thinking about the Changer's breathtaking promise that he would meet his father. That night? Already it was late afternoon. How would it happen?

He was seized with a longing to be back in more familiar surroundings. His hand stole inside his tunic to finger the gold ring and the locket. Was he on the verge of unraveling their mystery?

Eventually the sun sank behind the tower. John remained in a solemn mood throughout the feast Vixenia had prepared. This was a pity because the feast was superb. Since Aguila's death, the nightly airborne table had never returned. But the feasts they had enjoyed so much had created a tradition, a tradition that Vixenia was determined they would always follow. And on this occasion, not only did they still have the wine of free pardon, but for the last time (though they did not then realize it) the fireflies attended.

Crowded round long tables placed end to end, they ate and drank as they toasted and welcomed the Regents. There were speeches, but more important there were songs, a song about the arrival of Mab and of the Sword Bearer, songs of the company's journey over the Northern Mountains, songs of the eclipse of the moon and their journey through the dark, a song about the Qadar and the lake of pitch, about the journey down the river, the sinking of the Tower of Darkness, the building of the castle, and finally, new songs about the battle with the efel spawn, the valor of Folly and of Aguila, and the rescue of Mab.

The Regents' eyes sparkled as the Matmon men clambered on the table to dance. The waning moon looked down on the courtyard, but beneath the canopy the firefly light created a magic that none of them would ever forget, even though they were never to see it again. John, though he knew he should enter into it all, was unable to do so. His thoughts were in turmoil.

He stole away to Bjornsluv's chamber where he knew he would find Mab resting on a couch. The old man looked no better. John had hoped the properties of the tower that had wrought so astonishing a change in Mab might have proved permanent. But it was clear that if anything he had lost most of the benefit even of Bjornsluv's ministrations.

The seer looked at him with perceptive eyes. "You seem troubled, Bearer of the Swift Sword," he said in a low voice.

"Yes, I am, Mab. And I'm puzzled."

"About your father, I imagine. I heard what the Changer said. I was glad—very glad he gave you the promise. But I shall be deeply sorry to lose you. You have brought me much happiness at the close of my life."

John sighed. "I wish I knew when I was going to see him. But Mab, it will soon be the tenth hour. Did he really mean *tonight*? And in any case my father's in another world. . . ."

"Problems of that sort present little difficulty to the Changer."

They lapsed into silence, each absorbed in his own thoughts. The look on Mab's face slowly became one of pain. Almost of bitterness. When he noticed it, John was troubled. He wanted to do something. To say something. But what?

"Mab, you—you look—you look *bad*. Can I get you anything? Let me get Queen Bjornsluv?" he said at last.

"No, John. There is nothing I need now—nor any way you can help." There was a long pause.

"Why not?" John asked.

"You know the prophesies, Sword Bearer. You know my life ends when the prophesies are fulfilled. The Regents have come. Only the Goblin Prince remains."

"No, no, Mab, *no*. It won't be like that. Don't worry about it."

But Mab was not worried. John was! He didn't want to admit what Mab knew. So he did his best to put it out of his mind. Still something else bothered John. He remembered some other prophecy, some unmet longing that Mab had wanted to happen. But the seer had said so little about it. Dare he say anything?

"Mab?"

"Yes, Sword Bearer?"

"Mab, may I ask you something?"

"Of course," but the voice sounded more weary than ever.

"Well, oh, but it's nothing. I'll ask you later."

Mab closed his eyes. Bitterness still clouded the tired and ancient face. John turned away, distressed. Two minutes later he crept from the room. Drowsiness overtook him when he reached his chamber. In spite of his agitation, he lay on his bed and fell asleep.

Old Nick was calling. Old Nick was standing on the wharf under the tower. He held out a thin gold chain with John's ring and locket, and he was laughing hideously. "Come an' get 'em, young John!" he cried. "Yer dad'll never know 'oo you are if yer don't 'ave proof. 'Ow can yer convince 'im without these? Come an' get 'em, young John! I'm waitin' down 'ere for you."

He struggled into wakefulness and found he was sweating profusely. "Just a dream," he muttered, but he felt for the chain round his neck to be sure.

A cry of despair broke from his lips. Feverishly his fingers tore into the inner pockets of his tunic to be sure. But there could be no doubt. The chain bearing the ring and the locket, which had been with him night and day as long as he could remember, were gone. There was no sign of them.

30

Ian McNab

John could hardly breathe. His heart, surging tumultuously, seemed to be pounding inside his throat. Rage made him tremble and sweat. *His ring and his locket.* It was no dream. Old Nick had them, had them at that very moment, down on the wharf below the tower. He ran out of his room, down the stairs and across the lawn. In seconds he was on the wharf, his naked sword gripped in his right hand. At once an agonizing pain pierced through his left shoulder.

And sure enough, Old Nick was waiting for him. He was wearing his greasy black suit again, with the red neckerchief and the bowler hat. In one hand he gripped a sharp and heavy iron hook while with the other he held out the thin gold chain from which John's treasures hung suspended. The smile twisting his lips could not conceal the triumphant malice flaming from his eyes. "Come on, young John. Come an' get 'em. Come like yer come fer th' football. I could've killed y' then. An' this time, ay, *this* time, lad . . ." he held John's eyes in his, "I really am goin' to kill!"

Dull red light still permeated the rocky cavern. The water was mirror-smooth. The perfect circle of the tunnel arch and its reflection might have been a painted backdrop.

Staring at Old Nick and breathing heavily, John felt he was seeing him for the first time. "He's not a person," he thought. "He's not even an animal. He's a thing—an evil—a *thing-evil* that has to be destroyed. And I'm supposed to destroy it."

The rage that was still growing inside him was now tempered by fear. He was no longer thinking of the ring and the locket, only of the vile thing he must do away with. It was dangerous. Its easy victories over Oso and Aguila had proved that. Yet he was going to do it. The prophesies said so. He was to kill the Goblin Prince with his sword.

Before he knew it, he was walking with catlike readiness toward Nicholas Slapfoot. As he advanced the sword began to hum and to throb with blue light. The goblin carefully placed the chain around its neck and took a firmer grip on the hook, all the time keeping its eyes on John. Steadily the distance between them lessened.

"Don't ever let him come into physical contact with you," Mab had often warned him, and the words now hammered themselves through his brain. John stopped when they were five yards apart. But when Nicholas Slapfoot sprang at him like a tiger, he was knocked on his back before he knew what had happened. Worse, the goblin was on top of him, crushing him with a weight which drove the breath from his rib cage. His sword had gone from his hand. Out of the corner of his eye he saw it on the edge of the wharf. He could reach it with his finger tips. The goblin was smiling down at him. "Ee bah gum, lad, that were right easy. I thought you'd give Old Nick a bit more compatishun than that. But it's just as well. We can 'ave a nice little chat now." The bowler hat had fallen, and his stringy hair hung untidily round his bald pate.

John's fingers were scrabbling for the sword. It turned a little, so that he could enclose the tip of the hilt with the ends of his fingers. But the strength seemed to have left his arms. He could not breathe.

"I'm sorry that it's come t' this, lad. I never like killing young lads. There's no pleasure in it. But needs must. You'll appreciate that. I can't afford t' overlook what you plan t' do t' me, now can I?" John had pulled the hilt an inch or so closer and was straining to get his fingers round it. "Answer me, young John. It's rude not to answer when I'm askin' you a question. Y' really don't expec' me t' overlook it, do you?" At last John had the hilt in his grip. His arm felt like a column of lead. But slowly he began to raise it. "An' such a nice lookin' lad too. I'd 'av thought you'd 'av real nice manners." He began to raise the iron hook, smiling broadly.

Awkwardly John was now lifting the sword. It was beyond Old Nick's range of vision. He managed to get it vertical, but then the strength left him and his arm fell drunkenly toward Old Nick.

The goblin screamed and fell sideways to John's left. At last he was free, but for a moment he could not move. He forced himself to roll toward the goblin and with a tremendous effort kept the sword pointed in Old Nick's direction. The sword met with resistance and the goblin screamed again. Leaning weakly on his elbow, John saw that the sword had penetrated the goblin's thigh, wounding it for the second time.

Their eyes were locked, each intent on destroying the other. They struggled to their feet simultaneously. And as they did so, the goblin swung the hook viciously at John. It caught the edge of his cape and tore it from his back, but the weight of the cape, which now hung from the goblin's hook, prevented Nick from using his weapon until he was able to snatch the garment from the point and fling it aside. By that time John was well on his feet and backing away.

Gone was Old Nick's bantering manner. John continued to

back up, keeping the sword pointed at Old Nick, who was now clearly unable to sustain much weight on his left leg. "Good," John thought. "At least he won't be able to leap at me."

All his fear was gone. He watched Old Nick like a hawk, wanting time to recover his breath and his strength. Old Nick's weight had crushed the feeling out of his limbs, but he could sense it tingling back. There was no longer a smile on the hateful face as the goblin said, "Very well, young John. Let's see what y' can do with *this*."

John backed up three or four paces, fearful of being rushed again, even though he knew it was unlikely. But nothing happened.

"Look behind you, young John."

Unwisely John did so and was stunned. Old Nick was ten yards behind him. And beyond him he saw Mab, leaning heavily on his staff, his face wet with the terrible effort of standing. Mab said, "Turn round again, John." And when he obeyed, Old Nick was exactly where he had been before. John hurled himself to the cave wall, and stood with his back to it. Old Nick would not be able to get behind him there.

But a horrible surprise awaited him. There were now two Nicholas Slapfoots. Identical Nicholas Slapfoots, one on his left and the other on his right. And as he glanced from one to the other he perceived a third, five yards in front of him on the edge of the wharf. Not the smallest difference could be discerned among them. A bowler hat lay a yard or two from each. Each protected and favored a wounded left leg. Each held a wicked-looking hook in his right hand. But when they moved, they did not each make the same movement or even move simultaneously. He now faced not one, but three assailants.

Were there really three? And if not, which was the real Slapfoot? He had almost decided that the one who stood where their struggle had started must be the real one when the one in front of him said, "I'm comin' t' get you, young John!" and stepped forward.

"Watch your sword, John!" Mab called softly. "It will vibrate and flash when you are near the real Slapfoot. The others are merely shadows. Ignore the voice. He can speak through any of them."

Four weapon-bearing figures froze into stillness. Though his shoulder still throbbed with pain John hardly noticed it. Mab spoke again. "I am not allowed to use my staff or any magic to help you. This is your own fight, a fight you must win."

Carefully switching his glance from one to the other, John pointed his blade at the Nicholas Slapfoot in front of him. Nothing happened. Again he turned it, this time to the Slapfoot nearest Mab. Again the sword registered nothing. But as he turned it to the goblin who stood where they had struggled together, a low hum was clearly audible.

"Ignore the others! *They cannot hurt you.* They do not exist." Mab's voice was low and urgent.

John's strength was fully recovered now, and crouching a little he advanced slowly and steadily toward the real Nicholas Slapfoot. Old Nick's voice sounded from behind his right shoulder, and for a split second he almost turned. But remembering Mab's words he forced himself to keep his eyes looking in the same direction.

At first the goblin did not move. The hook was at his side. The throbbing sword gripped firmly in his right hand, John advanced to within four yards of Old Nick, then to three. But Old Nick suddenly backed away, and as he did so a figure rose from the shadows to come between them. John's mind spun and he gave a cry of bewilderment. *It was Grandma Wilson!* Old Nick had seized her and was holding her in front of him.

"Mind you. Don't 'urt 'er now, John. She didn't die, y' know. Th' doctor made a mistake. An' she's been 'unting you ever since. Th' Changer just sent 'er 'ere. But she will die if you come any nearer with that there sword." He released the old lady and began to back up.

Unutterable love was in her eyes and her arms extended

toward him. The yellow streak was still in her white hair, and her best apron rested smoothly on her long gray skirt. A terrible sob shook him and his sword arm dropped to his side.

"It's not real, John! It isn't anyone. He's just pulling the image out of your own mind. Walk through it! It isn't there!"

He knew Mab's words were true. He also knew as never before how very evil the goblin was. He knew more. He knew the power of Old Nick was the power of an evil still inside himself, a proud and rebellious evil, an evil he must now destroy. His heart was throbbing again and his mouth was dry as he said, "You're not just *outside* me, but *inside* me, Nicholas Slapfoot. And the Changer's sword is going to destroy you. I can wait no longer, and neither can I!"

To walk unfeelingly toward his grandmother with his sword at the ready was unbelievably hard to do, even though with part of his mind he knew she was an illusion. He looked beyond her, focusing on Old Nick, shuddering as he reached her and half relieved, half distressed at the way she turned to a vapor which swirled around him as it dispersed.

Old Nick, still backing up, stumbled and fell. Swiftly John raised the sword high, gripped it with two hands and stepped forward quickly. The goblin's hook was held menacingly above his ugly head as he struggled back onto his feet. But John was too quick for him. With terrible power, power that was never his, he swung the sword in one awesome sweep, cleaving the head and neck down the center, cleaving the chest and the whole trunk. An explosion of red fire flung him to the ground but he leaped again to his feet, only to see a collapsing mound of ugly dark green slime slop sideways into the water.

There was a splash as it poured itself in and a furious boiling and bubbling in the water which lasted for more than a minute. More bubbles rose to the surface from time to time. Then there was stillness. The waters settled and were clear. He felt free and cleaner than he had ever felt in his life. All the pain had gone from his shoulder. And he was alone with Mab again.

"Well done, John-of-the-Swift-Sword. Very well done indeed!"

John swung round, panting, to see Mab on hands and knees by the water at the foot of the stone steps. "Oh, Mab! It happened so quickly. I'm glad he's gone. He was a thing, not a person—just an awful, awful *thing*. And it was sort of inside me too—I mean the evil!"

Mab struggled painfully to his feet. "I dreamed your dream, and when I awoke I knew I must find you. My old heart well nigh ceased to beat." He stepped forward unsteadily and pulled John against him. "I knew it was to happen. Yet I dreaded it. You have grown dear to a dying man, John-of-the-Swift-Sword."

For a few moments he held John against him, swaying a little, and then released him. "See," he said. "Look what I have in my hand."

Slowly he opened his hand to reveal a glowing pross stone. "It caught my eye from a crack in the rock by the waterside as the Goblin Prince was melting. Doubtless it was lost there the afternoon you first attacked him. Take it. Let it be a memory between us when we part. Take it and think of old Mab whenever you look at it."

John took the stone between his fingers. It glowed with its own soft light, a light which soothed and comforted him. "Thank you," he said softly, looking into the ancient prophet's gray, sweat-covered face. He looked away again, for a tear was coursing down one of the wrinkled cheeks.

John took Mab's arm. "We must go back," he said. "You must rest. Lean on me." They moved with painful slowness toward the stairs. Only then did John remember.

"Oh, Mab!"

"What is it, child?"

"My ring and my locket!"

"Your ring? You have a ring?"

"He had them round his neck! Mab, I must get them!" He had been too concerned about the battle to take much notice.

But now terror invaded his body. They were his only link with the father he had never met. Turning from Mab he ran back along the wharf. Mab followed him feebly.

At first he could see nothing either where the goblin had fallen or on the smooth rocky bottom below the water. Its depth was impossible to gauge, and the dim red light made him frown and screw up his eyes. Had the ring and locket been destroyed with Old Nick? He put the thought out of his mind. Then to his relief he caught sight of a red gleam. After moving his head up and down a few times he was sure.

"You swim, John-of-the-Swift-Sword?"

Ashamed to have forgotten the dying seer, John turned. "I'm so sorry," he said. Mab sank to the ground, leaning his back against the wall.

John untied the thongs of his sandals and shucked them. Next he pulled his tunic over his head and stood on the wharf again, doing his best to gauge the depth of the water and the position of the thin gold chain. Then he dived.

The water was cold but John was intent on what he was doing. He was an old hand at finding coins on the bottom of swimming pools, and there was no doubt in his mind that he would succeed in recovering his treasure.

It cost him three attempts. Each time he would wait on the surface, treading water while he recovered his breath. His third dive took him right to the spot. The moment he felt the precious metal safely between his fingers he rose to the surface. Joy and relief surged as he rose.

He heaved himself from the water and crossed to where the old man sat. There was no chain. Only the ring and the locket. He handed them to the seer and then reached for his tunic and began to pull it over his wet body.

"I showed them to you in the boat when you rescued me from the tower," he said, his voice muffled from inside the tunic. "I showed them to Folly . . . and to Vixenia too, I think. My granma was going to tell me what they were . . . but she died. I told you she died, didn't I?"

"No, John. I've never seen them before. You certainly told me your mother and your grandmother had died. And you said that your father was a drunk who didn't want you."

John sat on the rock and began to lace up his sandals. "There's a picture of a soldier in the locket—and a lock of hair. I keep thinking it might be a picture of my father. Maybe now that I've killed Old Nick, the Changer will come and take me to him. He said tonight. Oh, Mab, I wish he'd hurry."

Mab had already opened the locket and was examining its contents, his wrinkled face a mask. "I should have realized you did not come from a world near here," he said quietly, "nor from an age that is close to us in time."

"What do you mean?" John asked. "Isn't this place sort of connected with the real world? I thought it must be, sort of, like a world-inside-a-world."

"No, John-of-the-Swift-Sword. You have come from a distant world, and an age that is not now." There was a long pause, a pause John knew he must not break. At last Mab spoke. "How slow I have been! I should have known."

John stared at him.

"With the Changer, such things are a small matter." He sighed weakly. "Now I can tell you about your father."

"You know him?"

"Now I do. I now know who he is. Or rather, I know who you are. I have known about your father long enough. There are too many things I have learned in my six centuries here." The seer's voice was weary. He was still staring at the photograph and the lock of hair.

"John-of-the-Swift-Sword, you are known in your own world as John McNab."

"No, Mab, John *Wilson*."

"Wilson cannot be your real name."

"But it is. I've always been called John Wilson."

"Perhaps so. But your father's name is Ian McNab. Wilson

was your mother's maiden name. She and your father married against your grandmother's wishes. Your father knew nothing about your birth. He was away in France. The cable announcing your birth apparently never reached him. He only knew that your mother had died."

John swallowed and took a deep breath. It was a new thought. John McNab. And his father's name was Ian McNab.

"Will I find him?"

"Unhappily, yes. The Changer never lies. His promises are sure."

John struggled with a frightening thought. "You mean he won't—won't want me?"

Mab sighed. "Who would not want a son?" he said. "All men long for sons. And from what I know of your father . . ."

"What do you know about him, Mab? Tell me. Tell me everything you know." He shivered with fear and longing as much as with the chill of the water that still clung to him from his dive off the wharf.

Mab closed the locket, then spent almost a minute examining the ring. "Your father was born in the north of Scotland," he said at length. "Twenty miles northwest of Inverness. He spoke Gaelic as a young child and learned to speak English at church, listening to an English minister so that he spoke it with an English accent. When he was fifteen he came to England to find employment and for several years worked as a miner in Bolton."

John nodded eagerly, storing every word in his memory. "Is that my father in the snapshot?"

"Yes, and the hair is a lock of his hair. When the photograph was taken he had just volunteered to be a foot soldier in the Lancashire Fusileers. He had been married a week at the time."

"Let me look at it again!" John extended his hand for the locket and stared at the picture with a new eagerness. His fingers were trembling.

"Your father was a good soldier, but he drank too much," Mab said quietly after a moment. "He became a regimental sergeant major, but was demoted to the ranks for something that happened when he was drunk."

John felt a pang of fear. "What happened?"

"It is little worth repeating. What matters is that the Changer came to him then. The war was virtually over. He had become the personal servant of a British colonel in the Allied headquarters in Paris. Once he stopped drinking he was able to save enough money to emigrate to Canada and booked a passage on a liner, traveling between Cherbourg and Montreal."

John drew in a deep breath. "So he did go to Canada. Then that's where the Changer will take me."

Mab made no reply. His shoulders were hunched and he fiddled listlessly with John's ring.

"I just can't wait!" John went on excitedly. "I wish the Changer would hurry up and let me meet him!"

"Unfortunately, you have met him already." Mab's voice was low and bitter.

John seemed not to hear him for a moment. Then as the words penetrated, he said, "What did you say? I've already met him? When?"

It was then that a peal of gentle thunder shook the rocky walls around them, and a glowing blue mist drove out the red light until the two of them were alone in radiant blue.

"Oh, Changer. You have mocked me!" the old man cried, staggering feebly to his feet. "You asked me centuries ago if I wanted a son, and I told you I did. 'Then you shall have one,' you said.

"But hundreds of years have passed. I thought it a kindness that I should live so long. But you brought me here and made me live so many years that I am now old and withered and dry as a stick. You have even made me love the child."

His head was tossed back and his body became rigid. He clenched and unclenched his fists in a fever of pain. He swallowed, took a deep breath and continued. "I know not by what mysterious magic you placed centuries between us, but you mock me, Changer. You mock me! What good am I as a father when I stand before the gates of death? What use am I to my son? What joy shall I have when I love him for a day or two, only to perish and leave him alone?"

John trembled. His own face was now drawn and pale—just like the seer's. He felt the universe was turning in nauseating somersaults around him. Mab? His father? Or was the old prophet mad?

A sound of rumbling thunder grew in volume, and the voice that John knew to be the Changer said, "Peace, Ian McNab! Peace! Your days are numbered here, but you will not die soon in your own world. Instead you will pick up your youth where you left it, as you enter once again the world of men. I do not mock you, Ian McNab. I restore to you your earthly years and give you your son!"

A steel gray door appeared before them bearing the number 345. And as Mab stepped forward to seize the handle, he was changed. John struggled to his feet.

"Mab! What's happening to you?"

The wrinkles were being smoothed away. The white hair was curling and turning a reddish brown. Green eyes sparkled with life and wonder. Mab's face was no longer gaunt nor his frame fragile. His beard vanished and a red mustache sprouted on his upper lip. He stood before John in a Harris tweed jacket, a tartan kilt, gray woolen socks and brogues.

He released the door handle and with a cry of joy seized John in his strong arms, whirling round and round crying, "I am Ian McNab, your father, son! My son, my son, I'm your father!" until he was breathless and John was dizzy.

So much had happened so quickly that John could only gasp and laugh. His face was flushed and his eyes were round with wonder. John noticed he was wearing his green blazer and shorts and that he was smaller too. He was sure the Salford Grammar School cap must be on his head. He could also feel his glasses resting on his nose.

But he cared little about how he was dressed. His eyes would only look at the marvelous man in the Harris tweed jacket and kilt.

"You said he was . . . I mean *you were* . . . Scotch, . . ." John said breathlessly.

"Not Scotch, son, *Scottish* . . ."

"Yes, Scottish." John stopped. Then he laughed with nervous delight. "Are you really my dad?"

Ian McNab drew him closer to him again. "I'm your father and you are my son, the son I never knew I had until today," he said, his deep voice trembling with emotion. John leaned against him, taking satisfying breaths of Harris tweed.

Then he pulled away. "What's the door?" he asked.

Mab turned to look at the gray door again. "How old were you when you came to Anthropos?" he asked.

"Thirteen."

"Well, son, I'm not sure what happened. But ten years before then in your time I booked a berth on a ship bound for Montreal. I never took ship, for the Changer brought me here first. It's all coming back to me now. My cabin number was 345. Perhaps—who can say—there may be berths for both of us beyond that door. But what year will it be in our world?"

The thunder rumbled again, and this time it had a curious effect on them. It took away their excitement and made them solemn and quiet. From the rumbling came the voice of the Changer, "Go forward through the door. The year beyond it is 1929. Farewell."

Seizing John's hand Ian McNab turned the handle with his other. As he opened the door they heard a babble of men's voices beyond it.

31

Link between Two Worlds

They were still leaning on the rail around the stern of the boat long after midnight. Nearly all the passengers had gone below. The only sounds were the muted strains of the small orchestra in the first-class lounge, the soft wash of the sea along the liner's sides and the underlying throb of the ship's engines. Behind them the churning of the screws formed a broad pathway of luminescent green that mocked the faint stars above.

Ian McNab and John had filled the hours since their arrival on board with the endless business of exchanging stories. "I didn't want to know anything about your world," Ian McNab confessed. "Perhaps I knew, deep inside, that you came from here, even though I had no idea who you were. I'm not sure. But I pictured it six centuries into the future, and I dreaded to know what it was like. I knew it wouldn't be *my* world anymore."

He had said relatively little about his years in Anthropos but had questioned John endlessly about Grandma Wilson, Pimblett's Place and Salford Grammar School. "The old lady had changed a lot in thirteen years. I didn't even recognize her image at the wharf," he said thoughtfully.

"Why did they call you Mab?" John asked him.

"Because they couldn't say *McNab.* Mab was easier."

"And will you still be a seer? Will you do magic here?"

"*Miracles,* not magic. Who knows?" Ian McNab grinned. "I don't have my staff, you know, any more than you have your sword."

"Gosh. I never thought about them till now. I wonder what happened to them? And our clothes!"

"Think what a sensation it will create when someone comes across them," Ian McNab replied. "Can you picture them lying on the wharf—your sandals and tunic and robe, your sword and my staff—*but no bodies!* What a legend it will make!"

The thought kept them speculating for several minutes.

"Yes, and if time goes by more rapidly there than here," his father continued, "we may have become a legend already. Just think of it. Minstrels may already be singing about us!"

"Will we ever go back?"

"You might, but not me."

"Oh, Mab, I wouldn't want to go back without you."

"You wouldn't want me to die, would you?"

"Die? Oh, *no!* But why should you die?"

"I was pretty close to it when we left, Sword Bearer. I imagine we would go back in the same condition we left. Maybe not. Anyway I'm not about to risk it if I can help it. I'd better stay here."

John remembered that gray face of the dying seer and shuddered. "I never thought of that, Mab."

"We must look before we leap, Sword Bearer."

There was a pause. "Why do you keep calling me Sword Bearer?"

"Why do you keep calling me Mab?"

"Did I?"

"You most certainly did."

There was another pause. John felt embarrassed. "I can't get used to saying it," he muttered shyly.

"Saying *dad*?"

John nodded, and once again Ian McNab's arm pulled him against himself. "You will. Or perhaps I should say, you'd *better*. If you go on calling me Mab, I shall have to stick with John-of-the-Swift-Sword—and that's far too lengthy."

They had hardly known how to behave when they first had entered cabin 345. Ian had been surprised that though ten earth years had passed since he had left, he had the same cabin number as for his first trip. Fortunately their fellow passengers seemed either to know them already or else to be expecting them. There was an elderly fat man from Montreal and three younger men who were French immigrants to Canada, all of whom greeted them cheerfully. There suitcases were on their bunks so that they knew at once which ones belonged to them. To John's surprise, his clothes from Pimblett's Place were all neatly packed inside his suitcase. He never found out how they got there.

They had first entered the cabin just at the time when Cherbourg was disappearing over the horizon, and the other members of the cabin evidently concluded they had been on deck. John smiled when he thought about it. "I didn't know what to say when we went through the door. It was so funny to feel the ship going up and down with the waves and to meet strangers who knew our names."

Ian McNab was looking down at an old gold ring which he wore on the middle finger of his right hand. He had returned the locket to John. "The Earl of Orkney gave the ring to my grandfather for some service or other," he said, "but we never learned anything about its history." He paused. "I wonder whether we brought anything else away with us. Have you checked your pockets?"

John searched. From his blazer pocket he pulled two stones,

the smaller one the pearl-like pross stone, and the larger one the Mashal Stone. They stared at the latter in amazement. Even in the starlight it gleamed a radiant blue. John slipped the chain over his head. But to his disappointment he remained plainly visible.

Ian drew in a long breath. "I have a feeling that you, at any rate, will be going back some day. The stones are a link between the two worlds. We'll have to wait and see what happens."

The remainder of the voyage passed without incident, and eleven days later they arrived in Montreal. From there Ian McNab and his son John traveled overland to Winnipeg.

I suppose I ought to say that they lived happily ever after. For that would be true. But it would only be part of the truth.

They lived *eventfully*—or at least John did. As Ian McNab had suspected, John did go back to Anthropos, and the stones did have something to do with it. But that is another story. Is it not recorded in the Archives of Anthropos? If you ever get hold of them you may read it for yourself.

THE ARCHIVES OF ANTHROPOS

Gaal the Conqueror

When young Eleanor MacFarland runs away from home one winter night, John Wilson tries to find her. But as the boy follows her footsteps across a frozen Canadian lake, he mysteriously passes through an invisible door – out of this world and into the greatest crisis yet to face the land of Anthropos.

The two children suddenly find themselves swept into a conflict between the evil forces of the sorcerer Shagah and the rebels loyal to Gaal, Son of the High Emperor.

Here is another exciting book of fantasy in the *Archives of Anthropos* from the creative pen of John White. Coming soon will be *The Tower of Geburah* and *The Iron Sceptre* to further entertain and delight young and old readers alike.

86347 078 5

The Dragon's Back

Ian Barclay

A classic whodunnit!

"Just north of Brighton, beyond the downs and nestling in a fold of the hills, lies Kings Nympton, one of the oldest villages in Sussex . . . It's best known building is the Old Shot Tower, known today as The Old Nail Shot Restaurant. This is the reason why a tiny village of no more than a handful of houses, is known throughout Sussex and beyond."

So begins Ian Barclay's murder mystery. The story opens with restaurant owner Mike Main returning from a Far eastern holiday. He soon becomes involved in a dark and convoluted plot as he tries to unscramble mysterious activities occurring in his restaurant at night. A host of characters help the plot along: crisp and curt Major Bradford; Peter Hoskins, the slightly breathless vicar; Anna Richardson, an attractive local schoolmistress; Mervyn Lyle, a shady antique dealer.

Ian Barclay is an Anglican clergyman, an accomplished cartoonist and has written many Christian books. This is his first novel.

0 86347 031 9